A HEALER PRINCESS

A Sweet Fantasy Romance

THE DANCING PRINCESSES
BOOK II

ALEA HENLE

ISBN: 978-1-952735-09-7 (e-book), 978-1-952735-11-0 (print, as A.R. Henle), 978-1-952735-27-1 (print, as Alea Henle)

Published by Crabgrass Publishing

Editing by Rare Bird Editing.

Cover design by Augusta Scarlett

❀ Created with Vellum

❧ I ❧

Leander followed the hum of bees to the scene of the crime. Or the mystery. No one seemed sure which term applied.

He slipped out first thing in the morning, when the dew still lay thick on grass and late-summer flowers. The sun barely poked above the horizon and the air remained cool, almost still. The long swath of his mantle wrapped around him from mid-chest to lower thigh, with ample left over to toss over one shoulder and fall to mid-calf. The light green contrasted with the darker shade of his knee-length tunic. Although clean, both bore stains along the hemlines and the tunic an ill-mended rent from knee to hip on the side. He slung over his shoulder his usual work kit, a stoutly woven bag of dark gray.

His steady pace down the stairs kept him warm. Legs pumped, arms swung, and strands of wavy, brown-black hair got in his way since he hadn't visited his barber before being sent off on the trip to Yaras and the summer palace.

The air had a thickness, a degree of moisture beyond what Leander was accustomed to, fostering the cultivation of lush gardens every-where—even inside the palace. He passed three immense pots over-growing with scented greenery and purple flowers before exiting and crossing a courtyard. Few of the plants blooming grew at all in the winter palace gardens, and in far less profusion.

His environs were at once familiar and strange.

Simple gray-pebble mosaics laid out clear walkways to and from different parts of the palace complex. Much as he looked forward to viewing the many ornate, full-color mosaics for which the summer palace was famous—not to mention visiting the local palace library and librarians—better to get started on his investigation first.

He took three steps away from the library path toward the gardens, then stopped at the faintest creak of hinges. The hairs along his neck prickled.

Early-rising birds called overhead. Blue-and-white lakelurkers spread their wings wide as they soared over the palace complex. Many smaller birds with gray coats and speckled chests darted among the eaves. Another gave a ululating screech as it plucked insects from between the stones.

He strode off as if untroubled, only to whirl around.

His sister froze a few measures from the open door. Her solid body canted forward as she balanced on her tiptoes, hands raised. A pale-blue mantle covered her from neck to knee, but the hem of her matching tunic fluttered around her bare ankles and feet. She'd chopped her hair off at shoulder length a few weeks earlier and burnt the lengths as a declaration of independence.

Whether or not they shared a sire remained a mystery, for their mother hadn't let slip so much as a hint, but no one ever doubted their relationship. Both had round faces, snub noses, and medium-brown complexions, though her eyes seemed bigger and darker brown, especially when trying to convince him to change his mind.

He motioned for her to return to the room.

For a moment her body remained raised, then her ankles wobbled. She dropped, shoulders slumping.

"Keep to your studies." His lips twitched at the heavy droop of her body, every line suggesting dejection. "Enough progress, and perhaps I'll permit you to help later."

She maintained a woeful expression for a few seconds longer, then flashed a brilliant smile and skipped back into the building. The door shut with a firm click behind her.

No one stirred in this corner of the palace. All the same, Leander watched the windows two floors up until Edrena appeared and gave a wave.

Nodding, he continued on his way toward the middle of the gardens. He'd slipped a coin into a few servants' hands in exchange for directions on how to locate a specific spot amidst the palace's pocket wilderness.

All the servants gave the same direction: walk out a specific door and take the garden path directly ahead, never turning aside.

Yet what constituted directly ahead? The mosaic path gave way to one of gravel, then even the stones vanished leaving a track of trodden vegetation, narrow to the point only one person might walk at a time. It appeared to be a servant's path, a back way that courtiers likely never noticed.

By implication, the servants who'd provided directions still recognized him as one of them. That, or librarians ranked as servants at the summer palace. Denizens of the winter palace, servants and members of the court alike, considered librarians as necessary record-keepers and bloodsucking parasites determined to extract detailed stories from anyone foolish enough to fall into their clutches.

Still, the librarians had accepted him into their ranks and given him a place on the ground. Falfor, his mentor, had seen value in nurturing his intense desire to uncover answers.

Trees rose high to either side, their branches and thick foliage blocking out most of the growing sunlight—and also the heat—but many dripped water although it hadn't rained the night before. Though the path showed evidence of regular trimming by gardeners, they failed to keep up with the growth.

Dozens of different shades of green flourished along with sprays of small flowers amidst mosses marking the many places where the path crossed another or split in two. The crossings, even when at acute angles, he navigated well enough. The splits he found trickier to interpret and guess which counted as straight.

All the while, the moisture in the air condensed into droplets coating him, mingling honest sweat and the wooded garden's dampness.

This particular assignment involved direct service to the Terparchon. The chance of a lifetime—or a dangerous slide set to send him back to his former life atop the winter palace roofs. Probably both in one, all of which made it interesting, at least. A nice change from reading over reports from the chief librarian's official and unofficial correspondents and writing summaries and annotating reports.

Alas, sneaking out first thing meant delaying breakfast. His stomach protested, having gotten used to regular meals since promotion from mere scribe to third assistant librarian for court affairs, then second. He could practically taste getting the raise to first if he managed to navigate the tangle satisfactorily.

He only needed to figure out what would constitute a satisfactory result and how to ensure it manifested *without* lying or faking evidence or making a big fuss that turned out to be no more than a bag of wind.

First, however, to see exactly what it was he'd been sent to investigate.

The summer palace contained one of the odd geographical sites poetically called the Shadows of the Moon. One and all—no one seemed entirely certain whether there were twelve or thirteen—took the form of perfect circles of chalky white stone in the middle of otherwise lushly grown gardens.

Many Shadows lay within the shifting borders of Codaros. The winter palace boasted one. Although reportedly popular as a place to picnic on hot days, Leander never understood the fuss over the ghastly thing.

How had the makers managed such perfect circles? Where did the stone come from? How deep did it go? Why did the stones' color remind him of nothing so much as the layers of ice left by the worst winter storms, a substance known to cause frostbite within moments?

Hardly thoughts conducive to rest and relaxation.

Evidently, the Shadow at the summer palace had vanished overnight.

A very particular night, immediately following one of the killer summer storms that regularly rolled off the lake waters around this time of year. Even when the dancing princesses eased a storm's wrath, it still leveled much damage.

Still, if the storm were to blame—a lightning strike, perhaps—there should be bits and pieces of the stone left behind. Scattered debris or some such, and the spot itself, the Shadow, surely would be blackened or in other ways blasted.

Instead, it had turned to full-grown flowers.

This unsettled the Terparchon to the point she considered no one at the summer palace exempt from suspicion, except perhaps herself, and sent to the winter palace for a librarian to investigate.

Hence Leander's presence.

With the end of the path in sight, he twined his fingers together and committed himself to the service of truth and justice and asked that they guide his inquiry.

"May I not mar or stain any reputation unduly, but only gather and sift through what is known and suspected to piece a tale that rings with veracity."

Nothing and no one answered, as expected. Librarians regularly debated the existence of Truth, whether divine being or earthly force, separate from the messy realities they faced on most occasions. The discussions Leander had participated in—usually involving copious amounts of intoxicating beverages—never came to any conclusion other than a general preference that they serve Truth without ever having to discover the answer.

His breath escaped in a huff, a brief tremor of relief slipping over his skin—and another runnel of moisture down his spine.

Then he left the cool of the woods. The sudden press of sunlight across his body dispelled any remaining chill. He halted and blinked, shading his eyes with a hand.

In the moments of mixed light and shadow, a whiff of something bright and sweet reached him. A flower of some kind, with a buoyant scent and flavor that reached deep within him and struck an unexpected chord. As though the aroma touched his soul and extracted all weariness to leave him refreshed.

The instant his eyes adjusted to the sunlight, he pulled a thin stick of charcoal from his kit. He scribbled a few phrases on a piece of old parchment. Rubbed them out and tried again, and a third time, before he gave up finding sufficient words to describe the new, strange aroma.

Sweat trickled along his spine.

A wide clearing stretched out before him. Stone paths bisected swathes of well-trodden green grass and blue-green mosses. One traced the circular perimeter close to the edge. Others headed to the center and no doubt formed a cross shape, although he couldn't see the far side due to the upwelling of flowers at the center.

Such blooms. Stalks of deep blue with long blue-green leaves and topped with petals mixing dark blue and silver. The blossoms glowed with the beauty of a star-lit night sky.

All the while giving off an aroma that lured him close and closer. He crossed the clearing without any recollection of doing so. One moment he'd left the woods, the next he stood only a hand's length away from the flowers. They swayed in the breeze atop their slender stalks, rising nearly as high as his hips.

Even among the wealth of strange and lovely plants, these stood out.

He still held charcoal and parchment. Setting to work, he sketched the flowers with detailed notes that, as with the scent, were at best an approximation far removed from the visceral reality. He even bent to check the earth from which the stalks sprung, finding it a rich, brown loam.

"Pretty, isn't it?"

Leander jumped, elbows clamped tight against his side. His hands clenched around charcoal and parchment. Who'd managed to creep up on him unnoticed?

An elder stood there. Once a half-head taller than Leander but now stooped so they had the same height. Skin of light brown save for their bare feet, covered by such a thick layer of grass and leaf clippings as to appear green. A knee-length, once-white tunic likewise bore numerous stains of green. The elder wore it in an old-fashioned style tied over one shoulder rather than both. Lacking a mantle or a proper cord or chain at the waist, they used a length of fraying gray cord to belt the tunic across a rounded belly. Their bald head boasted big green-brown eyes, a nose as short as Leander's, and a scraggly beard. A long stalk of grass bobbed between their gums as they chewed.

Overall, the stranger presented as a man but might be an eleee, the term favored by many, albeit not all, who found the terms men and women inaccurate or insufficient. Some eleee were rumored to be able to change anything about their bodies that they wished, though surely no one willingly chose a body such as this unless they wanted to pass unnoticed.

"Beautiful. I've never seen the like." Leander tucked his charcoal and parchment safe within his kit bag.

"I wouldn't think anyone'd have." The stranger settled hands on hips, ducking as they scanned the blooms. "I only ever heard stories about magic flowers, myself, but these are even better than any tales."

Several golden butterflies danced across the petals. The other huffed and angled their body to face Leander.

With minimal movements, Leander mirrored the other's stance.

"You're that librarian sent to find out why this changed overnight?" The grass stalk jerked this way and that.

"Yes."

"Thought so." A short nod. "Came out to find you."

"Did you now."

"Figured I ought to tell someone where no listening ear might hear and start rumors." The other removed the stalk and brushed the tip against a wrinkled temple. "I wouldn't like that."

"A good librarian respects their sources." Leander's fingers twitched to retrieve charcoal and parchment.

"So I heard. Well, I got a little tale for you then." The elder stuck the stalk behind an ear and crossed their arms over their chest. "Mind, it wasn't me that saw this. We had us a couple three extra pairs of arms and legs to help tidy up some of the branches lashed down by the last big storm. One of them, he told me later about seeing someone running through the wood over here that evening after the storm and before anyone found the shadow changed."

"So this man . . ." Leander tilted his head and left an opening for the gardener, given their description of their laborers, to offer additional details. The other scuffed a knobby foot against the grass and said nothing, so Leander continued, "saw someone running away."

"That's about the size of it."

"Nothing more?"

"Not really. Just that I figured she might've been here when the change took place and might be able to help you figure out everything what happened." The grass stalk moved from behind the ear back to dipping and rising out of one corner of the gardener's mouth.

"Who did you say saw this?" Leander asked.

"His name don't matter. He were up from the town, cheap labor, and I heard got hired on with a trader a couple day back."

"Convenient." An apt word, for Leander didn't miss how little the gardener shared.

"That's what I thought."

"And the woman he saw?"

"He didn't know her," the gardener said with a shrug.

But their eyes glinted, and their lips twitched into a smirk for a moment before returning to work away at the stalk.

"*You* do."

"Maybe I do, maybe I don't." The other tilted their head back for a long moment, then gave a decisive nod. "It were twilight. He said she were short with plenty of curves, lots of black curls, and dark skin with glittery bangles at her wrists. Young and bouncy with energy even as she ran." A hand with dirty fingernails stroked the short gray and white hairs sprouting from their chin. "Only one I can think of fits that description. She's a sweet thing, too. I've seen her over the summers grow from a little toddler turning circles on the green to as lovely a dancer as you'd ever want to see. You treat her well, you hear?"

"Of course. Her name?" Flickers of energy surged through Leander's body. Young, bouncy, sweet, curved, lots of curls. The winter court held several matching such a description, but only one had come with the Terparchon to the summer court.

"She's one of them princesses, now. The youngest, though not the newest anymore."

"Good to know." Leander swallowed, mouth suddenly dry. More

warmth welled within him, beyond that of the air and the sunlight. "Her name?"

"That's enough for you to find her." The other grinned, showing every one of their remaining teeth. "No doubt she'll tell you all you need to know, mind she might need a push. You just talk to her daddy on the quiet, and say old Natter pays his debts."

"Much obliged to you." Leander smiled and nodded as the stranger turned on his heels and stalked away—quite fast at that. He hadn't missed the gardener's reference to himself—assuming Natter was, indeed, his name.

The old man had avoided offfering true details, the kind needed for any report. Leander extracted his parchment and took notes. If the tale were true, did Natter mean the princess well or had he a score to settle with her father? The gardener would bear further investigation in addition to those he'd so carefully kept from naming.

Still, he'd given Leander another place to start with his investigation.

And a reason to introduce himself to a certain princess. Unfortunately, as an inquisitor with questions rather than merely an admirer.

＊ 2 ＊

The youngest of the dancing princesses hated infirmaries and hospitals without fail.

Merely being within the walls of the palace infirmary made Danissa's skin itch, though any scratch might draw a healer's notice to hop over to try and make her feel better with some greasy, smelly unguent or another. To suppress any shudders, she sat on a three-legged stool with her back straight. She tucked her hands in her lap, wrapped in folds of her warm yellow tunic and bronze mantle in her lap.

The folds prevented the hems of her garments from touching the black and white tiled floor. Earlier in the day, she'd painted her fingernails and toenails gold, and adorned wrists and ankles with matching bangles. The color complemented her dark reddish-brown skin, but also made more noticeable how her toes curled up from her plain leather sandals, though they were at no risk of coming in contact with the floor.

The tiles appeared clean, yet appearances could be deceiving.

A length of bronze cloth matching the mantle kept her hair away from her face. More discreet than the twined cords of gold and silver that proclaimed her rank, the cloth had already begun to slip. She'd tucked the ends back under, but the cloth wasn't holding as well as it should. A few more shakes of her head and her curls might fall loose and heavy on her neck, not desirable on a sultry late-summer day with too few breezes carrying heavy humid air away. Yet to readjust the cloth she'd need both hands, with the attendant risk of her skirts falling far enough to brush the floor.

Thick walls and stout shutters covering the window kept the room cooler than the outside, but not by much. The chamber was simply too small for much air circulation. Instead of cool or space, it offered proximity to the healers' quarters—sitting adjacent to the healers' on-duty rooms—and privacy. As such, it was set aside for patients of high rank and station.

A slender bed of mattresses stuffed with fresh grasses topped a pedestal of stone, filling most of the room. A seascape mosaic stretched across the otherwise pale gray walls, depicting the most unlikely creatures dancing together beneath white-capped waves. A variety of fish, all somehow imbued with hands and feet, conducted a lopsided circle dance at the center of one of a long wall, under the indulgent eye of an immense crab. On the other, lake folk with human torsos and fish tails swam in a circle, each holding onto the tail flukes of the one ahead by their teeth, no less, with lesser circles of starfish and shellfish within. Matching wavy shells surrounded the high-set window in the narrow exterior wall and the door opposite.

Alas, the room did not smell of the great lake even though it lay in the second rank of buildings in the palace complex, and thus relatively near the shore. Only gardens, the first rank, and more gardens separated it from the wide waters.

Instead, the chamber had an ammoniac scent that Danissa detested. It brought memories of pain, shrieks, and loss. Of death and a beloved form lying still and unmoving on just such a bed as this, albeit in a larger room shared with other ill and injured moaning nearby. Here, all sounds from outside were muffled.

A dozen or so years had passed since that day. Danissa had visited infirmaries on several occasions. She should be fine, yet the merest hint of the smell had the power to bring tears to her eyes. Even now, moisture threatened to break free, held back now only by force of will.

Only love or friendship ever convinced her to overcome natural revulsion and spend time within ammoniac walls.

Today's visit came from a lesser force. She looked in out of a sense of duty.

But Ylena was running out Danissa's patience and willingness to subject herself to the torment of her surroundings.

Three years earlier, Danissa had witnessed the first dance of a bright-eyed, laughing woman bent on rising to success. Ylena accomplished her goals in record time, becoming one of the dancing princesses—the magical attendants who used their powers in Dance to protect the land from horrendous storms, quakes, frosts, and blights—and claiming as her favored partner no less than the Terparchon's son. Rumors had circulated recently that they would wed and be named heirs against the day the Terparchon and Marchon died or elected to retire.

Now look at Ylena. At best a shadow of the dancing princess remained. The woman propped up on bed pillows wore only a thin gray tunic marked with wrinkles and stains. Her pink-and-beige skin once glowed but now had a dull tinge. Blonde hair hung in thick, greasy hanks around her oval face and badly needed to be combed with cleaning earths and properly oiled. Strange, musty scents mingled with the otherwise medicinal aroma in the chamber.

Worst of all, there was no sign of a book or scroll anywhere in the room. Every princess had some pass-time with which they filled the hours when they weren't exercising or dancing—well, every princess save Danissa, who dabbled at each but committed to none—and Ylena loved to read and puzzle over old books in the library. She'd even purchased a few books on her own, which she kept and treasured over in her room.

Yet here she was with not a book to be seen, not even so much as scraps of parchment or a waxed tablet.

A lightweight length of linen covered Ylena's legs, one fine and the other heavily wrapped from knee to foot in bandages and healing ointments.

"How is your leg?" Danissa asked for the third time, having received no answer to her first queries.

"Fine." Ylena's monotone voice and slumped shoulders belied her word.

"Truly? They've set it right now?" Danissa peered at the straight line of bandages under the covering. Enough weeks had passed since Ylena's injury that she should be out and about, except that the bone had proved to be healing crooked and had to be broken again and re-set.

"Yes."

"Does it hurt?"A stupid question. Of course it had to hurt, as sure as waves crested in the lake and rolled on the shore. Danissa had broken an arm as a young child and recalled with more clarity than she liked days of moaning to her mother about how it ached. Equally, she remembered the patience with which her parents eased her, replacing the healing pastes with fresh, always carefully rebinding the bandages after. Sometimes her father, but more often her mother, who would always turn and give Danissa a big smile as she finished rewrapping, teeth flashing white against her lustrous onyx-colored skin.

Ylena didn't respond except to roll her eyes briefly Danissa's way. The movement was notable only because the dark centers of the other princess's eyes contrasted with the surrounding white.

That, and because she'd reacted to so little of late.

Yet it showed that something of Ylena's former liveliness remained, albeit altered. Danissa had never seen her make such a gesture before her injury—nor the many visitation days afterward.

Danissa stopped by the infirmary regularly because Jola, one of the other female princesses, had gone so far as to write up a schedule whereby each of the princesses, and the compeers who partnered them in their magical dances, had assigned days and times to ensure Ylena never felt forgotten. One of the other princesses had been unwise enough to groan in Jola's presence and earned a lengthy diatribe about the consideration they all owed to each other.

Under other circumstances, Danissa, too, might have objected to the rotation. Even without hearing Jola's lecture, pity and politics kept Danissa's mouth shut.

Pity, for Ylena being brought low and forced to watch another Dance in her place.

Politics, first due to Jola's royal connections, which equaled Ylena's. Second, because Danissa had made a point to avoid the other princess of late and refused to create conditions where the other princess had to track *her* down.

As long as Danissa was required to be here, she might as well dedicate herself to any means of restoring Ylena's vitality.

Unfortunately, a moment after rolling her eyes, Ylena sank in upon herself. Her body became very still, from head to toe. Mouth slightly open, she drew rasping breaths through closed teeth. Then, all at once, her body went limp and she gave a shudder.

The cycle Danissa found all too familiar, from visits here and incidents elsewhere. Ylena's expression reminded Danissa of a fleeting look that had passed across her father's face more than once. Quickly banished, for he'd shake his head—then flash her a smile when he noticed her watching him.

"What are they giving you for pain?" Danissa fought to keep her voice even and friendly.

Instead of seeing the other princess, she remembered her father. Still tall, although perhaps he no longer stood quite so straight, with long braided white hair in sharp contrast to the deep brown-black of his skin. He danced with as much grace as ever, yet he'd stepped aside to allow the newest compeer to take his place in partnering princesses in the Dances on a regular basis. Although he still came to practices, he spent more time observing and teaching than going through all the exercises.

This even though both of his parents, and his father's father, still lived and worked and loved in the very city outside the summer palace walls. Danissa had visited with them only two days earlier, and caught her great-grandfather—the mold from which her father had been formed, though the older man wore his colorless hair in short curls—pottering in the garden under her grandmother's strict eye.

Yet she'd caught her father once or twice drinking from a strange-smelling flask.

A hint of that same aroma hung about Ylena's room now.

"Horrid medicinal tisanes when I ask, though I must ask for they will give me nothing with which to dose myself. I'm not allowed any more until the evening meal." Another spark of Ylena's former self flared in her eyes. "What do they think I will do if they leave me the whole pitcher, drain it dry?"

The other princess waved her hand, a loose and careless gesture out-of-keeping with the disciplined woman Danissa had danced with two moons earlier at the summer solstice.

Bending closer, Danissa examined arms where the outer layer of skin had begun to hang more loosely than before, and pretended to ignore the grunt of displeasure from Ylena. The more noises and reactions, the better. Anything that freed Ylena from being a passive lump —and made the span of Danissa's visit go faster.

"What about dancing? Does your pain discourage you from keeping up exercises?"

"What of it?" Another hand-wave from Ylena, although this a hair more controlled and just as well—a princess could do damage with a careless movement. "What do you think I do, rise at midnight and parade myself along the halls?"

"Dancing is more than moving legs. You know that as well as I. It's arms and body and spirit, and you've still got all that haven't you?" Danissa sprang to her feet, tired of Ylena's self-pity. Let her tunic and mantle fall freely. Hands free, she held them before her face with fingers extended—then curled the fingers in. Drawing no more than a bead of power from within, the gesture summoned a quick, fresh breeze that blew the ammoniac smell out the window and replaced it with the full aroma of the nearest palace flower garden. The mixture of light and vibrant perfumes lifted her spirits. How could it fail to do the same for Ylena? "Have you forgotten that Felipa Danced the spring equinox with us, though seated in a chair the whole time so as not to risk her pregnancy?"

Ylena turned her head away, fingers ineffectually covering her yawning mouth. A pitiful show, for her fingers trembled.

"Or what of Yanna?" Danissa didn't wait for Ylena's yes or no. "My aunt, my mother's sister. Her legs don't work at all, they've been small and withered since birth. She gets around on sticks and had no qualms blowing me out of her way. Still does. She was one of the princesses when I was a child. Danced for several years. Father partnered her often, and never had anything but praise for her, though he said it was a challenge to keep up with her and devise ways to align himself best with her movements."

"What happened to her?" Ylena had turned away from Danissa, but tilted her head to glance back over her shoulder.

"You may have seen her around." Danissa stuck her hands on her hips, bracelets chiming. "If you did not, it is your fault for not having looked. She still dances on occasion, and teaches. She retired from being a princess because she tired of the traveling and wanted to remain at home with her beloved."

Another face passed before Danissa's eyes—not her aunt Yanna's strong, determined one with chin set, but her aunt Sunia's streaked with sweat and pain. Then her father's again, not so tormented as Sunia except the pain was such a new thing to see hanging about him.

If only he were not so slippery at escaping whenever Danissa raised the subject in any way whatsoever. She pressed her hands together, willing patience and dreaming of the right words to say to convince him to share.

Only to nearly leap out of her skin at the thump of Ylena's fists slapping her thighs.

Danissa dropped back onto her hard stool, fingers snatching her skirt and mantle and pooling folds so as to keep them from brushing the floor.

Ylena slammed her fists against her thighs again, then sagged and pulled her arms close. Though, tellingly, her fingers curved into claws. "I find it hard to dance, here." One claw waved at her injured leg. "I'm still so . . ."

Danissa waited for Ylena to continue before offering a guess. "Angry?"

"Do you blame me?" Ylena asked.

"No, not at all. I'd be the same."

"I understand your aunt was able to Dance even with withered legs, but will the Terparchon grant me such a chance?" Hands dropping to her lap, Ylena clutched at her sheet. "I don't know if I can still Dance, still channel more than a breath of magic, and I'm not likely to get a chance anytime soon. Not still penned in this bed and with the new princess in my place and dancing with my partner, so the Terparchon doesn't need me to make fives, sevens, elevens, or thirteens."

"Have you ever Danced as a one or part of a two or three?" The princesses usually worked magic in only in the larger numbers, on their own or each with a compeer in support.

"No. Is it even possible?" Ylena gave a loose shrug, but watched Danissa over her shoulder.

"I've seen it done, with more power than I ever would have guessed." Danissa didn't want Ylena questioning that line, so she continued quickly, "I wonder if you might Dance yourself well?"

Ylena bolted up straight, spine stiff and mouth open as though struck by a bolt of lightning. She breathed, but her gaze went distant and she seemed to have forgotten the whole world around her. Tears welled in her eyes, but didn't spill out.

Danissa counted thirteen, thirty-seven, sixty-seven, ninety-seven, before leaping back up. "Ylena?"

No response.

"Ylena?" Danissa pressed against the bed and waved a hand in front of the other princess's face

"That's what it was about. It must be!" Ylena grabbed Danissa's hand, pressing it between hers. Face aglow despite tears trickling down.

"What?" Danissa asked.

"An old codex in the library here. One of those the former chief librarian kept tucked away, it's so fragile. The new chief allowed me a peep at the contents of a chest as he was sorting it, as a favor for helping copy a fragment of another that was fading." Ylena let go, hands shifting as though to cup something only she could see. "I could barely read the lines, but it seemed to be a compilation of stories about Dances for very specific purposes. To lift the heart, to make whole the body, to ease pain and undo that which does not belong, and . . . I thought little of them then, but perhaps . . ."

"Find the book and we can try." As little as a half-moon earlier, Danissa might have scoffed at the notion. Every princess and compeer knew Dancing soothed the forces of nature. It worked on great and mighty scales, rather than small and personal, as the Terparchon and the former princess who served as her right hand so often reminded the princesses.

"Hardly likely." Ylena's hopeful glow faded, her mouth turning down in a frown.

"Why not? The chief librarian likes you." And enjoyed spending time with Ylena, but left Danissa mostly to her own devices. Just as well, too, for the times she'd followed Ylena to the libraries in either palace, she'd spent as much or more time gazing at the many cute librarians laboriously copying works as at the volumes.

"He may, but he'll not bring that chest or anything in it out of the library. Nor will the healers allow me to leave here anytime soon, even if I promise to behave, not after my bad behavior earlier."

A hearty sigh escaped Danissa, though she refrained from belaboring the matter. At least Ylena recognized her fault in hefting herself and her partially healed leg onto crutches and crossing the palace complex to confront the new princess who'd innocently taken her place.

"But you,"—Ylena grabbed Danissa's hands—"you could copy it."

"He doesn't think much of me. Remember what he said the last time?" The words still stung. "Too eager and apt to spill ink."

"You can change that. Do better and get on his good side. Praise books. Show how much you love reading—which you do, I've seen you devour the broadsides you sneak in from the city." Ylena squeezed Danissa's hands. "He loves to share the treasures of the library with those who will appreciate them. Please?"

Danissa grumbled and protested, but with less strength each round. She'd wanted to see Ylena returned to her former vigor and drive—though she hadn't bargained for that drive being turned on *her*.

Yet the suggestion that Dancing might help ease the suffering of those in pain, such as Aunt Sunia . . . Or Danissa's father . . .

There was no other way around it. Danissa had to know. For Ylena's sake, and her own, she would have to brave the librarians.

Leander donned his absolute best attire for a formal meeting with the Terparchon—his best and most uncomfortable. He'd purchased the tunic during his rush to pack, so fresh from the loom and tailor that the creamy yellow still gave off whiffs of goldflower-infused dye. The lightweight folds fell to mid-calf, kept in order by a stout cord of darker gold around his waist. He'd last worn the rich, red mantle for his most recent promotion. Although meant for summer heat, the cloth remained stiff and chafed where it rubbed against his skin. A brightly polished gold broach held the mantle at one shoulder.

Or should. His hands fumbled as he thrust one end of the broach pin into a hank of cloth rather than through. His fingers itched to rub his wrists, a sign of nerves, further hindering him.

The lack of light didn't help. They'd closed slatted wooden shutters over the window as a barrier to the sun's warmth. Only a few stray beams crept in around the edges and along a warped board. A basket of light-stones sat on the narrow, webbed bedstead his sister had claimed. They cast enough light for her to read the flimsy, faded chapbooks as she prepared for her exam, but otherwise offered limited illumination.

Although if he were honest with himself, the fault for his trouble in dressing lay more in the tremors rippling through him than the dimness.

The air might be cooler than outside, but a light sheen of sweat dampened his skin. He drew in a deep breath and choked on the musty scent, though he tried to pass it off as a fit of coughing.

"That's the third time, so now will you let me help?" Setting aside her much-used reading, his sister rose. Despite having tossed her sandals in a corner, she clomped over the floorboards with their thin reed covering and snatched the broach out of his hand, nearly scratching him in the process. Her mantle lay abandoned on the bed, the light pink fabric of her tunic billowing.

"Very well." He stood stiff and straight as she fastened the broach and ran her hands over the mantle to brush out the more noticeable wrinkles.

"Sandals, too." She settled into a heap as she grabbed the flat soles and laid them out for him to step on.

He considered protesting, but took his place atop the thin swathes of gilded leather without argument. Edrena's narrow fingers danced as she wrapped the ties over the surface of one foot, around the ankle, and crisscrossed up the calf to the knee where she bound them tight enough to chafe—but not fall. He gave a quick kick to the side and nodded at tension. It would hold. Quite the bother, especially as he'd seen several courtiers earlier going about the palace with less ornate sandals, but this was the style of summer footwear in the winter palace when he'd left and he'd hardly had time to obtain new.

"Can't you bring me too?" Edrena had her head down and she mumbled as she wrapped the other ties around his calf. "Just to see them."

"No." A softer refusal than the he'd given the first ten times she asked, but no less firm.

"I'd be silent as a night kisser. I could be your servant, carry your tablet for you and make notes."

A chuckle escaped him even as his nerves jangled over the approaching interview. The mere idea of Edrena and night kissers linked together tickled his fancy. She had a far ways to go to mimic the birds with wide wings and soft plumage the color of the sky at midnight, fierce hunters whose prey rarely had any warning before the birds plunged. "No."

"It's just I've never seen them closer than from above, you know, before." She tucked the ends of the ties under and leaned back to peer up at him.

From this angle, her face and body seemed smaller, reminding him of how little and delicate she'd been when he'd brought her down off the palace roofs where they'd both been born and raised.

Where their mother still worked and drank and danced with death.

"Have you not even caught a view from a crowd?" He frowned, crouching down to make them more on a level.

"That's different, it's too far to really see anything on the ground. Most people are taller than me, and even when they aren't I never manage to scrounge a good viewing spot." She rose onto her knees, a smile lighting her face. "When I pass the test, the Marchon's supposed to come and welcome us to the ambassadorial service. They say he loves peace weaving because he came from the last city the country swallowed in war." The smile turned to a pout. "But he won't have time to *talk* to any of us, and I've got so many questions."

"In which case, how would you manage to be night-kisser quiet?" He tapped her nose. "This is no time for you to be asking questions. This is work. If I do well . . . We might stretch to buying you a more recent set of chapbooks for your exam. But if I anger or disappoint the Terparchon, I could lose my place and we'd have to go back up on the roofs to work."

"You'll do it." She caught his chill hands and pressed them between her warm ones. "Didn't Falfor say you were the best he'd ever taught?"

"Yes, but he's no longer chief at the winter palace library, and even when he was, he used to come back from meeting with the Terparchon or Marchon grumbling about them wanting a different story than he had to tell." He gave himself a tap on the nose. "No, it will all go well. I need only find answers for them and the library."

"That's the spirit." Edrena leapt from the floor and clapped her hands. "You look so splendid. Don't muss the mantle, will you? I want it for when I pass the exam."

"Won't I still need it?"

"You'll have plenty more by then."

Her trust and surety lifted his spirits as he rose and faced the door.

The sharp knock before he even started to leave rattled him. Worse was the person who stood on the other side when Edrena pulled the door open.

Of middle height, the new arrival had hair of mixed white, green, and brown. Although pulled back in a short braid, strands had escaped to wreathe their round, flat-featured face. Their medium-brown skin held a yellowish tinge heightened by the intricately braided gold ribbons adorning the hems of their loose, ankle-length bronze tunic. Simple bronzed slippers adorned their feet, tied at the ankle with matching gold cords. No bracelets, but a pair of anklets on one leg chimed as they shifted in place.

"Leander of the Library?" The stranger gave a half-nod to Edrena, and a half-bow to Leander.

"I am he."

"I am Rik, an eleee in service to the Terparchon. If you will follow me, I will take you to her."

Leander squeezed Edrena's hand as he left, giving a nod toward the battered book abandoned beside her pallet. She rolled her eyes but didn't follow.

He was the one who followed, absorbing his surroundings but focused upon his escort. Rik's garb and demeanor gave mixed messages as to the eleee's place and position.

As a child on the roofs, it had been easy. The better the clothes— the fewer holes or signs of wear—the more power. While this held true on the ground, it proved insufficient to note subtle signs of relative influence. He'd had to learn to notice and analyze the details, and the process made his head hurt, the more so when he encountered a mystery such as Rik.

The eleee wore no mantle. This was the clearest suggestion that he ranked among servants who did physical labor, since mantles had a tendency to get in the way unless tied back to the point they became little more than an unwieldy over-tunic. Leander himself, following the practice of most of the librarians and scribes at the winter palace, wore a mantle formed of two panels tucked under one arm—his writing hand—and fastened over the opposite shoulder.

Despite the lack of mantle, the quality of Rik's tunic and jewels far exceeded Leander's and most of those he regularly dealt with. Servant with physical duties the guide might be, but they surely had power and influence.

All the more reason to drink in any word that dropped from their mouth as perhaps a hint at the mood of the court, in particular toward the task for which Leander had come.

Sadly, the guide instead took upon themself only commentary as to the physical layout of the court and how to navigate between the different sections.

"The palace forms a series of half-circles from shore to shore." Rik led Leander through an arch linking two tall buildings. "Note the colors lining walks. Yellow denotes the outer most circle, oranges the next, and on in rainbow order to purple closest to the shore."

The walks themselves were formed of gray stones only slightly higher than the mortar holding them in place, and worn smooth by the passage of feet over the years. The colors on the stones edging the paths came from paint, evidently reapplied as needed for the vibrancy varied widely. Similar to the winter palace, where lines and patterns painted along the base of the walls guided people through labyrinthine halls.

Nevertheless, this was a subtlety easy to miss, for every courtyard boasted at least one mosaic at the center even if only so small a design as a flower. The larger the space, the grander the scope and finer the colored tiles forming the image. Mosaics also covered many of the walls. They distracted Leander again and again with brilliant splashes of color.

Scene after scene, glorious mosaic after glorious mosaic, exalted the Terparchon's ancestors and Codaros's absorption of other cities and their tributaries as it grew from a trading city on the great river to a state of size and far-reaching influence.

Familiar, for similar scenes appeared on the winter palace walls but as painted images. Otherwise, so much was different. Ground-level walkways connected the many buildings rather than second-floor bridges all leading ultimately to the towered castle at the center.

They passed large courtyards and chambers crammed with clerks and secretaries busily handling the work of overseeing the land. A fine breeze and the design of the palace ensured air moved without ceasing through the halls and corridors, allowing the scents of the flowers and gardens to penetrate indoors.

It didn't hurt, either, that large urns planted with flowers bloomed in corners and alternated with water fountains and mosaics as the central designs of each large space. The plants matched the edging colors. The further into the palace, the more they encountered subtle flowers of blue and greens with modest blooms and intense odors.

Although the sun was about a quarter above the horizon, everything warmed to the point sweat began to seep through Leander's tunic and dampen the mantle at shoulders, back, and chest.

As they drew close to the royal buildings, finer clothes and jewels dripped from the courtiers and petitioners crowding chambers. Leander's finery diminished in comparison even without the likely sweat marks. Most people seemed calm and at ease in the heat, but perspiration marked his forehead and neck.

He'd never come so close to the heart of power in its full glory. At most, he'd seen them from the distance, the same as his sister. Or, in the library, in twos and threes on the occasions when the great ones came to consult with the librarians rather than summoning them as the middle-rank servants they were.

His mouth grew dry and his stomach queasy despite his having drunk much fruit juice and eaten little when he broke his fast.

It did not help when Rik led Leander away from the public halls through a small doorway so low he had to duck to get through. On the other side lay a circular stairway only wide enough for two very thin people to walk abreast. Leander followed Rik around and around, up two flights, before they ducked along a series of dim halls.

A gentle tap on the back of one hand startled him. After passing by so many glorious chambers, they'd ended in a narrow passageway with little adornment other than guards standing at either end.

Slanting light from windows helped illuminate the short stretch.

Glowing stones in baskets hung at center, the shadiest part—right next to a single arched wood door, painted a deep purple untouched by sun.

"You should bow when you meet her." Rik nodded to the guards in either direction before laying a hand on the metal latch. "But you need not kneel, for this is a private audience. Take a seat only if offered one and otherwise remain standing."

"I appreciate the guidance." Leander swallowed the lump in his throat, only to have another manifest in its place. "And what . . . How should I call her?"

"'Your Excellency' will do." A gentle smile warmed the guide's face. "You need not fear her. You have come to help. She appreciates that."

The door led to another hall also with guards, and beyond that a chamber neither particularly large nor fine. The chairs and tables all bore signs of repeated use—scars and marks on the wood, scrapes on stone.

No mosaics anywhere, only white-washed walls interrupted on either side by a simple door. Then again, few works of art could match the luminescent lake. The far wall lay open to a balcony, with long shutters folded back to allow an almost uninterrupted vista. A few roofs of those buildings closer to the sea than the royal residence interrupted the expanse, but they were easily overlooked in contrast to the wondrous swell of blue and green waters.

Even this high, the lake proved large enough to offer no hint of how far beyond lay the other side. Ships ventured to and from the port where the city curved around the palace, their many-colored sails shining as so many jewels or stars scattered across the surging waves and depths.

Alas, Leander could not allow time to enjoy the view. Or the light fragrance of the waters mingled with flowers from the gardens below, and the hint of moisture on the breeze.

Three people sat on cushioned benches with their backs to the lake. How could they look away? Perhaps long familiarity or the need to do business and awareness that it would distract them.

Or to see how much it distracted those they summoned before them.

Rather, those *she* summoned before her. The Terparchon. Daughter of daughters in a line tracing back to the first rulers over Codaros.

He'd seen her many times before, but never this close, at least not with his feet on the floor. There was one time, when he was young and still learning the roofways, that he ended in the wrong place at the wrong time. Hanging on the edge of a tower replacing a group of crumbling roof tiles with his leg-handler nagging him to work faster. Although nearly upside-down, all the blood rushing to his head, he'd glanced through a window and recognized the woman on the other side though then she was only a dancing princess and designated heir.

The strands of gray streaking the thick mass of dark hair coiled atop her head didn't show at a distance. They softened the harsh lines of her long and narrow face, along with the wrinkles or sleep lines marking her brow. Her burnished skin had a faint green cast, and her deep-set eyes opened wide.

A purple mantle stiff with gold thread and jewels draped over a table to one side. Several bracelets and other adornments rested atop it. Although he'd never seen her in such plain attire, she seemed comfortable wearing only a light green tunic. The folds covered her arms past the elbow and fell below mid-calf right where the straps on her gilded sandals began to wrap around her ankles. A single chain of twined silver and gold wrapped one ankle, though otherwise she lacked any jewelry. Without the bracelets and other anklets to distract, nothing hid the strength in her solid body—or the thick, almost winter-weight mantle of blue draped across her lap. Her hands tangled in the fabric, holding tight.

Standing or seated, she dominated the room.

Only after several breaths did Leander truly register the others present.

Rik stood behind the Terparchon, close enough to fall within her shadow. Catching Leander's gaze, he nodded.

Drawing in a breath so sharp it hurt his belly, Leander set his hands against his chest and bowed deep. Straightening, he shook for a moment, unsure of protocol but certain his place was to respond, not initiate.

"Leander of the Winter Palace, who came down from the roofs and stayed with his feet on the ground." The Terparchon's words nearly tripped over each other she spoke so quickly, but her warm tones filled the chamber.

He froze, hearing her speak not only his name but show familiarity with his origins. Swallowing hard, he bowed again albeit not quite so deep.

"This is Amara, a former dancing princess who remains to guide them and offer counsel to me." The ruler waved a hand at the white-haired, lavender-skinned elder in tunic and mantle of blue seated to one side.

The woman smiled and nodded, perhaps more, but Leander couldn't tear his eyes from the Terparchon.

"Rik, who serves various of my court by their own choice, because they will not take a different place." The Terparchon reached back over her shoulder, and Rik clasped her hand briefly. "And Idan, who has been a cherished friend for all my life, and only recently ceased to serve as a compeer partnering princesses in their Dances."

The elder to the ruler's other side, equally white-haired but taller and stockier and with skin of black that shone dark brown under the sun where exposed by his red tunic and gray mantle, likewise acknowledged her words. His full lips curved in a smile, but his dark eyes held a tinge of sadness.

"You may speak freely before them, but no others."

Her phrasing surely meant he could engage in questions and answers as usual in the course of his investigations. It was only his speculations and findings he should keep close. Given the expanse of the court, not to mention the royal family, he might face pressure from others on that point.

"What have you been told of your assignment?" The Terparchon's hands twisted the fabric in her lap, knuckles tightening.

"Your Excellency wishes to discover why a Shadow of the Moon has vanished, to be replaced by flowers such as no one has ever seen." Leander stood straight, shoulders back, rather than keep bobbing up and down.

"We must know if this is an act of war, an attack by however many persons, or a sign of some subtle plot against us. There are many tales flying about court. They have reached even me—that it was a lightning strike, the work of the strange sorcerer rumored to live on an island in the lake that moves around by their will, or . . ." Hands still knotted in the fabric, she rose and paced up and down the room.

Although graceful, as befitting a dancer, her movements somehow freed Leander from the need to focus solely upon her. Breath still high in his chest, he took in the concern clear on the others' faces. As well, the signs of nerves or unease. The former in the case of Amara, one of whose legs twitched; Idan exhibited the latter, the undertone of his skin taking on a dull cast despite the sunlight.

Whirling around, the Terparchon pointed a finger at Leander, dark blue fabric dripping from it as the rest of her hand retained a close grip on the mantle. "You are to uncover the truth, whatever it may be."

"As you command." This seemed to require a bow.

"Rik will take you to see the site." The ruler waved a hand at the eleee, who likewise bowed though with far more ease than Leander.

"I have been there already," Leander offered, rather than take Rik's time when it wasn't needed.

"Have you now." The Terparchon shifted from frenetic energy go stillness. "And what have you learned?"

"I never saw this Shadow before, but if it was at all similar to that near the winter palace then it is,"—he sucked in a quick breath—"much changed."

A snort escaped Idan. Rik's lips quirked. Amara said nothing, though her leg had ceased jerking and foot rested flat on the floor.

"Nothing else? You've heard nothing?" The Terparchon asked.

If they stood face to face perhaps they would be of a height, but from a distance she seemed to tower over Leander, and her words had added meaning. Certainty bubbled up within him that she had heard he had spoken with Natter, or rather Natter spoken to him. "I've met those who've offered information."

"And what did they say? That it was a lightning strike? That is the most popular explanation, or so I have been advised." Striding back across the floor, she settled onto her former seat. Again the thick fabric, which she had yet to leave hold of, draped across her lap.

Leander paused. He was chosen for a reason, and he must cleave to that. "If Your Excellency will allow, I prefer not to speculate when I have only begun my investigation. I prefer to gather evidence, consider the matter, and see what explanations best suit."

"And how long do you think this will take?"

"I have nothing but this to investigate. I hope to have some answer for you soon, but I cannot say when."

"You're an honest man, at least in this." Again she rose and moved about—stomped without any musicality or grace over to a far corner, away from the windows, open air, and sun and into the greatest degree of shade. "It happened in a night—a single night! This cannot be by chance or accident, even lightning. You do agree, Amara."

For a moment, the Terparchon loosened her grip on the dark mantle. The next, she swung it around to wrap the heavy folds across her shoulders. A pungent, preservative scent filled the room, the type used to keep unneeded clothing safe from insects while packed away. It made Leander's nose itch, and he had to fight the urge to scratch.

"I have not seen the change." Amara rose and went to the ruler's side, leading her back to her seat in the sun. "The Shadows are the work of magic. I know of nothing that might undo them save more magic."

"Idan?"

"This is beyond my experience and knowledge." The elder coughed and pulled a flask from the folds of his mantle to take a quick swallow. "Magic seems the likeliest explanation, but who and where and how are mysteries."

Behind them, Rik crossed their arms over their chest.

"You disagree?" The Terparchon twisted to face them, holding the mantle close about her.

"The Shadows disquiet me and most others. The flowers that appeared here are the opposite. Beautiful and with an aroma that lifts the spirit." Rik tilted their head back, chest rising and a beatific smile lighting their face. "Such loveliness has been known to conceal evil—and yet I cannot find the will to consider this scent and the flowers that produce it ill."

Leander inclined to Rik's view, though his task was to consider all explanations and evidence.

The Terparchon evidently disagreed. Body tight, she shook her head. "What if it is a slow poison?"

A new voice, deep and holding a growly edge, broke in. "You're worrying again."

On the far side, a door had opened. The newcomer drew the eye as much as the Terparchon. He topped her by a few fingers, his broad body heavy with muscles. Even though he wore no armor, he gave the impression of walking with helmet and breastplate. Instead a light-yellow tunic fell to his knees, mostly covered with an equally light golden mantle wrapped around the body twice and the loose end thrown over a shoulder. His short hair remained a bright, light brown and his skin the color of parchment, stretched taut over a broad face dominated by a long nose. A single piece of jewelry adorned him: a chain to match the Terparchon's around one ankle.

Leander recognized the Marchon in an instant. The Terparchon's spouse regularly visited the library in the winter palace and enjoyed good terms with both past and current chief librarian.

The Terparchon whirled, hands raised and body suddenly shifting pose. A power whirled about her, and sparkling energy filled the room. The hairs along the back of Leander's neck stood on end, and he wanted to sneeze.

Rik, Amara, and Idan all startled, but recovered quick enough to back away and leave the bulk of the room for the two rulers facing each other. Leander didn't remember moving, but found the wall hard against his back and nowhere to retreat. He could only stay in place, keep quiet, and hope to survive.

An instant later, the power doused, but the Terparchon remained stiff as she regarded her spouse.

"Too much, am I?" The Terparchon tilted her head to the side, regarding the Marchon through narrowed eyes.

"Did I say that?" he asked.

"You didn't need to."

"Your question is then answered." Despite the defensive tilt of the Terparchon's body, he strode closer to within arm's reach.

"What is your explanation for this, then?" She waved a hand off in the direction of the former Shadow, now flowers.

"I don't think it is an attack, although the guard are on alert and will remain so. Why should it not as easily be a compliment, instead? That bare rocks bloom under the light of your rule?" The Marchon touched a finger to her temple, trailing it down along her cheek to her neck.

"You've never liked the Shadows." The Terparchon met him gaze for gaze, though her throat worked and she swallowed as his finger continued to move.

"Your mother was obsessed with them. That's reason enough." The Marchon's finger reached the thick winter mantle and he grabbed a hunk of the fabric.

"I am not my mother." The Terparchon's lips drew back and she spoke through clenched teeth.

"No." The Marchon tugged on the mantle, then let go. "Investigate this change, by all means, but let it go while your investigator does their work."

The Terparchon regarded him for a long moment. Then, with a snarl-smile, her hands loosed all hold on the mantle and let it fall around her. Turning her back on the Marchon, she faced Leander instead.

His knees shook, but he stayed upright with his back against the wall.

"You are now in charge of this matter." The Terparchon waved a hand. "Go, and bring me back an answer."

Leander started to sway but managed to turn it into a bow. He kept his torso and head low, as senses and the needs of the investigation returned to his mind. "If Your Excellency will allow?"

"What do you require more than you have already been given?" she asked.

"Permission to ask questions of whomever I may consider connected to this or in possession of information that may help me find an explanation for you." He didn't move or glance up. His hands trembled, but he'd earlier decided what he needed to do right by the investigation, and he was a librarian. Truth mattered, and it would outlast any ruler.

"Rik will see that you have authority granted to you."

"Including the right to speak to the princesses?" Leander straightened, bobbing his head then lifting his chin and gazing straight at his ruler.

"Why?" Her stance had eased, and though the word came out with a sharp edge, her face was calm. He might even call the twitch at the edge of her lips a bit of a smile.

"Your Excellency has raised the involvement of magic. The princesses may provide some insight into how this might have been accomplished."

Rustling suggested the others in the room had shifted about, but he dared not move his gaze from the Terparchon.

"Amara knows the most, more even than I." The Terparchon waved a hand at the other woman, who nodded. "You may speak to her and the others as needed."

"Speak to the compeers as well," Idan offered from the far wall where he'd retreated.

"And the musicians, the healers, the librarians." Rik stood near Idan, giving a half-smile in Leander's direction. "The gardeners and cooks. There are many who use small magics in their work, even though none approach the extent and variety of what Dance magic accomplishes."

A short laugh escaped the Terparchon. She jerked her chin at the Marchon. "And I suppose you will tell him to speak with the guard as well."

"You've already suggested it. I should think he might wish to speak to anyone or everyone." The Marchon turned his hand out, openly smiling.

The Terparchon shook her head, but gave Leander a nod of agreement. "Very well, Rik will arrange for you to speak with those you choose—except my children. If their names arise in conjunction with this in any way, you will bring word straight to me."

"You don't think—" The smile dropped from the Marchon's face.

"No, I don't think they're involved, but this is new. Nothing of this kind has ever happened in all the centuries that the Shadows have graced the land. Has it?" Again she pointed at Leander, this time without the dripping folds of fabric, much more at ease despite the concern clear on her face.

"The chief librarian is having the records searched, but no word of anything had been found before I left to come here," Leander said.

"You see? This is unknown territory. It is reason to worry." The Terparchon wove her hands together. "I need to know if we are in danger."

All heads turned toward Leander.

$$\text{❧} \quad 4 \quad \text{☙}$$

Danissa slipped out of infirmary, with its thick, cooling walls, into the full heat of day. Something she did many times and rarely minded, for she enjoyed heat, yet the switch drained energy from her. Her mantle drooped around her, becoming twice as heavy in the blink of an eye. Her tunic dampened with sweat. The smooth roundels circling her wrists and ankles slid and rubbed against her skin.

Her hair cloth unloosed, setting her locks free to curl wildly about her face and shoulders. The weight heated her neck. Rather than continuing forward across the courtyard, she shifted sideways. An alcove offered shade and a stone bench. She settled down, enjoying the comparative cool. Above her curved the roof, complete with down-spouts on either side to redirect rain water to nourish plants or join the rivulets trickling through channels around the edge of the square. The slow-moving water filled the air with a soothing chime.

Although the alcove lacked decoration, save for lines of blue-tinted tiles marking the pipes, the courtyard offered a restful scene. First and foremost, an array of large stone planters allowed a dozen mid-high trees and bushes to rise and provide shade in the open plaza. A warm breeze rustled the leaves before slipping through Danissa's hair.

Every wall bore numerous small mosaics. A green-and-purple fish here, nearby a stand of gray rushes with blue star frogs peeping through, a yellow sun-watch flower blooming in a far corner. The sheer variety should clash. Instead, the different parts offered reason to take one's ease. To sit and gaze about and absorb.

Likely the hour was the only reason she had the space to herself. At this time of day, most people took rests, alone or in company, and those who did business sought out cooler or more pleasant places than even this courtyard.

Danissa had traveled back and forth between the summer and winter palaces all her life, and no longer questioned why the court spent summer in the high heat and winter amidst cold and ice. She'd Danced through too many summer storms on the lake and ice storms in the mountains or along the river, easing and reducing damage, to wonder why the Terparchon insisted on residing where she might monitor dangers.

Yet in moments such as these, driven to refuge from the heat in an alcove, she sometimes wondered what it would be like to spend the whole year in a single city. Perhaps spend a summer where she was not constantly tying up her hair to keep it off her neck.

Digging fingers into her hair, she wrapped the cloth three times around before knotting it and tucking the ends under. A few strands stuck to her sweaty neck, but most now flowed out from the back of her head and down past her shoulders.

As she realigned herself with the breeze, the warm sweep wicked up moisture from her neck and shoulders and cooled her. She slumped back against the stone. Her stomach reminded her she hadn't eaten since breaking her fast, but the mix of warmth and cooling wicked away energy. So easy to sit and rest.

Only to catch her breath at the sound of a well-loved voice . . . and the strange odor she had come to associate with her father and the flask he'd started keeping with him.

"Keep this secret."

The scrape of wood against stone, followed by the shuffle of sandals paired with heavier footsteps, alerted her to the presence of others. A few flashes of light orange through the nearby tree indicated someone had left the infirmary but not gone far.

A second voice followed her father's. Both spoke low, but clear enough for her to hear.

"Are you sure you don't want at the least to tell your family?" It took a moment for her to identify the speaker, but by the last word she recognized one of the oldest, most respected of the court healers, one who traveled with the Terparchon rather than residing permanently in winter or summer palaces.

"No, that's the last thing," her father said. "They can't do anything, and I don't want them worrying, not Danissa, not my father or mother. It may be nothing, after all."

Danissa's breath caught in her lungs. Her mouth gaped open as a fish's, and her hands pressed against her chest. Any urge to cry out and alert them to her presence faded away, strangled by lack of air and the blow of his words.

"Hardly nothing since it drove you to consult me." The healer clicked their tongue. "I will continue my research. There may be some other tactic to make things better."

"The draft helps." Liquid sloshed around something, too much to be the flask her father now so often carried.

"The longer you use it, the less it will be of any use."

"If I'm lucky enough to reach that point, I'll welcome it." Her father strode off across the courtyard carrying a jug. Rather, he lurched for the first seven or eleven steps—right foot quicker than the left—before finding a comfortable pace.

The healer evidently watched for a moment before returning to the infirmary, with the attendant scrape of the door against stone.

All unwitting, leaving her to take apart their words and make them into sense.

Her father would consider himself lucky to reach the point the draft—the medicine?—became of less use?

He wasn't old! His father and his grandfather still lived. His hair might have turned white, but so did most in his family. She expected nothing less for herself, with a few gray strands already despite not yet attaining two decades.

Father—ill.

Dying.

Every fiber of her longed to rush after him. To ward, guard, nurse . . . to care and show her love.

But he didn't want her to know. Her in particular yet also the rest of their family, most of whom lived nearby in the city around the summer palace. She hurt for them, but more for herself. She was the one who'd spent her life with him on the court rounds. Dancing with him as a child, then a talented youngster cultivated as a future princess, and at last the triumph of becoming a dancing princess, and getting to Dance with him and see his pride and pleasure.

Except he stopped joining in the Dance. Only weeks—days— earlier, he'd ceded his place among the compeers to the newest. Let another partner *her* instead of himself. True, Stevan had been a pleasure to pair with, but he wasn't her father.

Who'd begun drinking medicine.

And keeping secrets.

Danissa had planned to wait a day or three before braving the library in search of the ancient text Ylena remembered—thanks to Danissa's questions.

Had Danissa's fear pushed her? Why else had she even mentioned the possibility to Ylena, when it led in directions she preferred not to go—the power in a princess Dancing alone or with only a compeer. Especially not with someone in the palace to investigate and determine what happened. If the truth were known, several would suffer. Better to stay away from the library and keep to her more usual haunts.

What was important was finding the scroll, the spell.

What might aid Ylena's recovery surely could help Danissa's father.

With a broken cry, she leapt from the alcove and lurched off across the courtyard. Away from the dancing pavilion, the royal quarters, her father's rooms and her own.

Toward the library.

She raced from courtyard to courtyard, passageway to passageway. Darted around the cooks, cleaners, sewers, and all the others who thronged the compound and were out and about in the heat of the day. No one stopped her. Most stepped out of her way, likely recognizing her as one of the princesses—or merely someone embodying trouble who might as well go be that elsewhere.

Her breath came in pants, feet and legs aching from slamming against stones and spinning about corners. Such different exertion from even the most physical of Dances. A jolt of pain broke her stride, as she bit her lip on a particularly heavy stride. The harsh taste of blood filled her mouth.

The physical pain subsumed under the fear quaking her heart.

Her need carried her all the way to the final courtyard and the door . . .

Only to stop and realize what a picture she would present—upset, clothing in disarray, and hair threatening to slip loose again.

Hardly the best way to encourage the chief librarian to allow her access to his cherished treasures—much less help her locate one among them.

The more so when he already had cause to think her clumsy or careless.

Running fingers over her hair, she adjusted the tie. Her hands quavered as she adjusted her tunic and mantle, stroking out the wrinkles from the soft fabric as much as she could.

The library loomed high above, with tall, arching windows to catch sunlight and ensure scribes could read the treasures held within. The long, rectangular courtyard thus appeared far grayer and gloomier than that near the infirmary. It lacked any mosaics on the walls, although the paving stones formed a pattern of scrolls and books around a simple fountain of water cascading over a series of shells.

Bending low, she dipped her fingers in the uppermost shell to wash her hands and cool her brow. It eased some of her tension.

But not enough.

Every muscle and sinew in her body still quivered with energy. She vibrated with the same charging, incessant feel as right before a storm.

Again, not a good way to approach the chief librarian.

The sun still shone high and the full weight of its heat pressed down. She hoped her father had retreated to somewhere cool to rest. Others certainly had, for the courtyard lay empty save for herself.

She'd have no problem if there were people present, save that their absence allowed her to have actual space. Ironically, this was not something accorded to princesses often enough. When she visited fetes or fairs on behalf of the court and was asked to dance, too often the crowd gave her barely room to breathe.

Not so now. The ground was not to her taste. The dancing pavilion had a mosaic, but it was carefully crafted to be flat and as even as possible, the tiles aligned with the mortar holding them in place. The stones paving the surface here were rough, with most of the pebbles and tiles sitting above the mortar.

Still, faced with the need to ease a body vibrating as surely as plucked string, the best thing to do was the one thing she'd done all her life.

Dance.

She neither sought nor expected magic in this. Lacked a compeer to partner her, or other princesses to weave about the area with her.

No, this time she danced as she had as a child unaware of power and proper channels. Instead of seeking to gather and focus magic, she moved to join all the elements about her—sun, breeze, earth—and to express all the tangled emotions surging within her chest.

Eyes narrowed to little more than slits, she traced the length of the courtyard with her arms, shoulders, torso, and head drifting this way and that. A slow, sensuous promenade wherein each and every sore muscle had a chance to be stretched and relaxed. Although she didn't seek power, trickles of magic slipped up from her feet, down through her head, and in along her arms to fill her with warmth.

No instruments played, but she had the twin beats of her heart and footsteps.

Step-by-step, her stride quickened and heart followed. Reaching the far end of the courtyard, she crossed the narrower side with two great leaps.

Then twirled her way around the remainder of the perimeter— head back and arms out. Soaking in light and shadow, heat and cool, and bringing them to unity within her body.

Only to stop before the arched entrance to the library. Eyes almost closed, she twirled in place. The frenetic energy drained from her into the earth and air. A sense of well-being pervaded her, turning her body buoyant to the point she walked on her tiptoes. Even her fear for her father shifted and weighed less upon her heart—present but less immediate.

A high ululation trilled above her deep, heaving breaths, the usual method of showing appreciation from a distance, though more so in the winter capital.

"Beautiful." A clear, resonant voice rang out in the emptiness.

Danissa jerked, heels dropping to the pebbles with a thud that jolted her teeth and nearly made her bite her lip a second time. Her tunic and mantle clung to her body, and tendrils of hair had escaped and lay plastered against her cheeks and forehead.

All of which left her in a less-than-generous mood, the more so as her unanticipated audience stood in the center of the archway leading to the library. She'd have to go around, or through, the watcher to reach the door.

Room existed on either side. The stranger appeared average in most ways. Taller than her, but not by much. Slightly more breadth to the shoulder and chest, and a hint of curve to the belly although the latter might be the drape of yellow tunic and red mantle. Dark brown hair hung around their face, several strands clinging to sweaty skin a few shades lighter. Matching scruff marked lines of beard and mustache against a round face set with wide eyes and short nose.

The tang of goldflower hung about the watcher. Fitting, for their skin glowed with the autumnal red-browns of the plant's leaves right when the hips were harvested for scent.

Her favorite perfume, particularly when worn alone or layered with honest sweat from work or dancing.

Irritation drained away, even as she drew in deep breath after breath to capture every last iota of that wondrous smell. She narrowed her eyes, scanning over the gentle face. They struck her as familiar, but as someone out-of-place. The lack of recognition itched at her, but she quashed it and inclined her head toward her unexpected audience.

"I danced for myself, but I am glad you enjoyed watching."

"Very much." They took the last step down, warm brown eyes now on a level with her. "I'd never seen . . . a princess dance so close."

"And now you have." The other had seen princesses dance and perhaps even her before, given the half-slip. That must explain the familiarity. They'd been in the audience sometime, somewhere she'd noticed them. Yet that answer left her unsatisfied. It didn't fit. Although quite appealing seen close, the stranger wouldn't stand out in a crowd.

But she'd have to leave the mystery for later or never, as she had other needs to pursue.

True, her dancing had left her even more in disarray, but calm enough to at least beard the chief librarian and ask for the favor for Ylena without mentioning her own need. This was not the time to be distracted.

"If you will excuse me,"—she nodded her head, a pointed glance at the door behind him—"I must see the chief librarian."

The stranger shifted to one side, but held out an arm partially blocking the way. "You won't find him there."

"What?" Danissa stopped only a step away, close enough to feel heat from their body separate from the warmth of the air.

"I already asked after him, but I was too late. He's gone off with the first librarian to meet with a seller of books . . . or to another library nearby. They didn't leave clear information, only word that they would return in a few days."

The regret in the other's voice resonated with her. Her shoulders slumped as she stood one foot poised to rise into the library—as fragile as a flower petal or leaf torn from a stalk to be tossed by a capricious wind. If both the chief and first librarians had gone, what worth even entering? The library operated on a fairly strict hierarchy, insofar as she'd observed, and the more precious an item, the fewer allowed access even from the ranks of librarians.

Of equal consideration, Ylena always dealt with the chief or first librarian. Would any of the others know what codices she'd viewed?

From despair to hope to somewhere in between. Worse, left on a knife's edge to wait to find out which way matters would fall.

It was too much.

Sinking down onto the stoop, her head drooped into her hands. Her shoulders heaved as her lungs labored for air.

Splashes echoed in the distance, and a breeze blew a few drops over to her, making her realize how parched her lips had gotten.

A modest clay cup appeared before her. Water rippled within, reflecting on the bright blue enamel around the rim. Lines carved into the sides gave it a shell-like appearance. No doubt it was one of the simple stock kept by the most popular fountains for drinking.

"It's fresh." The stranger knelt before her. "You looked as though you might need some, after your dance."

"Am I to take water from a stranger?"

"Would exchanging names make us more familiar?"

"It might." She appreciated the twinkle in the other's eye. "I'm Danissa, a woman of the court."

"And I'm Leander, temporarily a man of the court." He moved the cup closer to her. "May I offer you water?"

"Thank you." The cool fluid slipped down her throat and into her belly, reminding her she hadn't eaten for some time. Yet the water eased her aches and dryness, balancing the moisture she'd lost during her exertions.

As she returned the cup to him, she noticed subtle black ink stains on his fingers and palm.

"You're a librarian?"

"Yes, but more normally at the winter palace." He offered her a hand.

"That is where I've seen you before!" She hardly needed help, but she slipped her fingers into his anyway as she got up.

"You noticed me?" Leander ducked his head, glancing sideways at her with a shy air. The sight made her giggle.

Flashes of memories fell into place from the occasions she'd accompanied Ylena to the winter palace library and noticed Leander sitting at a table copying. Or searching for a book on the shelves. Helping someone or making notes on a wax-covered tablet. And often glancing sideways at Danissa in just the same manner.

"Of course." Her turn to watch him out of the corner of her eyes. Close enough to witness a warm blush spreading across his cheeks as her own warmed as well. "What brings you here? Have you followed the chief to his semi-retirement here?"

"No, I am on special assignment. I thought to consult him, but . . ."

"But he's away." A flicker of unease itched at her. The chief librarian had moved from the winter to the summer palaces well over a season earlier, so why had not the young librarian followed then? Except, her reasons for finding the chief librarian returned and overran her interest in Leander. Her shoulders and back curved, disappointment settling into her bones.

"Did you need to speak with Falfor?" Leander asked.

"Oh yes,"—a laugh escaped her—"though it's not certain he will speak to me."

"I am sure he would. He has always had a fondness for all the princesses."

The look in his eyes made clear the chief librarian wasn't the only one, but even open admiration didn't raise her spirits much.

"Not me." She tilted her shoulder, lips quirking to one side. "I might have almost knocked a vial of ink over an irreplaceable book."

"Someone so graceful as you?"

"It's easy to be graceful when I'm dancing." She sucked in a breath of heated air and fisted her hands. "But I must find a special book and I need the chief librarian's help. I don't even know what it is, save that Ylena, one of the other princesses, remembers seeing it here in an ancient compilation of special dances, and as Ylena cannot come here to search herself, I'm doing it instead. And I *do* need it so."

"A compilation of dances included in a codex. That should not be impossible to locate, even with Falfor away." Leander offered a hand. "If you like, I would be pleased to help you find it, as I can."

"Would you?" Elation at not having to wait, and perhaps not needing to face Falfor's disapproval of her—but above all to not have to wait . . .

"I cannot guarantee how much time I'll have until the task that brought me here is completed." Leander frowned, then cast his hands to the side. "But the summer palace library isn't that large even with the volumes Falfor brought from the winter court. I doubt I will have time today, but perhaps I can steal an hour or two tomorrow."

"That would be wonderful." Danissa stood tall, shaking her head so her thick fall of hair loosened and swayed. "If there's any way I can thank you."

"Hold your thanks until I have done something worthy of it." He sucked in a whistling breath. "First, I do need to ask for your help."

"Certainly. Whatever you wish." She clapped her hands.

"I'm investigating the destruction of the Shadow of the Moon. I would appreciate anything you can tell me about that night." He gazed at her expectantly, eyes dark.

All her joy and elation vanished and a lump formed in her belly instead. Recollections flooded through her. A fellow princess exuding anguish and anger. A strange dance on poisoned earth. A compeer lifting the princess high. A streak of lightning . . .

And the solemn promise they'd all shared—princess, compeer, and witnesses—to keep it secret from everyone else—most especially inquisitive librarians such as Leander.

A princess danced for Leander.

One step out of the cool library antechamber into the warmth of the day and there she was. For those sweet moments, nothing existed save her grace and movement. The heat that set sweat pouring down his forehead and back? A minor irritation. The good yellow tunic and red mantle sopping up the moisture to the extent he'd have to arrange for a special launder? A trifle. The sandals holding his feet to the stone floor below could not weigh down his spirits.

He stretched out his arms to either side, fingertips brushing the warm stones forming the arched entrance. The hint of roughness affirmed he hadn't been swept up into a heat vision. She was actually there in the long courtyard—shining against the gray stone walls.

A princess clad in yellow and bronze as though dropped from the sun. Although she lacked a circlet or broach of silver twined with gold, there was no mistaking her. A slick cloth wrapped around her head, but a glorious array of curls peeped out here and there. Her tunic must have twice the fabric in his, her mantle likewise. Both rippled and flowed around her lithe limbs. Her head tilted back, face turned to the sky so the sunlight brought out the red undertones of her deep brown skin.

He barely heard the chime of water trickling through the shell-form fountain, or even the press of her sandaled feet on the pebbled walks—his heart beat too loud in his ears.

A precious moment to keep inside, whatever else happened. He'd seen the princesses dance before, from far away or up above.

Never so close.

Never had the breeze roused by her passage whip by him.

And of all princesses, that it was *she*—Danissa—who'd visited the winter library several times in company with Ylena, the one princess all the librarians knew since she wanted to read anything and everything. He'd have watched in awe were Ylena dancing, but his heart caught in his throat to see instead Danissa, who rarely sat still even in the library but flitted about.

Who smiled back at him when she caught him glancing her way.

The youngest but not the newest of the princesses—the one he most needed to speak with—but he would give himself the gift of time.

Of these moments watching her.

Duty would call soon enough.

She twirled, her tunic and mantle belling out around her legs, and came almost near enough to touch. Stayed there, only an arm's length away.

A trill burst from him, tripping off his tongue, in celebration of her grace. "Beautiful."

"Oh!" She startled, casting a wary glance his way.

He remained still, quelling urges to reach out for fear of alarming her.

With a shake of her head, she granted him a gracious nod and kind words. "I danced for myself, but I am glad you enjoyed."

Encouraged, he ventured closer. All of a step down to put them on a level—enough to see they matched in height gaze for gaze. Blood pounded in his veins. His hands trembled until he grabbed his tunic and held it taut to reduce the vibrations.

Brown eyes met his, heat flaring between them.

Or not.

"You will excuse me." She pointed at the door behind him with her chin, making clear she expected him to move along. "I must see the chief librarian."

Leander blinked twice, her words sparking curiosity. He moved to the side, one slow step at a time, but extended his arm to block her way. At least he could serve her in a small measure, saving her from spending time on a futile search. "You won't find him."

He went on, offering the same explanation he'd received only minutes earlier on inquiring after the chief librarian. His previous disappointment flared again but quickly subsided. Falfor would return, after all, albeit not in time to offer guidance on Leander's interviews. The first—two princesses, one compeer, and three gardeners—had gone well enough, but Leander had left each with a nagging sensation that he'd have learned more if he'd only been more up-to-date on court gossip.

His regret paled in comparison to that which he'd unintentionally triggered. Indeed, all thoughts of his own situation dropped away in face of Danissa's shock.

She'd paused at his words, body still close enough for her every breath to disturb the air flowing between them. Her eyes opened wide, mouth drooping and shoulders likewise. Such a picture of sudden despair.

Her body swayed. He braced himself, arms out to catch her. Instead of falling, she folded inward and sank down onto the library stoop. Head in hands. Shoulders and chest heaving. Perspiration—or tears?—trickled down her face.

For a moment he wavered, then, catching sight of the fountain, tripped over to it. One circle, eyes always at the base, and he located the discreet cache of cups. All modest works of clay with a single touch of bright blue enamel around the rim. Grabbing one, he filled it from the top of the cascade. Drops coated his hands in the process, cooling him as he returned to Danissa's side.

Squatting next to her, he offered the cup.

She stared at it as though she'd never seen such before—or perhaps in amazement at his effrontery.

"You looked as though you might need some," he said, "after your dance." *And disappointment.*

Yet she hesitated still.

She thought him nothing but a stranger, even though they'd seen each other a dozen or more times in the winter palace library. All those smiles he'd thought meant for him turned to dust.

"Would exchanging names make us more familiar?" He knew her name already, but he could at least ensure she acknowledged him this once.

Then his heart thumped as she introduced herself only as "a woman of the court." Not as a princess, although they both knew he was aware of that, but neither did she add anything else to her name to indicate rank or distance.

"Leander." He gave as much of a bow as he could. His thighs and calves ached from maintaining the awkward position, for the pebbled walk was slanted beneath his feet to direct rainwater to the drains at the center. "Temporarily a man of the court," as the libraries weren't part of the court but rather the palace structures.

At least she took the water from him after, swallowing gulp after gulp.

Then handed the cup back to him, evidently expecting him to return it to the proper place for her. Which he did, intending to go on except he was weak and glanced back.

In time to hear her ask if he was a librarian.

All those quenched hopes flared again. Turning around, he offered her a hand up, admitting he worked at the winter palace.

"That is where I've seen you before."

Oh, there'd be no end to his dreaming now. She'd recognized him in some measure, and slipped her hand in his as she rose.

"You noticed me?" He slapped his other hand across his mouth, too late to keep the question back. His cheeks flamed beneath his cool fingers.

"Of course." She blushed, gaze meeting his for several breaths.

He maintained the gaze for as long as he could, before ducking away sure every inch of his body had turned hotter than ever before. Though he managed to speak, his voice and hers chattering over their mutual disappointment that Falfor was absent. A distant section of his mind stored the details away, at least so he hoped, but otherwise he luxuriated in the moment.

Until the meaning of her regret truly dawned. "You're looking for a compilation of dances included in a codex."

At her nod, elation flooded through him. She needed assistance of the very kind he was trained to provide. "I would be pleased to help you find it."

Alas, even while basking in the warmth of her appreciation, his other pressing tasks could not wait. Duty called—and involved asking her for answers. For the library, for himself, for his sister, he couldn't set that aside to charge forward on her behalf.

He would do what he could for Danissa, but he had to fulfill his reason for being in the summer palace first.

"I do need your help." He swallowed, mouth suddenly dry.

She clapped her hands, all smiles and delight at giving return for his pledge of assistance.

Until he mentioned the destruction of the Shadow of the Moon.

Danissa stilled in place, mouth gaping open and eyes wide.

"You know of it." How could she not?

"I doubt there's any one unaware." Her mouth snapped shut and she swallowed, a too-wide smile curving her lips. "I've seen the flowers. They're lovely and that scent . . ." Her gaze turned distant, inward, and a shudder rippled from her head to her toes.

"Then you will understand that the Terparchon is concerned about the sudden change." His fingers itched for his tablet and stylus to take notes, save to do so he'd have to look away from her and their close proximity.

"Yes, of course. . . ." She settled her hands against her midsection and tilted her head inquiringly at him, back straight and shoulders tense. "Was it not lightning?"

He blinked. "Was it?"

"That's what I've heard from everyone." Her gaze turned distant.

"Let's take things a bit at the time." A heaviness grew in his stomach, for their meeting had already taken a different flavor than the other interviews he'd conducted. Excitement, nerves, thrilled fear—all these he'd encountered, but not, until this point, such wariness . . . toward the subject or toward him?

Leander needed to help her be at ease, to feel comfortable confiding in him and trusting that he would use any information she provided for the good of the land. Perhaps if they left the library courtyard, went elsewhere, she'd lose some of her stiffness.

"Would you prefer to stay here or walk about?" He nodded at the passages leading off to different parts of the palace complex.

"Dance is not an option?" Her smile retained a forced quality, but a hint of sparkle glittered in her eyes.

"You might be able to speak while dancing, but I cannot. I'm not even much good at dancing." He offered her his arm.

Danissa's face eased at his confession of being a bad dancer, and she laid a gentle hand on his forearm. Warmth bloomed where their skin met, a welcome heat. "Then let's walk."

He made no protest when she chose a side way, still too thrilled at her touch. A few steps through a shadowed arch, and they emerged into a long, narrow garden. A single line of fruit trees, none particularly tall but all with wide branches supporting a wealth of dark green leaves with five points apiece. Pale green fruits clustered in groups of three and five amid the leaves. A light breeze rustled through the space, the whole offering much shelter from the hot sun.

A thin line of cobbles ran around the perimeter of the garden, only wide enough for one. Most of the earth lay bare, save for a few clumps of grass where a break in the leaf cover allowed more sun to penetrate —and patches of mosses where the sun might never reach.

"This is lovely." A deep breath brought a faint sweet scent that he couldn't identify.

"It's one of my favorite gardens. I found it by accident when I was young, on my second or third visit. I've never seen more than one or two other people here." Rather than walk about the edge, Danissa guided Leander on a winding route back and forth between the trees.

"A good choice, then." A favorite place likely meant being here brought her comfort. Indeed, her shoulders and back seemed less tense as she drew in deep breath after deep breath. Alas, time to return to the topic at hand though he kept his tone as light and casual as he could. "Many people reported a strange lightning strike hours after the storm. Did you see it?"

"I . . . Yes."

He studied the ground so as not to trip on any exposed roots, gazed on the interlaced tree branches, looked anywhere and everywhere except straight at her face. Yet in the process, he managed to always keep her in the corner of his gaze.

"How would you describe it?" he asked.

"A thick bolt, cutting through the air fit to crash into the earth."

Her hands traced a jagged form in the air that he failed to visualize. Still, she'd further differed from others he'd spoken with. He'd started at the dancing pavilion, where he'd found few princesses or compeers, and spiraled outward through those he met by chance and tracking down the people they suggested he speak with.

Some saw a flash and most heard a crack of thunder so loud it drowned out all else. None said anything about the bolt itself.

"How far away could it be seen?"

"I don't know. Far." Her free hand fluttered in the air, but the fingers resting on his arm pressed a little heavier.

"Then, how far away were you?"

"Far." She led him on a stark angle between two trees whose trunks had inclined toward each other.

She hadn't offered any details about the distance, in contrast to the bolt. The librarians under whom Leander served had taught him that one of the best ways to figure out who told the truth and who lied was to ask questions. Lots and lots of questions about details, and to keep wrapping back to key elements but inquiring about them in different ways. The more details a person shared, and the more the details agreed, the likelier they were telling the truth. Liars had to make up details, and sooner or later they'd either get caught in contradictions or exhibit a noticeable pattern of providing generalities.

Before he could inquire further, a red and gray form whirled in from the side.

"Danissa! I've been looking everywhere for you!"

After a moment's surprise, Leander recognized the newcomer as one of the princesses he'd met earlier. In every way, she was unmistakable. A tunic and mantle in odd shades of gray fluttered around her tall, thin figure. A wealth of red hair topped her long, pale face, the skin showing an unhealthy grayish cast. Dark brown eyes squinted at him, causing wrinkles to wreathe them.

Jola had pled a commitment elsewhere but promised to speak with him later. A common enough occurrence that he'd taken little notice. Nor would he have considered the interruption cause for note—except that she didn't look his way at all.

"Jola, what—" Danissa dropped hold of Leander's arm, leaving the skin where her fingers had rested to cool.

"There's a Dance planned. To ward off fires in the Silver Hills. All princesses are needed for practice." The other princess turned to Leander without meeting his gaze. "You do understand, librarian."

Whether he did or not, Jola whisked Danissa away so fast he scarcely caught a breath.

Danissa left nothing behind but the fading sensation of her touch.

He'd seen her dance close up, spoken with her, touched, flirted—and been seen, touched, and flirted with.

That much he had for their next meeting, with the knowledge that he might be able to help her after his work on the inquiry was done. He had reason to speak with her again.

But first, he had to continue interviewing her, for surety flowed in his blood that Natter hadn't sent him wrong.

She definitely knew something about the destruction of the Shadow of the Moon.

Information he had to elicit from her, and hope that in so doing he didn't have to destroy the fragile connection aborning.

Given a choice, Danissa would never have run from Leander. She detested running.

Dancing involved attaining alignment between body, music, and power. While a dance might include steps that appeared to the unaware eye as similar to galloping, in truth they relied upon connection to and reinforcement of musical beats and pulsating power.

Running, on the other hand, called for getting from one place to another as fast as possible. It did not require grace or carefully calibrated balance. Those who raced across long distances might achieve and maintain a rhythmic pace.

Regardless, this particular run bore no semblance whatsoever to dancing. Jola yanked Danissa in her wake, a firm hand clamped firm around Danissa's wrist as they went on a pelting, twisting sprint. A dash down one passage, and then a sudden lurching change. Another shift in direction, then a bolt across a courtyard.

Danissa's feet hit the ground heel first with a heavy grind that set her teeth rattling. Her sandals offered no cushioning whatsoever. Worse, one of the ties holding the leather to her feet had begun to work loose so that an edge of the sole flapped with every step.

Her legs ached, and sweat covered her body. Her soaked tunic clung to her skin to the point she looked forward to the next opportunity to strip and toss it in a laundry pile. Her mantle had also got wet enough she'd have to send it to hang in the laundry steam room until clean.

Danissa detested running.

The more so when there appeared to be no true need. She'd run if late to participate in a Dance, but not for practice.

A group of servants carrying covered baskets stopped and laid them down long enough to press hands to lips, heads turning as they drew to the side and watched. A trio of courtiers, in elaborate mantles and hung about with enough jewelry to chime as they walked, retreated against a wall and stared at Jola and Danissa with surprise and burgeoning concern.

"Jola!" Danissa roused strength to yank back against the fingers clasping her. "We're drawing attention."

The other princess hesitated. Stumbled for a moment, even, though she regained her balance within a breath. A quick turn, and she stopped.

Danissa wrung her hand free from Jola's grip, alternating between massaging the sore wrist and her thighs. She dragged in deep breath after breath, glad they'd paused in the shade of an arched passageway between two buildings.

At the far end, a glint of blue beckoned—the distant lake. The air flowing about them with a soft whistle carried a hint of moisture.

No eyes watched them here, freeing Danissa to set her hands on her hips and glare at her fellow princess for several moments.

Though she always found it hard to be angry at Jola for long.

The older woman never appeared well despite dancing hours with ease. Part of the blame lay in her horrendous sense of color. Nearly every other princess, and countless servants, had offered suggestions— subtle, deferential, or with outright condemnation—yet Jola persisted in choosing horrid shades of gray, yellow, and green that gave her skin a pasty color.

In turn, the unhealthy cast of her skin made her eyes seem even larger.

It was Jola's eyes that caught Danissa, reminding her of her mother that last year as she'd withered away to nothing but big, dark-brown eyes set in a skeletal face. Otherwise Jola and Danissa's mother had almost nothing in common, in appearance or life. Still, Danissa cherished those fleeting moments when she glanced at Jola and saw her mother's face overlaid on the other.

As always, the sensation vanished quickly.

Jola leaned back against the wall, shoulders tight as she pressed against the cool stone. A shaky hand brushed drops from her forehead. The movement altered the angle of her face, dispelling the resemblance.

Freed to glance around and take in their location, Danissa scratched at her head. The movement nearly dislodged the cloth around her curls, but she rebound it tighter.

All the while summoning up a mental map of the palace and placing them on it in relation to the library and the dancing pavilion. The three points formed a distinct triangle rather than a line. Danissa had missed the signs, too busy tumbling along in Jola's wake, but the other princess had not taken them on any of the direct routes to the dancing pavilion.

"You said there's practice." Danissa peered down the passage at the distant stone facade of the princesses' residence.

"Yes, later." Jola stretched, the muscles and sinews in her back crackling. "When the afternoon bleeds into evening."

"Right before the Fire Dance?" Danissa asked.

"That's tomorrow." A wave of Jola's hand dismissed the urgency she'd shown earlier.

"Then what are we doing rushing about in the heat of the day?" Danissa had rushed herself earlier when it was equally hot, bustling from infirmary to library, but surely Jola hadn't seen that to throw back at her.

"Not here, not now." The older woman clapped her hands together, fingers wrapping tight as she cast sharp glances to either side. "Let's move on."

Without checking, Jola started off.

Danissa remained in the shade, rubbing her wrist. The muscles weren't particularly sore. She'd heal fast enough. It was being dragged away Danissa resented. Jola had rescued Danissa from having to answer unwelcome questions, but *she* and not the other should have decided when to leave Leander.

Jola deserved respect as a more senior and experienced princess than Danissa, but . . .

She wasn't behaving as herself, not at all. Jola usually granted Danissa equal respect. After all, Jola was the child of craftswomen in a minor city while Danissa had spent years traveling with the court before becoming a princess, in addition to growing up the daughter of the leading compeer.

True, Jola had taken on duties to help keep the princesses organized. Thanks to the older woman's insistence, Danissa had signed on for regularly scheduled visits with Ylena. Danissa would've done the visits on her own, albeit perhaps not quite so many and not on a schedule, but acquiesced to more after polite but repeated water-on-stone requests.

Grabbing and yanking was not at all like Jola.

Then again—for once Jola's ghastly color wasn't all due to her tunic and mantle. Part was really her. Every part of her vibrated as she half-pleaded, half-demanded Danissa accompany her.

Her eyes glanced this way and that without ceasing, teeth near chattering.

"What's wrong?" Danissa grabbed Jola's hand, pressing cold fingers between her warmer ones.

"Not here." Jola's spine creaked as she turned her head left and right and left and right.

"Then where?"

Jola froze for a moment. "My chambers."

Danissa gave the other woman another once-over, then offered her arm for support.

For a few moments Jola stared at the extended elbow as though she'd never seen such a thing before. With painful slowness, she wrapped her hands around Danissa's elbow and forearm. Her cool fingers slipped and caught in folds of Danissa's mantle, as both were covered with a degree of sweat, but the older woman's nerves seemed to steady with support. She didn't lean on Danissa, even though she clutched.

Their first steps went awry. Both were too used to leading in movement to cede to the other, but by the fifth step Danissa settled into the follower role. The necessity of deferral and adapting her movements to Jola set her teeth until she made a dance of it. A minor dance of shifting forward on tiptoes then subsiding and waiting for another step forward. The challenge amused her long enough to see them over into the nearby residence hall and up one flight of stairs to Jola's chambers.

On entering, Danissa stopped half-over the threshold. She'd never visited Jola before, nor considered the import of the other princess enjoying a room at the end of the building closest to the royal residence, right at the corner with large windows on two sides. Even with the shutters closed over to keep out the day's heat, sufficient light trickled in to reveal a large, welcoming space.

The impression of size proved misleading on second view. It was likely no larger than Danissa's, merely lighter and with the furniture arranged to allow for that. The bed and reclining sofa formed an L set almost-but-not-quite against the exterior walls to catch any breezes slipping through the shutter slats.

Danissa's sandals scuffed against the stone flooring as she drank in the surroundings.

Jola tottered over to sit on her bed. A plain blue blanket covered the mattress resting atop a rope-strung bed frame. Shelves along walls held shoes and a paucity of trinkets and baubles, far fewer than Danissa's rooms. Then again, Danissa and her father had the luxury of storing some possessions with their family locally.

Other shelves held Jola's clothing. A wooden frame stood near the window. Garments that needed time to lose their wrinkles hung from the top rail, as did an ample supply of lavender sachets to keep away insects.

The greatest luxury lay tucked into one corner: a private water closet well hung with dried flowers to ensure a pleasant scent.

There was no sign of dust anywhere, yet the rooms had a hint of disuse.

A blue-glazed pitcher of water sat atop a tray on the low table between the sofas, with two crystal goblets beside it. No condensation clung to the pitcher's sides, but it was full. A thin slice of waterfruit floated at the top, the orange and green streaks giving off a faint sweet-sour aroma.

One glance at Jola and Danissa gave up any hope the other would take upon herself the usual hosting duties. Danissa lifted the heavy pitcher and filled the goblets halfway.

"Here." She passed one over to Jola before taking the other and settling onto the vacant sofa. The fabric groaned and condensed beneath her, adjusting to her proportions.

At the first swallow of the warm water, Danissa turned her face away, unable to hold back a grimace at the heavy tang of fruit starting to turn. She drained it nonetheless, not willing to waste it or wait between summoning a servant to provide a replacement.

Setting the glass back on the tray, she pulled up her feet and lounged along the sofa's long expanse.

Jola drank in slow, steady sips without any reaction to the heavy fruit taste. Her feet remained on the floor and shoulders hunched.

Danissa waited until the older princess had finished her drink and put aside the goblet before speaking. "Now, why did—"

"Don't you know who he is?" Jola interrupted, the bones in her neck crackling as her head swung around. Her eyes flashed.

"Leander? A librarian from the winter—"

"The librarian summoned to investigate the destruction of the Shadow of the Moon." Jola leapt to her feet, pacing around the room in a swirling pattern.

"Yes, I figured as much." At least this time Jola let Danissa finish her thought. Watching the older princess trace swirls made Danissa's head swim. She sat back up, swinging around to let her legs dangle off the side of the sofa.

"Yet you talked to him as though he were anyone."

"I've seen him before, in the winter palace library." Not merely seen but admired, though Danissa kept that to herself. "It doesn't hurt to be polite. It's not his fault he was given the task."

"He's a danger."

"No. We just tell him it must've been lightning." Even to her own ears, Danissa's voice weakened by the last word. His soft, resonant voice rang in her head, asking question after question.

About where she'd been when the lightning struck.

"It's not that simple." Jola settled on the sofa beside Danissa, vibrations pouring off her body to jangle in Danissa's bones and teeth.

"It can be." Danissa flinched at the pleading note she hadn't intended.

"Don't you see? We're in the greatest danger here." The other princess hunched and stared at Danissa.

"But we didn't do anything!" They'd only watched.

Danissa and Jola had both stood on good ground covered with healthy grass under an uneasy sky. Fresh from passage of an immense storm, clouds lingered and concealed most of the night sky. The pungent scent of downed greenery filled the air as Gisela, the newest princess, danced on the Shadow of the Moon.

One of the dozen or so Shadows of the Moon. The old Terparchon, the current ruler's mother, had regularly danced on any Shadow she passed near. Sometimes, in her nightmares, Danissa still heard the old Terparchon cackle as she did so.

A decade or more Danissa's elder, perhaps of an age with Jola, Gisela's face had twisted in agony as she danced over the Shadow. A sickly gray-green seeped up from the stark, white stone of the Shadow, tainting her light-brown skin. Once-graceful movements broke into jerky motions. The longer she remained atop the Shadow, the more she sickened.

"Exactly." Jola's fingers twitched until she wove them together. "We didn't intervene. We didn't report it. We didn't do anything."

"Except, I went for Stevan." Danissa shivered, the muscles in her legs quivering at memory of racing through the gardens to find the newest compeer. For a moment, her neck warmed with the heat of Stevan and his brother Brenn hot on her heels as she led them back to Gisela.

Stevan had braved the poison of the Shadow, joining Gisela in a Dance.

"We watched," Jola said. "We were there."

Sparkles of light and fire flickered in the air around Gisela and Stevan until the moment he'd lifted her high. Then they coalesced around her arms as she reached up and summoned lightning to strike the Shadow.

"We should've said something right away." Jola rubbed her hands together and breathed on them. "The Terparchon would've been angry, but surely she'd have remembered the odd charge in the air after the storm, and forgiven us. Eventually."

"Maybe, maybe not." Danissa tucked her hands beneath her thighs, warming them another way. "But Gisela and Stevan . . . Gisela was, is, still so new to court and Stevan so new to being a compeer . . . What might she have done to them?"

Danissa had mostly stayed away from the others ever since, other than a brief meeting to promise silence. Gisela and Stevan likely hadn't noticed, too wrapped up in each other. A lovely pair who exuded the joy and happiness of love's first flush to all who looked upon them.

Much though Danissa enjoyed dipping her toes in the games of love, seeing them even from a distance made her wonder what it would be like to slip further under.

Regardless, she had no desire to see the two questioned and punished for an act that saved Gisela—and destroyed a landmark Danissa had always feared and hated.

"It's too late, any way we look at it." Jola wrapped her arms around her torso as she rocked. The sofa legs creaked beneath. "She walks the halls at night, you know, pacing back and forth."

Danissa rubbed her head, for this didn't match her memories of the intervening nights. No one had paced up and down the corridor, and certainly not Gisela.

Then again, Jola's rooms had an air of disuse.

No doubt she'd spent those nights with her regular compeer, Nefeli, who was also the Terparchon's eldest child. Although the two women had not taken public vows, they were known to keep close company under most circumstances.

Surely Jola hadn't meant Nefeli marched up and down halls.

Her mother on the other hand . . .

"You mean the Terparchon?" Danissa licked her dry lips. Leaned over and poured some more of the sweet-sour water and gulped it down despite the bitter taste that remained.

Jola nodded, bouncing up and down with the movement until the sofa's creaky protests prompted her to rise and pace herself. "Even the Marchon can't get her to stop, she's so worried. Keeps repeating something about her mother never forgiving her."

"The old Terparchon never would have anyway." A cackle resounded in Danissa's ears, dispelled only with a sharp shake.

"What?"

"Never mind." Unlike Danissa, Jola hadn't grown up with the court and had joined the ranks of the princesses after the almost-bloodless coup that had transferred power from the old Terparchon to her daughter and son-in-law.

"We have to keep quiet. We promised." Jola settled back on her original sofa, hands clasped and pleading eyes turned toward Danissa. "And we did nothing wrong."

"If anything, Gisela and Stevan did something right." After lightning struck the Shadow, the rock had crumbled away to reveal two bodies well enough preserved to suggest they'd been murdered centuries before. Then they'd turned to dust and blown away with the wind.

"But our only security is in silence." Jola turned a long finger on Danissa. "Stay away from Leander."

"I'll have to talk to him. He's asking us questions." Danissa leaned back against the wall, startled to find the stone cool. "He's supposed to ask questions."

"Then tell him about the lightning and nothing else. That's all he needs." Jola leaned forward and grabbed both Danissa's hands. "We have to stay strong. Brenn won't be in much danger, for what could he have done? He's no dancer. But you and I, we could've intervened."

"And we'd have been wrong to do so." Danissa shivered. "The Shadow always was a blot."

"But it was the Terparchon's blot."

And around and around they went, agreeing on so much.

Yet every time Jola repeated the simple warning for Danissa to stay away from Leander, something in her resisted.

She wanted to see him again. Talk to him.

She had to. He promised to help her find Ylena's codex. That was her only reason.

Or was it?

✵   7   ✵

Leander wished for a princess on a falling star.

White light flashed across the sky, arcing from high above only to fade as it neared the waning moon. No other stars moved, content to shimmer in their scattered array against the wine-dark expanse.

A clean knee-length tunic covered his body as he leaned against the frame of the open window: the same dark green he'd worn that morning.

He'd left it hanging from a hook in the wall when he dressed to see the Terparchon. Somehow, in the space of a day, someone had laundered and dried it, returning it to his room softer than before and carrying a whiff of salt-scented soap. The ill-mended rent had vanished, redone to the point he'd hardly recognized it as being his except that the new, tidy stitches replacing his traced the exact same jagged line from one knee to hip.

Likewise, someone had worked similar miracles of cleanliness and tidiness on his mantle. On all the clothes he'd brought with him, in fact. Earlier in the evening, a twinkling-eyed person a good decade his elder appeared at the door and whisked away Leander's formal wear as well. The stranger smiled and told him the clothes would be popped in with the royal family's and princesses' and compeers' attire for laundering.

"It's no trouble," the elder had said as they gathered the elegant tunic and mantle with Edrena's eager assistance. "The court pays its launderers well. Has to, with all the tunics and mantles the princesses go through. These'll take longer than the others, but like as not we'll have them back before you need them."

And they'd toddled off with Edrena's soiled tunic as well despite Leander's protests.

They left behind fresh pitchers of water for their use, the liquid cool enough beads had rolled down the outside of the clay jugs well into the evening. They'd even provided a new, unmarked wax tablet on which to take notes, without removing the old one in case he hadn't yet transcribed the information onto parchment.

All this care was intended to make things easier for him to do his job, no doubt, but he wasn't used to such efficiency in service to him. Rather, he rendered it to those who wandered into the library.

Then again, he'd been summoned to provide service by finding an answer for the Terparchon. So this was not so much for him as for her. That he found easier to accept.

The problem being he wasn't completely sure what question she wanted answered.

As a result, sleep eluded him. He stayed up well past the long, lingering dusk when the folk of the summer palace came out to play and laugh. Past the withering of their voices as most returned to their chambers to sleep, and into the comparative tranquility of full night.

Strange and familiar sounds occasionally broke the quietude. Distant calls heralded night hunters flitting about on soft wings. Snores ranged, with gentle huffs emanating from the pallet in the corner where his sister slept while a louder honking irregularly resounded from down the halls where others slept. Further away, people not yet sleeping continued to chatter, and assorted footsteps betrayed various people of the court moving from one place to another. Headed for trysts, no doubt, or returning from the same.

The air had turned distinctly cooler than the day, a welcome change albeit nowhere near the chill of summer nights in the winter city. A breeze rustled, hinting at the greater gusts high above. Wispy clouds raced across the sky, leaving the bulk dark save where stars glittered or the half-moon glowed silver.

Down below, from the not-too distant earth, came an answering glimmer.

Something in the gardens in the summer palace gave back light to the sky.

Based on the location, the most logical source was the former Shadow.

Why would the flowers shine?

A good question, but first to confirm whether or not the flowers gave off the illumination.

Slipping from the windowsill, he pulled on the simplest of his sandals. He snatched his sheathed knife from under his pallet and strapped it about his waist.

Nabbed a newly cleaned mantle, too, in case the ground proved far cooler than three floors up.

He regretted the delay a moment later when his sister roused.

"What're you doing?"

"Go back to sleep." He wrapped the mantle around his shoulders. "There's nothing wrong."

"You're off again? Where?" Edrena shifted from sleepy to awake faster than ink dried on a page, a gift he envied. One minute lying prone with an arm thrown above her head, the next she'd bolted upright. Leaning over the edge of the bed, her hands scraped along the floor as she searched for sandals.

"The gardens. I won't be long." Leander grasped the door handle but didn't open it.

"The gardens? Gardens." She wiggled as she fastened one sandal, the bed creaking. "Wait, the Shadow? Are you going there again? You've got to take me this time."

"I'm only off to check something." The words tripped off his tongue, lacking any strength.

"Let me come too. I won't be any trouble. It's not as though I'd be studying now, at night." Another creak and scraping sound, and she'd got both her sandals on.

He opened and closed his mouth once, twice, without managing anything more than a hissed indrawn breath. Better to have her here, safe inside, or safe with him?

She took his moment of silence as assent, as it probably was, and snatched up a thin gray mantle to wind over her tunic.

Slipping her hand into his, she followed—for a wonder—as he led the way out of their chamber and down the hall. Carefully placed luminous stones and baskets of moss offered sufficient illumination to ease their path down the stairs. The closed stairway was warm when they entered, but cooled as they descended thanks to a steady flow of air from a window at the bottom.

Once out into the full dark of night, he made her wait until their eyes had adjusted to the limited light from partially hidden moon and stars. She shifted her weight from foot to foot, energy fairly vibrating off her. Only when his sight had settled into the thousand shades of gray tinted with muted colors did he lead her to the narrow path he'd followed the morning before.

Birds called in the distance, night dwellers with low hooting exchanges, but they paid him and Edrena no mind. Many of the flowers had closed their petals tight, their narrowed lines making the path appear different. Their scents lessened as well, though the air was heavy with moisture under the cover of the trees. Even less light penetrated here, making the task slower as he sought the gaps between bushes. First he followed the mosaic stones, then gravel.

Why view the site by night? Because the change had happened in the dark. Yet Edrena's presence hot on his heels set his fingers tightening on the hilt of the dagger at his belt, though they were alone.

A few paces before the gravel disappeared into a narrow earthen trail between bushes, wide enough only for one, Edrena skipped around him and darted forward. No chance now to turn back.

So easily she followed the trail that he remembered only because he'd walked it so recently. She had keen eyes, better sight than him perhaps, but still . . .

"You went out to see the Shadow today, didn't you?"

She didn't say anything, yet paused long enough to toss her head.

The dim light obscured her expression, but the angle of her body shouted her answer for her.

"Can you never obey?" A futile hope. She had so little fear that he feared for her.

"When it really matters." She forged onward. "And when it makes sense."

"And who decides?" Might as well make her admit the answer.

A highly visible shrug, due to a fortuitous beam of moonlight between clouds and a break in the tree cover overhead, showed the glee on her face. "Me."

"How will you manage when you pass your exam and have to obey all embassy rules and the laws of whichever country you're stationed in?" He followed close, keeping two steps back so as neither to lose her nor step on her heels.

"That's different."

"Oh? Many of the rules and laws may strike you as having no sense." A hint of the celestial scent reached him, driving out every mote of drowsiness. "You won't be tempted to bend and break?"

"Of course not. It will be my task to represent Codaros."

Such surety. A promise he could only hope she'd manage to keep.

"Though some of the laws of the other lands are so silly." She stopped and leaned in, voice dropping even though no one else could hear. Her eyes glinted in the limited light. "Did you know there's a city where no one's allowed outside during the hours of dawn and twilight?"

"But you'll follow that if you go there?" He asked.

"Yes." Her shoulders slumped, then she bounced on her toes and started off again. "Maybe I'll at least find out the reason why."

The path widened, and the light floral perfume strengthened. Tension drained from his shoulders and back. He breathed deep, grudging every exhalation because it was time not spent inhaling the aroma.

"It smells even better than before." Edrena shifted to walk beside him, slipping a hand into his.

When they reached the edge of the clearing with the former shadow, words fell away.

Even from a distance, the flowers glowed as though a miniature sky in reverse: midnight blue stars against soft silver. His feet sank into soft mosses and patches of grass in turn. They swallowed up any sounds of footsteps. Edrena traipsed along next to him in silence, the warmth of her hand in his and faint whistle of her breathing the only indications she hadn't slipped off to wander on her own.

A number of other figures stood out against the wide circle garden. The light of the flowers called forth subtle resonances in them, for every one boasted a faint halo of silver-and-blue.

Edrena, too.

And him.

Some of the others nodded. Others paid him and Edrena no mind. No one moved close.

He stopped where a walkway traced a circle around the flowers. The firmness of stepping stones beneath him helped him avoid swaying under the influence of aroma and light.

Despite being the source of most of the illumination, each petal, leaf, and stalk showed clearly as they swayed in the breeze.

And perfumed the air.

"What are they?" Edrena's voice dropped to the merest whisper, fingers trembling against his.

Not from fear, not her who once climbed an icy tower to refasten loose roof tiles. Something in her voice sent a rill of warning through him. His hand tightened.

"No picking any."

"I wouldn't!" Then, after he gave a soft huff of disbelief, she leaned against him. "I only thought it for a moment. But you didn't say what they are."

"No one knows, yet, or if they do they haven't told me." He bent and leaned forward, amazed at the details visible despite the depth of night. "Flowers out of legend."

"Magic." Edrena knelt next to him and likewise curved in to sniff. One of the blooms swayed toward her.

"Undoubtedly." Leander drew her away, just in case. "But good or ill?"

"They must be good." Edrena wriggled, fingers twitching and reaching for the flower which appeared to return her interest.

"So I hope." He pulled her further back. "Until we know, caution is the wiser choice."

She quivered, but settled against him. "I hate it when you're right."

"I hate it when I'm wrong."

"But just look at it, it's so much better than the Shadows that it *has* to be good. I mean, think of the one near the winter palace. You can see it from half of the palace roofs, and it's always awful." Another wriggle and she burrowed her face into his chest for a moment. "Even snow never sticks to it, or ice. Nothing does."

"True enough."

Her qualms passed, sooner than he wished, and she drew away with a promise not to go too close. He twined his fingers together rather than hold on.

He had to trust her sometime. She'd surely pass the exam at the first opportunity, and be off on her longed-for adventures.

Easier to let go when he stood close enough to the flowers to breathe in their heavenly perfume.

At least Edrena kept to her word, when he checked as she turned a wide, wandering circle. She stayed not only a couple arms' lengths from the blooms, but also from the others watching, as he, in quiet.

Were the flowers good? Perhaps even having a positive influence upon Edrena.

What of the disappearance of the Shadow, might that be good or evil?

Then again, those weren't questions he'd been tasked to explore.

Or were they?

Something every successful librarian learned, the sooner the better, was that people did not always come to them and ask for what they really wanted. For varying reasons. Sometimes they didn't realize. Others weren't ready to admit their underlying desires or they thought they already knew where and how to find the answer and came asking for that rather than their true goal.

The librarian's task was two-fold.

First to ascertain, in so far as possible, what a person truly sought, and where and how to help them discover the answer. Danissa's desires from earlier in the day being an excellent example, for she'd admitted looking for a codex though likely truly sought information to help her achieve . . . whatever it was she ultimately wanted.

Therefore, Leander had to consider not merely what the Terparchon had asked of him but how.

Her first words referred not to good or evil, but safety and danger.

Perhaps she'd been honest in her desire—or in her fear—and her advisers, instead, had raised the issue of good and evil, of the Shadow versus the flowers.

But he had a second task: to document the events for the library's records of the land, for later generations to consult and remember times before.

The flowers did not strike him as evil any more at night than by day, although the lovely smell might have something to do with it. Could be ill in pleasant disguise.

He preferred Edrena avoid drawing close enough to touch or be touched, as a precaution.

He'd lost track of her, but found her quick enough. She stood partway around, talking to someone only a little taller and also attired in gray over a tunic with a pink tinge. A corded belt emphasized their waist between the swell of breasts and hips.

Following the stepping stones, a sense of familiarity grew. Closer proximity allowed recognition. Although he had yet to speak with her, she'd been pointed out as the newest of the princesses, Gisela.

But she couldn't hold his attention for long. As he meandered near, the aura around the person between him and Edrena flared into a silhouette he couldn't mistake: Danissa. Not after studying from a distance for so long, then watching her dance earlier.

His feet stepped off stone onto grass and moss, uneven surfaces that made him sway.

Or was that merely her proximity?

"They are lovely, are they not?" He stopped out of arms' length, waiting a sign to draw any nearer. "And the scent is nothing I have ever come across before."

"I've never seen anything similar either. Nowhere, not here or in the winter gardens or anywhere between. The gardeners say the same, though one or two hints at having smelt something similar once upon a time. None have managed to say where or when." Her voice fell on his ears, as soft as his as though she spoke only for him to hear. She tilted her head. A shiver rippled along the lines of her body, visible thanks to the strange halos cast by the flowers. "Did you follow me here? To get your answers."

"No, I didn't know you were here until now." Though he might have ventured out, had he known. "I came to see the flowers by night."

"Oh." Her eyes met his, flashing warmth despite the dark, as though she'd heard what he hadn't said.

"That's all. Questions are for daylight. This is,"—he moved one step closer, aligning his body so he faced the flowers at the same angle —"something different."

"It's a moment of dreams, of balance." She shifted toward him, hand brushing his. "Of light and dark, warmth and cool, and all things being possible."

"Exactly."

Shoulder-to-shoulder, they gazed on the glowing blossoms as the scent of the flowers twined around them.

❧　8　❧

anissa dreamed of a warm hand enfolding hers, and woke well-rested despite how late she'd gone to bed the night before.

She preferred not to probe why the light pouring in through the windows onto her bed had an extra clarity and the cool air an added sweetness. Credit the early morning for the quality of the light and the scent to late-summer blooms. If she happened to leap from under the blanket with a decided bounce, that spoke only to her eagerness to start the day.

The hour of sunrise always struck her as the most magical in the day. When most of the world woke and everything burgeoned with possibility.

Cold creeps formed across her body as the breeze picked up. Although the air warmed slowly, what counted as warm in winter near froze her in summer. She snatched a light tunic in a warm pink, the soft fabric eased the chill as it covered her from shoulders to mid-calf. With a red cord binding her waist and two matching bracelets on her left wrist, she was dressed enough to leave her room.

Under most circumstances, she'd never do so in such informal attire. Only to visit one place, not far.

Her father's rooms.

She'd been a princess for nearly a year, yet she still sometimes walked through the door to her chambers in either palace and looked around for him. They'd shared his suite for so many years that her feet automatically turned left after she went by the stairs at the wide hall of the compeers' quarters. A simple mosaic covered one side of the hall, portraying a landscape of hills and valleys pierced by the occasional river and lake. The stone floor chilled her bare feet, prompting her to hasten her steps.

Almost to the end of the hall, she came to an abrupt stop. The second-to-last door opened, and a bald man with extremely fair skin emerged. He wore a simple dark blue tunic tied at both shoulders, and carried a slatted bucket. From the sloshing, it was still half-full.

He likewise stopped at the sight of her, a smile stretching his face wide and amusement in his eyes. With his free hand, he motioned for her to turn around. "Other end, princess."

"Thank you, Pavlos."

Her heels hit the floor harder as she switched direction and stomped to her father's new quarters. The location was better, closer to the royal wing. His new rooms also had features the former ones lacked: a nicer view, his own water closet. Highly suitable for a retired compeer and counselor to the Terparchon on their own or with partners.

But not a parent with child, for this suite lacked any equivalent to the alcove in which she'd slept for years.

She rapped lightly, in case he had taken to sleeping later.

"Come in, come in." His voice rang out, a good sign.

Yet when she entered she didn't see him at first. A rug of woven rushes covered most of the floor, soft but with a prickly edge that made her miss her sandals. A green sofa suitable for lounging rested against the far wall beneath the wide window, shutters tied back to offer a view of the lake. Another sofa, upholstered in purple, stood at right angles against the wall shared with the next-door suite.

Usually she found her father on one or the other—the green sofa if he wasn't expecting her and the purple if he was.

A new chair had appeared in the room, set opposite the purple.

Although supplied with ample cushions in green and blue, it was a *chair*, a style of furniture rarely seen in these parts.

Her father sat in it, feet not bare but slid into blue slippers that didn't go with his red tunic or silver mantle. His white hair hung in a long braid over one shoulder. At first glance, his hands lay in his lap but on closer view they held his medicine flask.

An expression of surprise crossed his face.

Whiffs of fruits made her nose twitch. Sweet starmeg, peppery redberries. She blinked at the rectangular blue-enameled tray sitting on a low table between chair and green sofa. At the center sweated a pitcher with slivers of precious ice beside two round mugs. Warmer water filled a shallow vessel for cleaning one's fingers. A small yellow plate held several fresh-baked rolls on one end of the tray, balanced by a matching plate containing redberries and spears of starmeg— arranged around a dollop of yogurt dotted with honey.

Service for two—but she wasn't the guest her father had expected.

"Am I interrupting?" Danissa refused to glance at door leading to his bedchamber in case he had a guest there.

"Oh no, no." Idan set the flask aside on the floor by the chair leg and rose with care. He shuffled forward with a big smile and arms out. "You are always welcome."

She snuggled into his hug. This was the safest place in the world. His arms couldn't keep out pain. She knew that too well, since he'd held her years earlier as they watched her mother, his beloved, die. All the same, her father ranked as her retreat, her steadfast, her solid ground.

Did his body feel thinner than before? His cough more insistent and his heartbeat faster?

His hold on her seemed tighter, as though he feared slipping away.

She pulled back longing to ask, but he'd lifted his head to look over her shoulder.

The door remained open behind her. The scuff of feet against the stone prompted her to glance around as well.

"Another for breakfast?" Pavlos asked, both hands now empty.

"You'll stay?" Idan pulled back from Danissa, cupping her head.

She searched for any sign of discomfort or wish that she hadn't come just then, and found none. "If I may."

"Another mug, if you please, Pavlos." Idan waved. "But we have food enough."

"Won't be long." The other man tripped off, closing the door as he went.

"I was hoping I'd catch you sometime today." Idan bent and tugged at the table to move it close to both sofas. Sweat beaded his forehead as the legs squeaked but barely shifted.

Danissa leapt to help. Her hands curved under the table rim, lifting it just high enough to slide across the flat rushes, without making it clear she was doing more than him.

The table dealt with, she reclined on the green sofa making sure to arrange her body with her head at the far end. The better to watch him as he settled back into his chair.

His words from the day before weighed on her. Why didn't he want her and the family to know? *What* didn't he want them to know?

She hated secrets.

Hated holding them herself or having others keep them from her.

Words trembled on her tongue, none suitable for the occasion. All weak, nothing more than pleas for him to share.

Her father held secrets often, but those were matters of state. Or, before she became a princess, details of Dances to which she was not privy. She'd teased him about his closed mouth before, not expecting him to spill anything to her.

She swallowed the pleas. He wouldn't bend to that. She'd have to figure out some other way to entice him into sharing.

If he noticed her abstraction, he made no sign. Indeed, a bright smile made his white teeth flash in the morning light.

"Word has come from the hillside." He raised a finger. "A fest tomorrow, to which we're bidden."

"Another? Weren't we there only thirteen days ago?" She lifted the cool pitcher and poured sweet water into one of the mugs. After her father nodded for her to pour for him as well, she filled the other and handed it over.

"Ah, but that was for your uncle's younger daughter's first child, safely born. This is for your great-grandfather's birthday."

"They always have a lot of fests in the summer, despite the heat. I used to think they were all to celebrate us." Chilly water slid down her throat, easing the tightness in her torso. Her eyes fluttered closed as she envisioned the hilly climb up to the family house and fields. Her, as a young child racing ahead of her parents' more decorous pace. She'd trudged at her father's side, hand tucked securely in his, after her mother's death. In all cases, dozens of family members greeted them with a thousand hugs and smiles, kisses and tears.

"They were. We celebrate life and those who are among the living." Her father raised his mug in a toast to the empty sofa. "Since you and I are often far away, when we are near they have even more reason to take any excuse to celebrate. Although in this case, they would hold the fest even if we weren't present. Since grandleether's death last winter . . ." He pressed a hand to his mouth, tears trickling down his face.

She wept a tear or two as well, though not so many as him. Her great-grandleether had always seemed ancient and distant. Other than sitting Danissa on their lap and stroking her cheeks when she was small, the old eleee had rarely done more than smile at her.

But her father remembered his grandleether when they were more active.

"Grandfather is now eldest." Idan wiped away the tears. "So the celebration of the eldest moves to his birthday."

Instead of drinking from the mug, he set it back on the edge of the table and reached for his flask. A strange, sharp scent made her eyes smart for a moment.

He took a sip, recapping the flask and restoring it to the floor nearby.

"What are you drinking?" She tilted her head and scrunched her face. "It smells awful."

"Something a cook whipped up for me." He wiped sweat from his forehead. "Seems my aging bones don't deal with heat so well as I used to."

Danissa fanned her face, driving away the last wisps of the smell. Something in his words struck her as off. He sat hunched in the chair, so different from all the times she'd caught her great-grandfather lying out in the sun in the morning or even at midday. He didn't do so for long, saying only fools considered the sun a harmless friend, but he enjoyed basking his bones in the heat. Sometimes her father's parents joined him.

These were only three examples counter to her father's claim of suffering in the heat.

"What's in it?" She swung into a seated position and reached for the flask. "It reminds me of the tisanes Aunt Sunia drinks."

And that her mother had tried as well, though the tisanes helped her aunt more than her mother. They'd fallen to different doses of the same poison, or so Danissa heard every time she asked, always with a sign not to speak of the one who'd arranged the poison even though the old Terparchon was dead herself by that time.

Her father winced and rapped her hand, moving the flask to the other side of his chair, out of reach. "It has some of the same ingredients. We're neither of us getting any younger."

"I know." She settled back along the length of the sofa, sipping water. "I miss her and Aunt Yanna."

She'd have no trouble sharing what she'd overheard with either of her aunts. The notion of confiding in her father's family, dear though they were, gave her less comfort. They'd never dealt much with the court other than selling their fruits to grace palace tables, concocting perfumes to tempt the pickiest of noses, and hosting other branches of the family active in trading around the lake.

Indeed, they still gazed on her father with bemusement that he'd been snatched up as a compeer, and exhibited confusion when she became a princess. His work as a counselor to the Terparchon they understood, but for them dances were magic-less communal affairs rather than powerful rituals.

Then again, most of the court held similar views on dance. A handful of courtiers at best appreciated the power and complexity the princesses worked in their underground chambers.

"I miss your aunts, too." They sat in silence for a few breaths before her father heaved a sigh. "Only another moon or so until we leave."

"Time for two or three more fests up into the hills?" She rubbed her hands, wondering what other reasons the family would give as added reason for her and her father to climb up. It was a game of sorts, for everyone knew they'd make the trek anyway, if not quite so often.

"That too." He laughed, skin crinkling in deeper lines around the corners of his eyes and across his forehead.

A knock interrupted the jollity.

"Enter and be welcome." Idan waved at the door, although only Danissa could see him.

She remained stretched out along the sofa, expecting Pavlos back with a third mug.

A newly familiar voice set every muscle in her body afire with energy instead.

"Have I come too early?" Leander asked.

"No, no come along in. We're in luck, my daughter is joining us." Idan rose and clapped hands with the younger man before turning to indicate the purple sofa. "Please, take your ease."

The night before, shadows had concealed most of Leander. Danissa had stood next to him drinking in his presence and voice without truly seeing him. Morning light revealed him in full color. Health bloomed on his warm skin and gleaming hair. He stood straight, body shapely under green tunic and mantle, sandal straps wrapped around muscular calves. One arm held a scroll. A canvas pouch slung across his chest evidently contained heavier items, and a knife hung from his belt.

Seen so close together, Leander and Idan had similar sizes and builds. Yet the contrast made inescapable how much Danissa's father had withered. His shoulders were rounded, and folds of skin sagged at his neck and along his arms.

"It's a pleasure to see you again." Leander bowed to Danissa, then turned to her father. "We met by chance yesterday."

He glanced back her way, meeting her gaze. Neither mentioned their midnight encounter watching light glow from the flowers.

They'd said nothing there she'd be ashamed of sharing. All the same, Danissa preferred to let the memory belong only to them rather than reducing it to a fumbling description. Words couldn't encompass what had passed between them in silence in the garden.

Strange to have such a meeting with someone she'd known less than a day. Then again, he'd come across her at the end of her fruitless search for the chief librarian—and the codex.

"I didn't expect to see you again this soon, but here you are on breakfast terms with my father."

"He's been kind enough to offer advice on subjects with which I am less familiar." Leander started and broke eye contact with her to smile and nod at her father.

"It's nice to see you getting along so well." Amusement warmed Idan's voice. "But sit, Leander, and enjoy the food."

With exquisite timing, Pavlos arrived as Leander settled onto the purple sofa. He sat rather than reclining, sandaled feet flat on the rug. His gaze heated as he traced the lines of her hips and legs, stretched out on her sofa, but he remained in an upright position. The scroll and satchel he bestowed on the sofa next to him, on the far side away from Danissa.

Pavlos had brought additional fruit sticks and honeyed yogurt as well as a mug. Idan settled back into his chair as Pavlos adjusted the set of the table and tray. The servant also rearranged the food within reach of Idan and both guests.

Danissa stared at the rushes in the rug and the lines tucked under and over each other. Unlike the night encounter, her memory of the day before was fragmented. He'd questioned her about the Shadow until Jola snatched her away, then let it be at night. Before the questions, though, how much had she shared about her need to get into the library, find codex, find spell . . . Everything mixed up with her father's secret. She didn't want him worrying over her—likely he desired the same.

Until she had something to offer, she'd maintain silence.

She filled a mug for Leander, then leaned over under the cover of the noise and pitched her voice to reach only Leander's ears. "Don't tell my father about the codex."

Leander jerked his head slightly, then smiled at her and nodded slightly as he accepted the mug.

As Pavlos left, drawing the door closed behind him, Idan proved not completely unaware of exchange.

"So, tell me how you met my daughter." The amusement in her father's voice set Danissa's muscles twitching as though on pins and needles.

Leander sipped water, throat moving as he swallowed, then set the mug aside. His head tilted back, a distant expression on his face. "I saw her dance. She thought herself alone. She was kind enough to forgive me for staying to watch."

"You Danced on your own?" Idan asked.

"Only a few steps, nothing connected to Dances. It suited my mood." She shrugged and dipped a slice of starmeg into the yogurt.

"Dances can be beautiful,"—he leaned over to pat her foot—"but I've always thought you loveliest when you dance for pleasure."

She blushed and smiled at him, kicking out a foot. That way she didn't betray the second surge of delight at Leander's soft-voiced "I agree."

"Now." Idan clapped his hands together. "How fares your investigation?"

Leander raised his eyebrows and popped a redberry in his mouth. His shoulders stiffened. He didn't look at Danissa, but a ripple of unease stroked up her spine.

"Oh, she can be trusted." Idan patted her foot again. "All of the princesses can, though not all the compeers."

"Father!" Danissa laughed because she always did. Her father had teased her aunt Yanna about it for years, then shifted to teasing Danissa when she became a princess.

Leander set his plate aside and picked up his tablet, pulling a stylus from his belt pouch.

"It's a joke!" She swung her legs around as she sat up. Was he actually writing it down?

"Is it?" Leander asked, stylus at the ready.

"The best jokes have at least a grain or two of truth." Idan turned his hands out to either side and shrugged. "I trust all the princesses with the good of the realm. I cannot say the same of all the compeers."

"You name no names." The younger man wrote, but in a compact style Danissa found unreadable especially when peering over from the side.

"I have no proof, no surety." Her father scowled. "But neither can I see them doing anything to turn the Shadow to flowers. If that changes, I will entrust you with names and speak them to the Terparchon, but until then I must hold my counsel."

"I value your insight into the court here." Leander wrote more before returning to his meal.

Danissa set her plate aside, appetite gone. She lay on her side on the sofa. Ran over the names and faces of the compeers, remembering the times she'd danced with them in practice or Danced in power. None struck her as untrustworthy. Her father was privy to information she was not, as a royal counselor, but she'd never realized he wasn't truly joking.

Finding one secret seemed to be a thread leading her to others—or rather reminding her of the others he'd always kept from her.

"I will share what I can, as will Amara and Rik. You can trust Danissa also, as I do in most things,"—her father's hand wrapped around her foot again as he smiled at her, his fingers cool against her skin—"but beyond us you would be wise to keep your own counsel."

"Mine is the task." Leander inclined his torso.

"Just so." With a last caress, her father returned his hands to his lap. Something about her expression must have alerted him to her unease, but he misconstrued it for he added in a confiding tone, "Leander is investigating the change in the Shadow."

"We spoke yesterday about it, but were interrupted." Leander turned to her, lips twitching. "I hope we may continue at another time."

Danissa bobbed her head, then bit her lip. He meant to ask her more questions about the lightning strike and what she'd seen. Nothing she wanted her father to hear. The older man might catch some hint in her voice or pose to show she chose which truths to share. Which secrets she kept due to promises she'd made to others. Above all, the mere thought of picking her words with ever more care made her shudder. Later would be better. "Perhaps after today's practice?"

"Of course." Leander turned to face Idan. "You wished an update, for the Terparchon."

She slumped back, one arm falling to hang loose off the side of the sofa.

As Leander spoke, he dropped a hand. The table offered cover, blocking her father's view. In that space, his fingers brushed hers and gave a quick squeeze. The touch sent a thousand jolts through her, that she fought to keep from her face. He understood and wouldn't press her here.

Delight and fright filled her in equal measure.

Too many secrets. If she couldn't bring herself to spill hers, how might she challenge her father over his?

Or, worse, she might pry his from him—and lose hers likewise to a certain quick-minded librarian.

の　9　の

Many things surprised Leander in this, his first visit to the summer palace.

Seeing a princess dance so close he could touch her.

The heat.

Mosaics instead of paintings on the walls.

The sprawling mass of the summer palace with its many courtyards and fountains, all aspects that those members of court who traveled mentioned whenever returning to the high reaches of the winter. Their tales and descriptions proved mere shadows of reality.

Then there was the food.

His imagination had run short of the mixture of sharp and sweet filling his mouth. The short, thin slice of starmeg—notable for the five-point starry marks scattered over the green flesh—had seemed solid when he picked it up and dipped it into the yogurt, but one bite and the whole dissolved into a thick, cool liquid.

He dipped his fingers into the shallow bowl, although the starmeg left no residue behind. Rubbing his hands against his wrists, he waited until his skin dried before touching his clothing. No need to mar his mantle or tunic even if he did have access to better launderers than ever before.

If only Leander also had access to a chair or bench.

Idan sat on the only chair in the room, a solid affair of wood and woven slats beneath layers of seat and back cushions. He'd left the two sofas for his daughter and guest. This could be taken as a gesture of hospitality, except the way the older man leaned back while grasping the chair arms suggested he required the support.

His daughter clearly did not. She reclined on her side, propping her head on one hand. Curls spilled through her fingers. Bare toes dangled over the far edge of the sofa. In between, her body rose and dipped in a sensuous line of hills and valleys. Dipping a redberry into the yogurt, she leaned back and dropped the fruit into her mouth. One swallow, and then she licked her lips as she returned to her former pose.

Fortunately, Leander's mantle and tunic pooled in his lap as he perched on the other sofa, hiding the ways he reacted to her presence. No position offered him sufficient comfort, regardless of how firm the sofa frame or plump the cushions.

How was he supposed to recline and move between eating, drinking, taking notes, and rolling out the materials he'd brought with him?

Best to remain upright.

His fingers still tingled from brushing Danissa's. Her quick glance at him had begged him for discretion in her father's presence. At least she'd offered a time for him to continue, though not a place.

Natter had suggested Leander ask Danissa while her father was around, if she proved unforthcoming. But it was too soon. He'd keep that in reserve.

His feet twitched, toes cold despite the frenetic energy roiling along his legs.

What had he got himself into?

"Other than the princesses, have you anything to report?" Idan waved a hand, sending a faint whiff of astringent air across the narrow space separating them; Leander's eyes watered. "Others you've spoken with?"

"I consulted the library." Leander patted the soft roll of parchment at his side. "But Falfor and his second are away to obtain a compendium of strange flowers in hopes of finding more about those that appeared where the Shadow was."

Idan nodded, stroking his chin.

In contrast, Danissa's body stiffened and her eyes went wide. She subsided back into her relaxed posture with a huff. "Our library's not good enough?"

"The summer palace library is much smaller than the winter. They evidently determined they'd find more or better information off in Erevestis." Leander sipped cool water, swallowing a faint wish he'd had a chance to accompany them. The city, located a few days journey further along the lake shore, on the far side of a wide river, reputedly boasted several libraries and several merchants who dealt in books and other valuable goods.

"Any news?" Idan asked.

"Not as yet. In addition, I've spoken with a number of servants, in particular most of the gardeners, from Teden to Seyara to Natter and on." He angled his head toward the mug, gaze darting back and forth between father and daughter. "None of them admit to so much as recognizing the flowers."

"Wait, Natter?" The older man lifted a hand, the muscles in his neck tautening.

"Yes."

"It's not a common name." Idan rose, wavering a moment before he stomped around the sofas to the window. His back rounded as he laid his hands against the stone windowframe.

Danissa abandoned her languid pose and sat up, exchanging puzzled glances with Leander. "Father?"

"Hush." Idan's whole body shook. Silence fell, broken only by his harsh breaths. A choked laugh escaped him, and he turned around to totter back to his chair. "Has it been that long?" He addressed the question to the floor, then glanced at Danissa. A fond smile stretched his lips. "I suppose it has."

"Who is Natter?" Danissa asked.

Leander sat back, fingers itching to remove tablet and stylus from his satchel, but the sounds of writing might distract them.

"An old . . . rival, I suppose you'd call him. Would-be rival." Idan snapped his fingers and turned up his nose. "Natter paid no attention to me at first, even though your mother and I were an established pair.

Quite unusual. Most other would-be beloveds accepted the first "no," although a few required a second because they came back to see if either of our minds had changed."

"Ick." Danissa mirrored her father's expression, reclining back.

"Too right." Idan patted her feet. "Your mother showed little interest in him, but he hung around until she finally had to tell him outright to go away. Even then, he blamed that on me though he went." Tilting his head to the side, he licked his lips and gave a sharp shake. "Was encouraged to go."

"Officially?" Leander broke and retrieved his stylus and tablet to make notes.

"Oh yes." Idan smiled. "Larissa was a childhood playmate of the Terparchon, and although she preferred not to ask favors, she did so in Natter's case."

"Where and how?" Leander had heard of many people sent off on journeys to other places in hopes their behavior would improve, but the approach failed as often as it worked.

"I don't remember the details."

"When was this? I never heard any of it." Danissa crossed her arms over her chest, glaring at her father.

"You wouldn't. You were young, barely toddling. He ignored you, except when your mother was around."

"Then you would say that the Natter you knew had a grudge against you?" Leander asked.

"Definitely."

"I will take that under advisement." Leander pressed notes in the wax covering the wood slat. "If this is the same Natter."

"It's not a common name—and the Natter I knew is most definitely in palace complex, off in the gardens." Idan waved a dismissive hand.

Although inclined to agree with the older man, Leander could not rely on his assurance. Perhaps the two might be brought face-to-face, or some other measure. If the Natter who'd courted Idan's beloved, Danissa's mother, was indeed the same as the one Leander had met, that cast a different light on the gardener's suggestion that Leander question Danissa.

Which he still needed to do, regardless, for the more he remembered her earlier answers the more incomplete they seemed.

His companions had gone along a different line of thought.

"Did mother have many suitors?" Danissa's fingers danced over the food tray before she selected a slice of starmeg.

"Oh yes. Too many for my taste. Some more serious than others," —the older man's expression grew distant, lips curving—"but she chose me in the end and I always counted myself fortunate for that."

"She used to say you chose her, and she never wanted you to regret that." Danissa gulped down the starmeg as though swallowing anything else she might have said.

"We chose each other." Another fatherly pat on her foot.

Idan's room lacked signs anyone but himself occupied it. The beloved and mother both remembered so fondly had left no traces visible apart from the effect on those who'd known her.

Leander swallowed a slice of starmeg, filling his mouth with the sharp, sweet, coolness rather than give in to the urge to ask about the absent woman.

Or the mutual choosing that softened Idan even in memory.

His head turned, gaze settling on Danissa at the same moment as she shifted to look at him.

An itch along the outer edge of his neck prompted him to tear his gaze away—and find Idan watching both of them with raised eyebrows.

A deep, resonant bell tolled in the distance. A matching vibration rippled up Leander's spine.

"There goes the warning. Practice is being called." Idan clapped.

Danissa was already in motion. Her hands fluttered as she settled her tunic and mantle and ensured neither had any crumbs or juice marks. She glanced anywhere but at Leander as she hustled over to give her father a hug.

Leander rose, but remained on the far side of the low table and food.

He had his reward when she pulled away from her father and had to face him to say farewell.

Except she didn't say anything. Only stared, hands wrapped around the folds of cloth hanging about her sides.

"We'll speak after your practice, as you suggested." A promise, and a hope.

A hint of heat flashed in her eyes, but she nodded. Her feet tapped out a quick rhythm as she fled and the door closed behind her.

Desire to see her dance again welled in Leander's chest, making his ribs hurt. The first taste the day before had only whetted his appetite and appreciation. But work came first, and he had more to speak about with Idan.

Without the distraction of Danissa, Leander made quick work of more slices of starmeg and redberries. Then he set the food aside after topping up his mug with water one last time.

Idan ate little to nothing, nor drank water, but instead retrieved a flask from beside his chair and took a swig.

An astringent smell wafted over, making Leander's nose and eyes smart. He wiped his eyes, barely able to see Idan cap the flask until the third pass.

"My strengthener." Idan replaced the flask on the floor. "One of the chefs makes it for me."

"It's an intriguing aroma." Leander blinked a few more times, sight finally steadying.

"Smells of an infirmary, you mean?"

"That wasn't quite what I had in mind, but it does have a medicinal quality," Leander said.

"To drink as well, but I've gotten used to it. Now,"—the older man pointed at the scroll still resting on the sofa next to Leander—"is that for me?"

"To view, yes." Leander cleared away food and drink, ensuring no crumbs or anything sticky remained on the table. Picking up tray, he paused until Idan told him to set it in the hall outside the door.

Settling back into his seat on the sofa, Leander unrolled the scroll. The parchment whispered as he laid it out. Magic flickered at his fingertips, then the corners settled flush against the table. Bright colors laid out a map of the palace buildings, gardens, and city. Most of the drawings had been traced in charcoal then re-inscribed with deep black ink in flowing lines. A few elements were later additions in a harder hand but thinner ink.

"This is the most recent in the summer library's possession, and I am on my honor to return it directly."

"Two years old, at the least." Idan bent forward and tapped a small square near the lake shore. "This was torn down after flood damage last summer. The Terparchon and princesses Danced that storm, but the water had to go somewhere and she decided the building could be sacrificed. About time, too, for it had fallen into decay after the tower burned in a different storm."

Someone had scratched in a very faint note to that effect, in charcoal rather than ink. The note described the building as a place of retirement, but included no mention of what replaced it.

"It's a swimming area for the children at the children's palace now," Idan chuckled, "although they allow older visitors if accompanied by a child."

"How old must one be to require an escort?"

"Fifteen, why? Do you desire an escape from your labors?" Idan straightened, head tilting and one eyebrow lifted high.

Leander raised his hands in denial. "My sister is here with me, but she is just over that."

"If she wishes to swim, an invitation can be arranged. Lessons too, if she does not know how to swim." The older man settled back in his chair. "I have been known to visit there, thanks to the children of friends."

Leander expressed proper appreciation for the offer and promised to pass it on, then turned back to the map. He traced the lines indicating the walls surrounding palace and the three pairs of gates.

"Those are patrolled regularly, day and night."

"What would you guess the odds to be of someone slipping past unnoticed?" Leander asked.

"Not impossible, but difficult." Idan hesitated, eyeing Leander over fingers woven together. "More than eyes and arms guards those walls. The princesses Dance them twice every year."

Leander waited, but Idan offered no further details.

"The garden with the Shadow isn't particularly near the walls." Leander tapped the spot on the map. "Given those protections, it's very unlikely someone from the outside got in, destroyed it, and escaped, all without leaving any sign or anyone taking any notice."

"Correct." Idan coughed. Bent and retrieved his flask for another swallow.

The scent again stung Leander's eyes, though not so fierce as before. The scroll rolled back up with a snick. Librarians had three minor magical abilities—to return items to where they belonged, to recreate knowledge that had been lost, and to preserve information for future generations—of which Leander had been introduced to two.

Laying hands on the parchment, he whispered "home." The word triggered a small magic invested in the scroll, not him. The roll trembled as he recalled the shelf from which he'd plucked it. The scroll dissolved under his hands and reappeared on the shelf in his mind's eye. A feeling of completion ran through him indicating success, though it was the first time he'd ever worked the spell with materials from the summer library.

In the map's place, Leander set two lists facing Idan, one several pages long and the other short, pulled from his bag. The long had some light marks on it beside some of the names, the short none.

Idan leaned forward. One finger ran down the lists, page by page, then he leaned back and tilted his head inquiringly.

"The long list is everyone who lives or works in the palace this summer, the short those visitors known to have been around the days immediately before the change." Leander didn't need to see the lists to review the names as Idan picked up the pages and flipped through them.

"You're thinking one of the court did this," the older man said.

"I'm not drawing any conclusions yet. There are too many unknowns. The gardeners I've spoken with don't even recognize the flowers that bloom in place of the Shadow." Leander set his hands on his thighs and shrugged. "If someone is behind it, they are likely of the court or among the servants. But names alone, should I ascertain them, will not necessarily provide the answers the Terparchon seeks. Her concern seemed to be for the land's safety."

"Codaros has many enemies and few friends. It used to be worse. Matters have improved under Chloris and Lorenz, but bad blood remains." Idan continued to sift through the pages before letting them flutter back onto the table. "She worries."

Leander took a few moments to realize the names Idan had used belonged to the Terparchon and Marchon. He'd rarely heard them used since they took control of the country. "I hope I may set her mind at ease."

"Word has come from nearby Shadows within Codaros, and one without, that they are unchanged. I am sure other rulers are also interested in learning more about the change, although no one has yet managed to pick any of the flowers and take them away for study. They fade into nothingness when plucked." Idan shivered, then stared at Leander. "You have perhaps the trickiest path to trace. I, too, hope you may set her mind at ease—but only if you speak truth."

"I will offer no lies, nor any comfort unless I find it."

"Exactly." Idan slapped his thigh. "She prefers to face her fears and her enemies head-on."

Leander bowed in acknowledgment. The Terparchon wanted truth. And worried for the country. Invasion, poison, danger . . . that something more might follow upon the change in the Shadow.

"I have, perhaps, grown to be more like her in the years I've spent in her service." Idan coughed again.

Leander jerked, frowning.

"Until recently, I partnered my daughter in Dances as her compeer." The older man leaned his head on his hands, gaze fixed on Leander. "This suited both of us, but it wasn't our choice. Princesses and compeers are paired at the discretion of the Terparchon, and Amara who so often stands for her in running practices. The needs of the Dance rule, although Amara takes personal preferences into account."

All interesting information, as Leander had never particularly considered the matter of matching princesses and compeers. His feet twitched, toes growing cold and not due to any draft along the floor. His mouth became dry and he swallowed hard.

"Who my daughter Dances with is not her choice, but in all other matters she is free. I do my best not to constrain her."

The sight of Danissa twirling around the courtyard the day before flashed through Leander. "Freedom suits her."

"Whomever she chooses, it will be her choice. It must be. I will not abide anything else."

Leander squirmed, trying not to show discomfort that Idan read his desires, though he had no argument with Idan not influencing Danissa. Leander would rather win or lose her regard in his own right. Swallowing again, he set his shoulders and stared back at the older man. "I have responsibilities that constrain my ability to make any choices, or seek any. My duties to my sister, the library, and the Terparchon come first."

"And that is as it should be, for now." Danissa's father smiled, eyes brightening, neither of which gave Leander any great comfort. "I will give you one piece of advice: if you would have my daughter choose you, you must find a way to bring all those into harmony."

❧ 10 ❧

Sometimes Danissa preferred *practicing* to Dancing.

Newcomers thought the practice chamber was an enclosed circle. Although windowless on the main level, glass windows ringed the second level along with a discreet walkway. Seven more windows glinted from above, inset at the center of the gilded wooden ceiling. Those who worked and danced within for long hours knew the design included discreet spiral elements encouraging the circulation of air. Fresh streams cascaded down from certain windows. Sour flowed out through others.

Quite unlike the underground chamber below, where fresh air always seemed to remain just out of reach of nose and mouth, regardless of how much desired during Dances.

One of the male-presenting princesses joked that they could measure the success of any given Dance in the stench of the room at the end, and the quantity of perspiration dripping onto the floor.

There was a reason they wore simple, undyed tunics and sandals to Dance, with no mantles. How they looked mattered less than their movements—and the lack of dye made the tunics easier to clean. Likewise the sandals, although they sometimes wore out in a single Dance and had to be tossed.

In contrast, she had more freedom to decide what to wear to practice. Older clothes, of course, for they would wind up only slightly less in need of washing than her Dance attire. For this practice, she'd selected a well-worn pale-blue tunic that fell to mid-calf, covered by a simple mantle once a favorite for it was the gray-blue of the lake waters and embroidered along the edges with a design of waves and fishes. Alas, the mantle also bore a large stain across one shoulder and over the front where a servant had spilled a half-full platter of grape-stuffed fish. The launderers managed to remove most of the fish smell so only a hint remained, mixed with an ashy, soapy scent, but nothing could completely remove the stain.

A trio of gold and silver chains clattered about one wrist, matching cords about her waist, and a similar anklet above the opposite foot. Her hair she'd pinned ruthlessly to keep off her neck and shoulders. Thin sandals protected her feet and the practice floor. Bright paint blazed against the wood planks, dazzling in images representing different types of dances. Waves for storms, flowers and leaves for abundance, and of course flames for fire.

This would likely be a hard practice. The Terparchon hadn't called for a Fire Dance in several years. Several princesses, including Danissa, and most of the compeers had never done more than a desultory stab at the steps. The previous afternoon had ended with Danissa dripping, despite practice being cut short so that half the princesses could attend a banquet celebrating some visiting emissary or other, from which Danissa counted herself fortunate to be exempted.

Everyone had returned today dressed expecting to sweat. All wore only two layers of thin fabrics. Princesses marked their status with twined cords of gold and silver about their waists while gold and copper denoted the compeers. The presence of more warm bodies hardly altered the morning chill hanging in the chamber despite the rays of sunlight streaming through the eastern windows.

A ghastly mantle in green-and-purple in one corner attracted little more than raised eyebrows and rolled eyes. Jola stretched near Gisela and Stevan, the newest princess and compeer. They were sensibly clad in matching shades of light blue that managed to flatter both Stevan's height and ruddy skin and Gisela's shorter, curvier form and light-brown complexion.

Over on another side, Danissa couldn't miss Heron, the tallest and quietest of them all in pink and red. The brown-haired and brown-skinned eleee was the only princess not born in Codaros. They'd visited the summer palace while on a trading venture from Sirasas several years earlier and somehow become princess. Danissa was certain her father knew the full story, but he'd never shared it with her. Begs and bribes went nowhere with him.

Danissa turned around again and again, the skirt of her tunic belling around her legs. All the princesses and all but three of the compeers were in sight. Among the missing were her father, the Terparchon, and Amara, who regularly put the current dancers through their paces in practice when the Terparchon couldn't do so herself—and the Terparchon's children, compeers all.

Only one musician was visible this morning: Rik, a former compeer who managed to have a thumb in nearly every pie. They wore no mantle, only a tunic as they settled onto a cushioned chair and placed a tall drum before them.

A pat and a twirl roused a bang and a rattle. Then Rik laid a hand atop the skin of the drum, stilling the noise.

"There's time yet," they said, as all heads turned toward them. "Take your ease as you can, for soon you will dance."

Danissa settled into a spot near Heron. She traced the outline of a curved shell painted in purple and blue before starting a few desultory stretches. No sense getting too much into things, for Amara was sure to have them do more warm-up exercises before they began practice. The retired princess always seemed to assume no one had stretched or done any movement since the day before—might as well live down to expectations and save her energy.

She rolled her arms in modest snake movements, keeping her muscles limber and countering the remaining morning chill.

A stir of air announced an addition to the ranks lining the walls. Idan entered with ease, though his ever-present strengthener flask hung on a cord from one wrist. He wore light layers, too, in shades of orange, but the glorious embroidery of flames surging from the hems of his mantle suggested he was sticking to his recent retirement. No one practiced in such a lovely garment.

Danissa twitched and rolled her shoulders and hips to try to smooth out the nervous energy surging through her body. Dual desires struck her: to rush to him and stay away.

When he spotted her and smiled, she waved back.

His brows rose, face wrinkling in puzzlement.

The conflict subsided. Sandals barely brushing the floor boards, she crossed the expanse in no more than a few leaps and ended in his arms.

"How's my ray of sunshine?" He stroked her cheek, knowing better than to disturb the pins in her hair.

"Well as ever. As though you hadn't seen me already this morning." She pulled back and wrinkled her nose at him.

"I try never to presume." Idan wrapped her in another hug, squeezing tightly. The rough edge in his voice suggested he was thinking of her mother.

"Keep holding on." She rested her head on his shoulder. "I'm not ready for the Dance."

"No one ever is ready for fire." Idan squeezed her one last time before letting go.

A rill of energy fluttered across the floor and set her toes twitching. His, too, no doubt.

"Last I heard, there's still a messenger due from the hills with more detailed word of the situation. Any Dance will wait on that, so you may do the same—and have longer to practice." He coughed. Lifting his flask, he gulped down a mouthful.

Danissa fisted her hands at her sides, watching his throat muscles flex as he swallowed. She drew in a deep breath and let the medicinal smell sear her throat.

A boom drew all eyes to Rik, hands raised above the drum. They hit the edge with the heel of their hands a second time, and third.

The flutter of power built to a low hum. It wouldn't rise much higher, due to the paint in the floor and other precautions, but the presence of so many princesses in one place always woke the land in some measure.

With a rustle better fitting to three times as many feet stomping, the Terparchon entered in company with others. Her purple tunic and mantle glittered with embroidery, and the bangles around her wrists and ankles chimed, but she was attired simply enough to make clear she meant to join the practice.

As were her children, all in light color tunics and mantles scarcely less fine than their mother's. Gold and copper cords around their waists marked them as the missing compeers. Their father, too, wore matching cords over a plain gray tunic and mantle. The Marchon rarely joined practices or Dances. The mere fact of his presence set Danissa and the other princesses and compeers on edge.

Not a good sign for the situation in the east and the rumored fires roaming the hills.

Amara wore darker shades of gray than the Marchon as she entered with two more retired compeers carrying drums . . . and Leander of all people.

Blinking didn't dispel his image. He slipped along the wall before coming to a rest only a few arms' lengths from Danissa and her father. He met her gaze and nodded, moving on to do the same with Idan.

Her father showed no surprise at the librarian's presence, but she had no chance to question him.

Amara called them all to the floor to begin stretching. Rik started a slow, soft rhythm.

Perhaps Danissa allowed Leander's presence to distract her at the start. Maybe she glanced at him once or twice, or five or seven times, only to be caught out more often than not. Once by her father, otherwise by Leander.

She thrust awareness of him away while on the floor. Beads of moisture accumulated along her skin as she worked through a series of sun stretches. Bowed low. Rose with the sun. Swayed. Triumphed with the blaze of noon. Then sank and descended.

From sun stretches, Amara set them to warming legs and arms, torso and back. Every muscle was needed as they turned to practicing fire steps. Occasional groans and creaks punctuated the silences between drumbeats.

Danissa had no chance to glance aside. Her whole being focused on internalizing the beat of the drums—as the other former compeers joined Rik. Each drum had a slightly different sound, harder or softer or more mellow.

The drums shifted unpredictably between heavy spates of thundering beats when their different sounds melded into one and softer, slower stretches where the various drummers conducted conversations in rills, slaps, and bangs.

The dance matched the mixture of music. When the drums spoke to each other, Danissa focused on replicating exact steps and arm movements in quick succession and high precision, while trying to match her body and heartbeat to one or another drum. When the drums thundered, she had to shift to improvisation involving leaps and falls, rolls and lifts.

All while avoiding the other princesses and compeers.

Danissa counted herself fortunate in her compeer. She'd danced with her father until his retirement but he'd ensured she had another born compeer to partner her. Stevan could sense where she moved and align his body to best manage the power flowing through her. He'd rather be with Gisela, but they were too new at being compeer and princess respectively for Amara or the Terparchon to let them partner with each other.

Poor Gisela had the worst of it, for although partnered with the Terparchon's son, he was a taught compeer and only approximated Stevan's innate speed and precision.

The practice held Danissa tight, helping her ignore everything else when on the floor. Except, Amara had them rotate. Only seven of the thirteen pairs on the floor at any time, with a new pair slipping in while another shifted out.

When she took a turn off the floor, she busied herself in drinking water and walking about the perimeter so as to keep her muscles loose and limber. Alas, wherever she went—unless she wanted to stare at the wall—she had a fine view of Leander making a similarly lazy circle around the edge. He watched the action in the center but also spoke to other princesses and compeers.

And never glanced her way.

She had agreed to speak after practice. He clearly intended to keep to that.

Unfortunately.

Danissa had assured Jola that she could face Leander's questions and give nothing away. She remained certain.

Yet when the practice ended, she fled to the baths. Normally she'd stay to talk to her father. Not this time. Too hard to face Idan talking about anything except what she most wanted to—or Leander and the counter task of avoiding what she least wanted to.

The heat of steam didn't ease the turmoil roiling her belly. Nor the usually relaxing rhythm of having her skin oiled and scraped. Or the soft, sweet lilac perfuming the oil, her preferred scent. Gnawing the edges of a hard biscuit helped a little, but not enough for her to finish it.

She still had half of the biscuit in hand when she left the baths, neither the first nor the last princess to do so.

Pulling on a clean tunic and mantle in a plain, soft orange to match her father's earlier choice, she tiptoed through the pavilion halls, sandals in hand rather than on her feet.

Alas, her first choice of exit came to an abrupt stop—blocked by Leander talking to Stevan and Gisela.

Before they could turn around, and Stevan at least surely knew she'd nearly stumbled on them, Danissa fled in the opposite direction.

Speeding through the halls, the familiar mosaics on walls and bright floor patterns blurred into a gray mass as she headed for the door on the far side. A new, thin coat of sweat dampened her skin as she ran.

She burst out, letting the door slap closed behind her.

Then stopped.

Sunlight bathed her in warmth unfiltered by glass window panes. A pair of light breezes wafted up the scents of the gardens and the kitchens, giving her a whiff of flowers one moment and meat roasting another.

Before her lay the great plaza. It stretched far and wide before the central palace building, with an excellent view of the lake. An old mosaic covered the breadth, portraying the first Terparchon's selection of the first Marchon. Shutters covered the many tall, thin doors opening out from the palace onto the plaza, and the space was empty of awnings or decorations apart from the intricate mosaic on the floor.

Both were signs the Terparchon had no immediate plans for court festivities.

Under the circumstances, the plaza should be empty. Without awnings, it offered very little shade and most avoided it especially during the height of the day. The sun was approaching its zenith and Danissa should head for her rooms to rest until the cool of late afternoon and evening, especially with a Dance looming.

But the plaza wasn't empty. Someone sat at the far end, dangling feet off the side and resting arms on the lower protective railing as they gazed over the calm lake waters.

A clear sky lent the waters an extra tinge of blue. Ships braved the waves, sails high and oars out. A few distant ships were smudges against the horizon. The closer ones sailed to or from the city harbor, which didn't seem to interest the watcher at all.

Such intense focus despite nothing remarkable in view.

"What are you looking at?" Despite the soft scuff of Danissa's feet over the warm plaza surface, she managed to sneak up on the other.

The watcher started, gasped, and scrambled to their feet. Dusted themselves off, brown eyes peeping through a shock of shoulder-length brown-black hair. Their light pink tunic and matching mantle enhanced the rosy undertones of skin only a little darker than their eyes. Although familiar, no name popped into mind.

"I'm sorry, am I not supposed to be here?" The other had a high voice, suited to their appearance of youth.

"Well, it's not usual, but I don't think there's a law against it so long as you don't linger long or seem suspicious."

"I wanted to look from a roof, but no one will let me up to the highest rooftops and the rest haven't a clear view."

"View of what?" Danissa asked.

"There's another country across the lake, isn't there? Or two? More?" The youngling clasped their hands tight together, bouncing on the tips of well-worn sandals.

"Yes. Codaros only stretches to the promontory there"—Danissa pointed at the land jutting out into the lake far along to one side, then halfway around the other side—"and beyond the island near the far harbor."

"Oh." The stranger shaded their eyes, leaning forward so sharply Danissa wasn't surprised when they stumbled forward.

Whatever attracted them still didn't show to Danissa. The height of the sun had started to raise a haze in the air, blurring longer views. The light and heat pressed on her. The remaining traces of oil on her body mixed with sweat to become less sweet. Tunic and mantle began to stick to her body at certain points.

The other's clothes likewise clung to their skin and ample sweat glinted on their forehead. They evidently hadn't brought any water or other drink with them, an error for this was one of the few plazas lacking a fountain. True, Danissa lacked a drink as well, but she hadn't planned to stop here.

"You shouldn't stay here too long, under the sun."

"I know." The youngling shuffled away as Danissa accompanied them on a wavering track toward the opening between the dancing pavilion and the main court. "Oh, to see better. Farther. From the roofs of the winter palace, you can see three countries. Three! And here are two more, only I can't see anything."

"Come back at dawn, and you may see more. That's the best time. Sunsets are lovely and make quite the play of light on the water and hills." Danissa pointed at the far shore, where the haze had grown and blurred hills and water. "I prefer sunrises with their softer mix of light and shadow. Rise early, that's the best thing."

"I wish I could, but my brother would be sure to catch me sneaking out. He sleeps too light, even when he's snoring." The youngling threw their whole body into the sigh, shoulders rising high then slumping. "The only chances I have are when he's off at business."

"Then ask him to bring you."

"And lose his sleep? He needs it. He works so hard, and worries so over me. He frets when I study too hard—I mean to take the exam to join the ambassadorial service—but also pushes me when I slack off. I can't do anything that would cost him rest."

The push-pull of care going either way reminded Danissa of her and her father when she was younger and thought herself so important in making sure he took care of himself, not realizing how much it was the other way around.

"Some of my family lives up on the hill on the other side of the city." Danissa waved at the palace looming over them, blocking the view. "From their veranda, you can see the far side of the lake, when the weather is clear. My father and I plan to go there tomorrow for a fest. If you're available and your brother agrees, perhaps you might come with us as our guests?"

The invitation slipped out, encouraged by the spark in warm brown eyes at the notion of climbing highland and seeing farther.

"That would be lovely!" The youngling clapped their hands to their mouth, hopping up and down in joy. The next moment, they leapt into action, racing across the remaining plaza straight for a figure standing in the shade of the dancing pavilion. "Leander, did you hear?"

"Yes, Edrena, I heard. It's a very generous offer." Leander wrapped his arms around his sibling, gaze meeting Danissa's.

The resemblance between the two became unmistakable viewed side by side. Danissa longed to assert she'd had no idea of the relation. But she disliked lying to herself.

Drum beats, slow and insistent, sent vibrations through the floor. These seeped up through Leander's feet to reverberate in his bones even as his ears pulsed with thump after thump.

His mantle and tunic hung heavy about him. His skin grew clammy, tunic and hair sticking as the air grew hotter.

Then again, two thirteens danced in various combinations in the room. A handful of musicians and others, not including himself, ranged around the perimeter. This late in the morning, heat was only to be expected.

Yet he'd found the chamber cool when he first entered. An oddity, considering the many windows on the second floor and the window at the apex of the ceiling which combined to let in light regardless of where the sun was. Even in the midst of the heat pouring off the dancers, breezes kept the air moving. One might fancy the breezes danced with and between the people on the floor.

And what a floor. Paint rather than tiles or stones covered wood planks with all manner of images, no two alike. Studying it for a month might leave much to be discovered.

Alas, he had no reason to pause and examine the floor with the attention it warranted. Rather, he circulated around the edges of the room. Stopped and spoke with those who'd stepped out of the dancing to rest and recoup. Not much, only a word or two—an introduction and making arrangements to speak in earnest later.

For all his determination, he kept pausing to watch the practice, so different from what princesses and compeers did in public. There they tripped measures that involved twelve or twenty-four bodies rushing this way and that, turning circles, forming squares, stars, forming bridges with arms so that others might pass under and through.

Here movements were sudden. Amara kept pushing the princesses to be jerkier and compeers to remain very still or vice-versa. Sometimes they barely moved, making small, labored gestures and rising to tiptoe. Other times they all burst into frantic leaps and turns.

The air got hotter, drier, and harder to breathe. A hint of smoke sent him reeling against the wall in a coughing fit.

A hand patted his back. Another thrust a flask before him.

He took a small swig and nearly choked again on the thick substance that filled his mouth. It coated teeth and tongue, and tasted horrid and medicinal. His saliva thinned it, and as drops slid down his throat they soothed.

Drawing in a deep breath, without a single cough, Leander turned to find Idan close.

The older man took a swig himself, then capped the flask. "This is why only princesses and compeers, current or retired, are allowed in the underground chamber when the princesses Dance."

"It . . . The power is stronger there?" Leander sagged back against the wall, letting the stones keep him upright. Strengthener the medicine might be, but his head still swirled.

"Oh yes."

"Is that why only seven princesses are on the floor at a time?" Leander waved a hand at the people gyrating.

"We prefer to Dance in smaller groups if we can. Best to let some rest and swap in and out as needed." Idan cupped his flask between his hands, head turning in a way that suggested he watched Danissa. "Most Dances are done with sevens or elevens."

"It's not what I thought it would be at all." Following Idan's gaze,

Leander drank in Danissa leaping around the floor with a young compeer at her side. The drummers pelted hands against wood and hide, raising such a thunder that he could barely think.

Then, in a moment, they shifted to tapping out a complex pattern leaping from one drum to another. On the floor, the dancers' exuberance contracted into delicate steps and gestures.

"What, you expected the same music and steps as at court balls or village squares?" Idan patted Leander's shoulder. "Sometimes we use those measures, but better to keep a distinction. No sense risking a princess accidentally sparking a fire or blowing up a storm with a careless run of steps at a ball."

No one who lived in the winter palace could doubt the power of the princesses. They shaped the worst winter storms, easing their strength and redirecting their wrath to places where it did the least harm. Without them, the roofs and chimneys would require two or three times as many laborers to keep hale and functional.

By the end of the practice, Leander gladly left the warm room for the comparative cool of the hallway outside.

There he waited for Danissa, who'd headed for the steam baths without a word to him.

And waited.

And waited.

Alone, until one of the compeers emerged from a door along with a gout of sweet-scented steam—and not just any compeer, but the one with whom Danissa danced. Stevan, the newest.

The compeer had an open face, skin with a red tinge enhanced by the heat but also gleaming with touches of oil. He stood a good half-a-head taller than Leander, in suitably long tunic and mantle, gray and blue respectively. His head turned this way and that, long brown braid brushing across his back, before his gaze settled on Leander.

Eyebrows rising, Stevan's sandals barely made a sound as he crossed the stone floor to Leander's side. "Who are you waiting for?"

"Whomever will speak with me."

Stevan took a moment to consider, then tilted his head to the side. "I'm here, and waiting too, so . . . What would you like to know?"

"In your opinion as a compeer,"—Leander straightened, though he still had to tilt his head back to meet Stevan's gaze—"why did the Shadow become flowers?"

"Starting with a hard one." The compeer rubbed his chin, lips quirking to the side. "I haven't actually been a compeer very long, so you'd be better off talking to Idan or Nefeli or one of the others."

"I will." He noted the names, though he'd need the Terparchon's permission to speak with Nefeli. "What do you think?"

Stevan ran a hand over the top of his head, loosing a gusty sigh. "I can't imagine anyone missed that lightning strike. I'd believe anything of it."

"It does seem to have been a massive hit." That was the one thing everyone seemed to agree on. Indeed, no one had admitted to having missed seeing it, although several hadn't realized where it struck until the next day or later. "Where were you, at the time?"

"Oh, ah, in the gardens."

Leander didn't hear anything, but Stevan turned to stretch out a hand to a woman exiting the princesses' baths. Closer to Leander's height, she had a curvy figure clad to match Stevan, head topped with dark curls and face featuring a hesitant smile. Her fingers twined with Stevan's as the two leaned in to each other.

"We're talking about the lightning strike, you know, the one that changed the Shadow when we were in the gardens, um, together." Stevan rested his cheek against the princess's shoulder.

No doubt the gardens offered many comfortable nooks for lovers to meet in.

"You saw the lightning, too, then."

"Yes." She turned out her hands, nestling next to Stevan. "I'd tell you more, but I'm a new princess and ill-qualified to say what changed the Shadow. I didn't even realize I had dance magic until the Terparchon found me, but . . . I'm not sorry the Shadow changed. I never saw one before this and it was"—she shivered—"disgusting."

A flicker of more curls around a corner caught Leander's eye. He sucked in a long breath, the temptation to follow her fighting the urge to slow down and ask more detailed questions of the two before him so as to check them off his list.

Temptation won.

He left Stevan and the princess, only belatedly recalling her name from a brief introduction as Gisela. They exchanged looks when he requested a further meeting, but neither demurred.

Indeed, Steven even offered advice on which way to go, which entrance to leave through.

The heat Leander expected, but brightness also struck him as he left the pavilion. Light reflected off the water, multiplying over and over. Even though he emerged into a thin stretch of shadow, he had to blink several times before his sight adjusted.

An immense plaza stretched out before him, covered with an intricate mosaic easily a match in detail and complexity for the painting on the pavilion floor. This portrayed stylized people and various symbols requiring proper attention to decipher.

Before he could lose himself in it, he turned around and spotted Danissa at the edge of the plaza talking to Edrena.

No doubt his sister had a good reason why this counted as studying. Leander dipped a hand into his bag and pulled out a flagon of lukewarm water. Took a swig and swished it around his mouth, restoring flagon to the bag.

He took all of two steps toward the two women, before the clump of heavy feet on stone stopped him. An older man in thick sandals ascended a stair from the gardens to Leander's side.

Natter wore a tunic as stained with green as before, but this time his legs and feet were clear of grass cuttings. He rubbed his hands and nodded at Danissa. "You found her, I see, but she's a sharp one. Chip off her father's block, flitting here and there."

"Nothing of her mother in her?" Leander kept his tone neutral.

"Not enough." He started, turning narrowed eyes onto Leander. "What'd you hear?"

"That you knew her."

"Knew?" Natter summoned up a glob of spittle and sent it flying down toward the garden. "Loved. No prettier than her daughter. Might be thought less by some were they set side by side. She was a wonder, though, my Larissa. All she had to do was walk through a door and all heads turned toward her, and her not a princess. So much life cut short. Poison. Aimed at the gal's father, so I heard,"—he pointed at Danissa—"but struck Larissa and her sister instead. My love died, her sister survived, Idan thrived. We lost more than we kept that day."

"So you knew Idan, too?" The reference to poison struck a chord, though Leander had no time to check the records. There had been a spate of them at the winter palace over the years. One of his fellow sub-librarians had investigated a suspicious incident recently, but was unable to identify the source of the poison.

"We never took to each other. He always was a wild one, and I've no hand for taming wilderness. I like my gardens neat and tidy." Natter met Leander's gaze straight on. "I get where Idan'd have you going, putting this on me, but his daughter was seen running from the gardens that night. That's truth, and no bark on it. Wasn't me that saw, but it was her."

The older man turned and disappeared down the stairs too late to hear Leander's whispered "I believe you."

Again, he found himself torn between following up, to see if he could get the witness's name out of Natter, or waiting and asking Danissa more questions.

He stayed since Edrena kept Danissa company. Hung back, keeping to the shadows, but some of their words carried.

Such an appealing idea, to go with Danissa and Idan to their family's home and spend a day with them.

Edrena jumped up and down in delight at the idea of seeing more countries clearly even if from a distance.

How could he deny her? It all seemed so simple. Wrap up questioning of Danissa and be free to enjoy time in her company.

When Danissa, following behind Edrena, laid eyes on him, the shock on her face made clear she hadn't realized Edrena was his sister. They resembled each other, but evidently not quite enough when met separately.

"Did you hear?" Edrena rubbed her hands together, every mote of her being vibrating.

"I see you two have met each other. Edrena, Danissa." Leander set a hand on his sister's shoulder, exerting gentle pressure until she calmed.

"Oh yes, and she's been so kind, offering a chance to see from a distance!"

"I'm glad." He eased his hold. "Now, go back to the room. Return to your studies if you want to go anywhere tomorrow. I'll join you shortly, but for now I need to speak with Danissa."

Danissa's arms pressed tight against her sides. Head high, she stared at him with no expression save a tic twitching in one cheek.

Edrena started to whine, only to stop an instant later. She glanced back and forth between them, mouth a round O. "You mean *speak* to her, as in ask questions? About . . ."

Leander pressed a finger to his lips.

"Don't ruin this for me." His sister scowled and pointed a finger at him. Then stomped off.

As her footsteps faded into the distance, Leander advanced as Danissa whirled around and retreated to the farther end of the plaza. She stopped against a stone balustrade no doubt meant to keep people from falling off onto the much lower hill.

An earthen beach stretched wide enough to allow children to dart in and out of the lake under the watchful eyes of adults. Farther along sat the stone foundation of a tower of some kind. All the stones showed signs of scorch marks.

Still farther in the distance, a blurry stretch of land topped with hills and trees jutted into the lake. Matching reality to the maps he'd recently scanned, it was a promontory dividing Codaros from the city-state the chief librarian had headed off to in search of a fabled collection of botanical books.

Leander had never been there. Never left Codaros for that matter, and only traveled away from Tharis, the seat of the winter palace, a handful of times.

"Your sister longs to travel." Danissa rested her hands on the balustrade.

"Yes." Something he both desired and dreaded. Wanted her to have her dream, but if—when—she achieved it, he'd have to wait, not knowing what happened to her wherever she went. Hoping she stayed well and happy and healthy.

"The ambassadorial exam . . . I've heard it's difficult. Intentionally so, to ensure only the best and most driven represent Codaros in the courts of our allies and enemies."

"She'll pass." He nodded as firm as if Edrena, not Danissa watched him. "And leave me behind." The words slipped out.

Sympathy shone clear on her face. He hated to destroy it, but duty weighed on him.

"I have to ask you more questions."

Danissa pulled her shoulders back, hiding her hands behind her. "You don't, I've told you—"

"Where were you when the lightning struck?"

Her mouth opened and shut. She licked her lips, bit the bottom one. Tension poured off her in waves.

"You were there, weren't you? What did you see?" He swallowed as hard as she.

"Nothing, anything. I just . . . stood there and it . . ." She cut one hand through the air in a slanted gesture as though something flashed very close, then returned it to behind her back.

"How far away?"

Mouth shut, she repeated the gesture, waving at the center of the plaza.

"That close."

She winced, wrapping her arms around herself and turning away, back toward the swimming area.

"You didn't do anything. But someone else did." A guess, but why else would she be such a mix of fear and protection? "Who?"

She hunched, turning more inward. A faint sense of energy sparkled in the air, similar to during practice.

Leander's lungs burned as he dragged in a breath tasting of smoke.

Danissa remained silent. He drew close, voice dropping although there was no one around to hear them. A breeze wrapped around them as though closing them off from the rest of the world.

"Tell me. Trust me. I'll arrange for you to be protected." He maintained several hands' width between them—space enough for her to move, to escape if she needed. "Who are you afraid of?"

Of all things, that broke through.

"I'm not afraid of them." She turned on him, eyes flashing despite sparkling tear drops in the corners. "They did nothing wrong. They were trapped on the Shadow. On poison. They had to escape somehow. I fear *for* them. No one will understand. They'll think the worst."

Leander closed his eyes and swallowed. She'd given him truth, but as a riddle to be pieced out. They—one eleee or two or more of any kind—had somehow gotten trapped on the Shadow. Had he ever seen anyone on the Shadow near the winter palace? Not to his recollection, and he certainly felt no urge to go on it himself. It was poison, killing them? And they somehow called the lightning to gain freedom.

The unknown *they* had that power.

Who? No one wielded magic on that level except princesses, and after the morning's practice, Leander would swear they did.

So she'd seen one of the other princesses. Two were eleee, so it could've been one of them, or perhaps two of the female or male-presenting princesses. The number didn't matter how many in the end, surely, for she knew them all. No wonder she was torn.

She shivered with fear or anger. Hands fisted at her sides. If her glance were a dagger, he'd be cut to ribbons for having pushed her to the point. Or she raged at herself for letting it slip. Most likely both.

He kept his distance, but extended a hand. "I believe you."

Then winced at the same words he'd used with Natter, though she wouldn't know.

His words surprised her, for she blinked and swayed before returning to a stiff stance. "What?"

"You witnessed another princess, or two, step onto the Shadow. Become trapped. Sickening, perhaps. Desperate to escape. Whoever they were, they Danced themselves free. Are you even allowed to Dance on your own?"

She didn't answer, but he'd heard enough earlier, during practice.

"Princesses Dance in most often in fives and sevens, so your father said. Sometimes in threes."

"I've never Danced in a group smaller than three or larger than thirteen." Danissa lifted her chin high. "There aren't enough of us to try any higher number. I always thought there had to be three or more."

"So it was one or two princesses who Danced." He kept his hand outstretched, even as his arms muscles began to ache. "Who?"

She gritted her teeth and shook her head.

"Would they want you to bear all the weight of questions?"

"I didn't do anything." Danissa drew in a deep breath and let it out with a whistling sigh. She glared at him. "I hated the Shadow, all the Shadows. The old Terparchon used to dance on them, smiling. I don't see how she could. But I only watched and . . . *They* did it all."

Based on her admission, the change was not the work of an enemy.

"I don't need the full tale for the Terparchon. I can answer her concerns based on what you've said." He moved one step closer, hand still open before her. "Trust me with the rest."

"Why?"

"The library records require a complete account, to document the workings of Codaros and its peoples." To ensure Danissa understood, Leander continued. "I want you to tell me the whole, share names and details, and I will add them to the records."

"Everyone will know."

"No." He stretched both arms out to either side, palms up. "There are other magics besides Dance in the world. Less powerful, but capable of keeping secrets until there is no longer any need. I know them."

She slipped further way, backing up step by step. Sweat poured down her face. Her hands were clenched tight.

He couldn't push her, not now. They both knew that she'd let slip too much. A few words only, still enough for him to guess and to focus on the other princesses. He'd get the truth one way or another. "Take a day or two to decide."

Dropping his hands to his sides, he bowed to her and started to turn. Then he spotted the promontory blocking any view of farther countries.

Edrena. The invitation to the fest. Without turning around, he said, "if you would rather Edrena not accompany you tomorrow, say the word. Or if she is welcome, but not me, I understand."

He couldn't resist twisting his head around for one last glance.

Danissa had her arms raised. Her hands shook, fingers unclenching. She didn't meet his gaze, but her voice came across clear enough.

"Meet my father and me at the front gate at midday tomorrow."

12

Why had she invited him?

If Danissa led the small troop trekking up the side of the hill, she'd not have to face so plainly the consequences of her impulsive offer.

Alas, she followed behind the others. The narrow track offered space for only two to walk abreast unless one struggled through the growth edging it, apart from occasional spots where manual labor had widened it enough for carts to pass. Long, straight, almost-flat stretches alternated with sharp turns and rises as the path wove back and forth up the steep hill to the plateau. Fields of hardy grasses with deep roots and scraggly plants that nevertheless boasted large pink blooms stretched far to either side.

Rain runoff had carved deep, uneven channels down the center. Marks showed where wheels had stuck in mud, although several days of hot sun had baked the earth enough that none of them risked getting trapped. Instead, gouts of dust roused after each and every step.

Another reason to regret walking last. She lingered even further behind, to allow the dust to settle and risk breathing less. A canvas satchel slung over one shoulder, woven in a simple pattern of jagged black lines against undyed threads, held a flask of water, her sandals, and a change of clothing. Though she rarely walked barefoot in the palace, she always did so when climbing the hill to visit family. Her toes dug into the warm earth.

Dust covered her feet and legs. Her light blue tunic she hiked to her knees, tucking the excess fabric under her belt. She'd wrapped her hair in a thin cloth with blue-and-white stripes, to keep dust from settling into her curls.

She doffed her mantle and tucked it into the satchel. So too did all the others, cause for joy and concern. Regular gusts of wind tossed and tugged at Leander's yellow tunic. The lines of his muscles and bones showed with every step, and the many puffs of air lifted the hem high enough to offer a clear view of a shapely backside.

Those same gusts and puffs showed her father as well—gaunt and lean in comparison. How had she missed the way he withered out-of-season? His predilection for long mantles, perhaps, or not wanting to recognize the changes.

Only half-a-moon earlier, he'd climbed this same track at a steady pace. He'd held tight to Danissa as they clambered up the steeper stretches, but as much for her benefit as his.

This time he leaned more heavily on Leander on those same parts. He might deny it if she asked, but the play of muscles made it clear.

Given the care with which he aided her father, Leander recognized it, too. He paused and engaged in a delicate dance of offering help without insisting, letting Idan decide when and where to take advantage. The gentleness of Leander's hands on Idan's arms and back. The phrases that floated back to her, mixed with laughter. Both carried satchels similar to Danissa's, albeit marked with different patterns, but over the course of the climb Leander's grew heavier and Idan's lighter piece by piece.

Yet Leander did all without ever glancing her way to make sure *she* noticed.

She didn't regret the invitation, not now.

Or not at all, or his half only. She wasn't sure which and preferred not to face the million thoughts and feelings swirling through her.

The only sure thing: pleasure in Edrena's enthusiasm.

The girl raced ahead to top every rise. There she'd turn to look at the view, beaming with every mote of her body. Her pink mantle and blue tunic tossed in the wind as she waited for the others to catch up. Once they did, she pestered Idan with dozens of questions, barely pausing for breath between them—and thus allowing him time to recover from his exertions as he chose which to answer.

Danissa only glanced back a few times. A beautiful the view, true, with palace, city, and gardens retreating and full extent of the mighty lake becoming more evident, but she'd seen it a hundred, a thousand times before.

Nor did she spend time studying the hillside and the farming complexes scattered across the various plateaus. The shimmering blue-white line of the river cutting through the hills as waters rushed to the lake, and the smaller swathes of streams where the land lay flatter. The lush growth lining streams, river, and lake, in sharp contrast to the sparser flowers blooming along the steeper, drier lands.

Rather, she watched the slowly shrinking distance between their party and the edge of the plateau. Searched for the rows of short, stout starmeg trees that signaled they grew close. Sniffed any downward breezes for hints of the flower beds.

Anything to hint they drew closer to the scattered cottages and barns at the periphery of the family complex—and the trellised patios and wide earthen plaza at the heart.

Yet with each steep section mounted, it wasn't Danissa who eased her father's passage but Leander.

She might have missed this with a word or two. He'd offered.

If Danissa were Jola, she'd have taken him up on that.

Then, again, neither would she have let slip that she'd been present at the destruction of the Shadow.

Because Jola *hadn't*. Danissa encountered the other princess lurking in the cool area around the dancing pavilion after Leander left her the day before. Jola'd wrung her hands red waiting and watching and trying to decide whether or not to sweep Danissa away from Leander again, or whether that would appear too suspicious twice in a row.

How could Danissa both wish she had and be grateful she had not?

Jola'd pulled Danissa into the comparative cool of the pavilion halls when Leander vanished from sight. Pressed mugs of water into her hands when the other princess determined Danissa required bracing.

"Are you all right? He didn't hurt you or threaten or or . . ." Jola hovered. Her pale lavender tunic and deep-orange mantle swayed with her movements.

"No." Danissa leaned back against the cool stone and drank deep. The chill water made her shiver.

"Oh, how fortunate. He wasn't so bad when he talked to me. Asked only a few questions, but"—Jola's eyes narrowed as she glared down her nose at Danissa—"he scarcely took his eyes from you when we were practicing. I think he likes you."

Danissa took another sip of water rather than answer immediately. Too often, words spilled out of her as earlier with Leander. Jola should be in no danger, as one of the other witnesses rather than an active participant in destroying the Shadow—but he'd figured most of it out though he still wanted the tale from her.

For the library records, as he'd said, or the Terparchon?

"You like him, too!"

Danissa froze. The surprise and horror on Jola's face hardly encouraged confession.

In a twist of fortune, good or ill, Gisela and Stevan hustled around the corner. The rustle of their sandals on the floor presaged their approach, giving Danissa additional time to think of answers—though nothing came to mind.

Stevan led the way, rushing up to Danissa and looking her over. "What happened? Are you all right?"

"Fine. Why, what are you doing here? Weren't you . . ." Danissa waved a hand and gestured in general, rather than betray that she had no idea where they'd been or what they'd been doing.

Alas, Gisela took up the accidental challenge. "We were over at the infirmary. We'd barely arrived when Stevan insisted we return. That he needed to leave, at least, and I decided to accompany him."

Danissa should've focused on the distance they'd crossed to come check on her, but a different detail caught her instead. There was no reason for them to be over at the infirmary unless . . . She turned to

Jola, nearly dropping her mug. "You put *Gisela* on the schedule to visit Ylena?"

The newest princess had, after all, taken Ylena's place among the princesses after her injury.

"Of course." Jola stamped, holding her head high. "Never alone, always with a third—it'll be you in another few days—but the two of them will have to get along well enough to Dance together when Ylena's better."

"Ylena was perfectly polite, although the first words out of her mouth when we arrived were to ask after you." Gisela nodded at Danissa.

Danissa's head ached. The codex Ylena wanted her to find, she'd almost forgotten amidst everything else.

"You aren't all right." Stevan stared alternately at Danissa's feet, then her face. "What's wrong?"

Stevan must have sensed something about how Danissa stood. They had danced together in practice earlier, with him focusing on aligning himself with her movements. From years of dancing with her father, she knew the connection took time to diminish after.

It was only fair to warn them. "I might've let something slip. No names, but . . ."

Jola squeaked and leaped back to shiver against the far wall.

"I'm not ashamed of what I did." Gisela sighed but held her head high.

"We did." Stevan put an arm around her shoulder. "Though you've never seen the Terparchon in a rage or you might not be quite so serene." He tilted his head back, gaze growing distant. Then his brow furled. "There's no triumph or gladness."

Danissa exchanged puzzled glances with the other princesses. She and Jola kept silent as Gisela asked what Stevan meant.

"Leander. The librarian," he said. "I think it will be all right."

"Such an optimist." Jola's mouth tightened, and she clutched her elbows.

Gisela laid a hand on Stevan's arm. He covered hers with his as he smiled at Danissa. "Leander has a good set of feet for someone who doesn't dance. I like the way he walks."

So did Danissa's father, also a born compeer, based on the rapport between him and Leander as they surmounted the second-to-last steep section.

The breezes grew more temperate as they climbed higher. The matching route down from the top of the hill—much gentler and easier than up from the bottom—appeared in the distance, above the trees massing at the perimeter of the plateau.

The wind carried a growing mix of flowers and food cooking. Most of Danissa's kin could likely pinpoint the differences between the various scents. To her, it all added to a whole that represented the family.

Edrena had slowed again, and Idan and Leander caught up with her. Idan pointed something out to Edrena, whose squeal carried despite the distance.

Then Idan and Edrena headed up not on the usual track, but a less worn stretch through the grasses and flowers. Although longer, it rose bit by bit and no doubt struck him as better suited to his condition.

Danissa followed, and Leander, who'd held back, fell into step with her.

He walked with an easy stride, taking the windward side and offering a bit of shelter from the cool breeze.

Quivers raced along Danissa's limbs. Her mouth was dry. She paused for a sip of water, lukewarm despite the casement of clay, then slipped the flask back into her satchel.

The air around Leander vibrated, adding to the ripples of sensation running up and down Danissa's arms. Yet he didn't so much as glance at her. His attention remained on his sister. If anything, he seemed to be resisting—with difficulty—the urge to run ahead and walk with Edrena and Idan.

Soft grasses grew in profusion along the gentle rise, with broken and flattened stems marking where others had walked before. Danissa tried to match her steps with where they'd gone, to keep from damaging more stalks. They scratched her skin, but only enough to clear some of the dust.

He could have joined the two ahead, but didn't.

Just watched his sister.

"When does Edrena take the exam?" Danissa asked.

"This winter. She's already reserved her place." Leander swallowed, throat working as a lump passed down.

"Will this be her first try?" Applicants were allowed only two.

He nodded. Silence fell between them, other than the crunch of grass beneath their feet, broken by a sigh. "She's wanted it ever since she first realized the lands across the river were different countries."

"She said three,"—Danissa hadn't puzzled that out—"but only two are visible, even from the north tower of the winter palace."

"Sirasas, Kitiva, and Orfelth."

"Orfelth? I've never . . ." She stopped in her tracks. She'd barely even heard the name. The city-state lay up the river from the winter palace, above the rapids. "She's seen it? From where?"

"From the roof of the main palace, and the towers." He paused as well, turning to face her. Drops of perspiration dotted his forehead, but his expression remained serene. The only sign of nerves or unease was the working of his throat.

"The roofs? No one ever goes up there!"

His belly jerked in a bitter laugh. "People live up there."

She'd never considered the possibility. If they did, and he knew, and his sister had seen . . ."Did Edrena? You?"

"She and I were born on the roofs. Enough live there to populate a small village." He started off.

She had to move quick to catch up, all the while trying to reconcile this piece of information. The winter palace occupied as large a footprint as the summer palace, but it was bigger. Far bigger, with more and larger buildings, many towers, and less space for gardens. All but one of the few courtyards were functional rather than meant for relaxation and enjoyment.

This did make for a lot of roofs, given all the towers and gables. Still . . . "Why would anyone live on the roof? Especially in winter, with all the ice storms!"

"Someone has to keep the roofs and chimneys in good repair." Leander had his head down, not gazing at Edrena, Idan, or Danissa. "Most of the roof dwellers love the heights and open spaces, although there are huts, with roofs of their own, for unpleasant weather."

"But that's no place to raise children." Danissa clapped a hand over her mouth. An unthinking thing to say, since he'd just shared that he was born there.

"The seneschal and their staff agree with you on that." He fumbled with his satchel and downed water. "Four times a year, guards visit the roofs and sweep up any children they find, no matter how young. They're taken down to the lower levels, to the children's halls. Usually one of the parents goes with them, until they're old enough to be on their own."

"But not the two of you."

"Our mother never told us who sired us. She may not have known. There was only her to go down, if the guards found us." His voice lowered and he slowed his steps, rubbing his wrists. "She loved the roofs, and refused to let either of us go. I know every place she hid us against the sweeps."

"You never tried to get away?"

"She was my mother. And she didn't leave things to chance." He stopped completely, lifting his head to meet her gaze, hands twisting as he rubbed one wrist after the other. "She hid us, bound and gagged. Over and over I swore I'd keep quiet—for she had me convinced she was in the right."

"Bound and gagged?" Danissa clapped a hand over her mouth. His wrists showed no sign of marks, but he kept stroking them.

"She didn't trust me. Us." His hands moved faster, pressing the skin harder.

"Why did no one else step in?" She laid her hands over his, warm against his cold fingers. He stilled, fingers of one hand wrapped around the wrist of the other.

"The chief roofer agreed as did most of the other roof dwellers, or if they disagreed they were too afraid of the chief and my mother to challenge it outright. Besides, children are useful. Especially when they're someone else's."

"Useful." Her mouth had gone dry again. How much did she want to know?

"When the high towers take damage in storms, wind or snow or ice, and it's too treacherous for larger, heavier adults to clamber up or set up a scaffold." He turned his head around, waving at the path they'd climbed so far. "This is nothing in comparison. We both did our first repairs at the age of five. I didn't think it a problem for me, or for her the first time. But the second, when a piece of slate broke off the peak of the high tower. She climbed and nearly slipped. Three times."

Leander trembled. Gaze distant, perhaps lost in remembering.

Danissa shifted to stand at his side, bracing him.

"I took her and turned us both in to the seneschal." He laid his head on her shoulder, voice a mere rasp. "Falfor, then chief librarian at the winter palace, was there. Happenstance I thought at the time, though I'm no longer so sure. He'd already caught me sneaking down to the library, and welcomed me there. He offered an apprenticeship. I haven't been back to the roofs since."

"Has Edrena?"

He threw his head back and laughed, though there was little mirth in it. "Not after I told her about the ambassadorial service."

They stayed in place, his hands still cupped in hers and bodies close enough their shared warmth rivaled the sun's heat.

"Why tell me?" Letting go one hand, Danissa touched a thumb to his cheek to wipe away a trickling tear.

"To share who I am, should you choose to trust me." Their gazes met, meshed for a long moment. He glanced away first, shrugging. "As well, so that you know why seeing other countries means so much to Edrena, in case you repented of inviting us."

"You realize she may never want to return once she leaves."

Another tear trickled down his cheek. "If that's what she wants."

His sister and her father had far outpaced them. They were little more than smudges in the distance, approaching the side entrance to the complex. Danissa wrapped an arm around Leander's waist and they started walking again. Soon, they sped to a pace where maintaining the contact was awkward. Her arm slipped, but he grabbed for her hand so they continued side by side.

She'd feared he'd press her for more information. Instead, he'd given her uncomfortable truths, albeit of very different kind from hers.

She wanted to regret inviting him, but couldn't.

13

Leander lost track of Danissa in the blink of an eye.

One minute they walked through a wide opening between low walls of piled stones stretching out to either side. The walls were decorative rather than defensive, reaching no higher than his knees. Brownish gray, with green marks in those places where water might gather and remain long enough to breed mold, they suited the environs. Two large buildings stretched to either side, both lacking windows but featuring many doors. These, combined with an equally large trellis overgrown with vines, marked out a large five-sided open area.

An empty area. No one was anywhere, although bangs and crashes from the buildings and farther in the distance suggested Danissa and Idan's family were about. Somewhere.

A lean black dog with a green spot on its head lay sprawled at the edge of the trellis. Sleeping and snoring, its whole body jerking with each snort. On second glance, the green spot turned into leaf fallen from the thick vines growing atop the trellis. Small purple and orange flowers from among the leaves contributed a soothing perfume that underlay the scents of bread baking and vegetables laid on a grill.

This high above the palace and lake, the air had a cooler edge.

Leander welcomed the warmth of his mantle over the frail fabric of his tunic. He bent to brush some of the dust from his feet and legs.

"We're home." Idan stretched his legs one at a time and shook them.

"Where is everyone?" Edrena asked.

"Give it a moment."

Danissa stood to the side and slightly behind Idan. She elbowed Leander.

When he turned her way, she lifted a hand and raised one finger. Two. Three.

The dog lifted its head and let out a mournful howl with a resonant edge that carried. Other dogs began to howl nearby.

But the animal didn't move. Danissa raised a fourth finger.

"They're here!" At least three voices yelled variants on the sentiment.

The next moment, people were everywhere. Tall or short, thin or stout, old or young, and all variations between. Most had some features in common. Falls of thick curls here, the same nose there, similar curves or straight lines.

And one and all gave the newcomers an exuberant welcome—with lots of hugs.

Hands waved. Voices cooed. Everyone seemed determined to hug almost everyone else as many times as possible. Danissa vanished into the center.

So many people. So many hugs.

People waved at Idan and several drew close enough to touch his hands or kiss his cheeks, but only two pulled him into a big embrace.

Edrena scooted over, pressing hard against Leander.

Three others also kept to the outskirts, avoiding the shifting, seething mass of people. An ancient elder tottered over to sit on the stone walls. A big bear of a human with a shaved head stood at the edge of one of the buildings waving a ladle and yelling unintelligible words or names, their deep voice booming over the rest of the crying, shrieking throng. A child half Edrena's age at best jumped up and down nearby.

No one hugged Leander or Edrena, but they kept *almost* doing so.

Clearly they had to remember they didn't know either of them and hadn't received permission for an embrace. Occasionally one or another of the younger women, men, and eleee giggled when they glanced at him, but made no more than jerky movements toward him before being swallowed back up into the hugging horde.

Falfor had hosted Leander to dinner several times, back before he half-retired to the summer palace, but always for small, decorous affairs. The same occurred with the new chief librarian except she invited groups of the sub-librarians together, which made for more noise as they subtly and openly competed with each other for her attention.

Nothing on the scale of this. Events involving a dozen people at most, not several dozen over.

As many people lived and loved here as on the winter palace roofs —maybe more.

All of his expectations about the fest and Danissa's family melted as though ice laid out in the summer sun.

Most spoke—or yelled—using the general trade tongue common in Codaros, at least in the winter and summer courts. Leander caught phrases in at least two other languages, only one of which he understood enough to have any clue what people talked about. Mostly the people seemed to call out names, although trying to locate anyone seemed a fruitless endeavor.

Again and again, someone burst from the mass with arms wide and nearly grabbed Leander or Edrena in an embrace only to apologize and turn and grab someone else.

"Do they do this all the time?" Edrena twitched and leaned forward without leaving her place at Leander's side. "There are places on the other side of the lake where just about every time you see someone you know at all well, you're supposed to hug them and kiss them on both cheeks. I hadn't realized it could be so . . . active."

"They're happy to see Idan and Danissa." Leander grew cold everywhere except where Edrena leaned against him.

"And each other. They're not just hugging Danissa."

A person who looked much like Danissa except their had hair gone half-gray and green approached Leander and Edrena with arms extended. A beige substance dusted their hands, flaking off when they dropped their arms to their sides. Little showed on their light-yellow tunic and mantle, but elsewhere many people bore hand marks on backs and shoulders. The stranger continued closer, nodding to Leander then Edrena.

"Forgive us our enthusiasm." The words were clearly rote, with no expectation of forgiveness being denied. "It is not only the arrival of my brother and his daughter that excites us, but kin from afar. I am Madane, oldest sister to Idan, and I welcome you."

"I'm Edrena." She mimicked Madane's gestures. "Leander is my brother."

"Some do not enjoy being hugged and passed around." Madane jerked her head at Idan and the ancient, both now seated on the low stone wall. "And we try to resist with strangers. But if you wish, we would be happy to welcome you, too, in our traditional way."

Edrena leaned forward, but didn't leave his side.

"Up to you." He wrapped an arm around her, giving a sideways squeeze.

With all the enthusiasm appropriate to someone who wanted more than anything to travel and meet other people, she approached Madane and was quickly embraced. An instant later, Madane left beige marks on the back of Edrena's pink mantle as the older woman passed her on to the next nearest relative.

Madane raised an eyebrow at him.

After a moment's consideration, he nodded.

He only remembered being hugged on special occasions, such as after completing successful repairs to towers and roofs, when the older and heavier adults couldn't manage it.

Had he hugged Edrena much?

Whatever he'd done, it bore no resemblance to this. Stranger after stranger wrapped their arms around his shoulders or waist. Pressed their fronts against his. Squeezed and beamed at him as they called welcome one way or another.

His body seemed all angles and sharp edges compared to the people gathered around him. Every time he tried to mirror their gestures, his timing seemed off. He grabbed too late, as they were letting go. Or too high or low. On several occasions, his elbows hit a back or shoulder. As often, hands or elbows smacked him in the back or arm because he moved too fast. He managed not to step on anyone's foot, though he came close, but two adults and one child stepped on his.

Not everyone resembled Danissa, but enough did that he nearly missed enjoying when he came face-to-face with her in the center of the crowd. Even with her, he lurched and almost held on too long.

Body aching and breathing uneven, he wormed his way to the edge of the crowd and snuck away. Cool air wafted around him, marking the difference from communal hug to self-isolation.

Others left as well, which eased his discomfort. Some headed off to unload a cart of some sort, others to cook or do various things in the buildings and trellis-covered areas. The youngest started a game that involved a lot of shouting and running around, and the three half-grown people overseeing the children happily added Edrena to their number.

She seemed much more at ease with touching and being touched than he, more than once skipping over when a child tripped or fell and setting them right with a smile and hug.

Danissa had gone off somewhere, for she was nowhere to be seen.

Leaving Leander nowhere to go.

He turned around once, twice, then noticed Idan waving from his seat on the low stone wall near not one but three elders. All had stark white hair, and far more wrinkles on their warm brown faces than Idan. One still sat fairly straight, but two were bent over. The smaller bent one held a gnarled but stout stick in one hand, the taller a cane with a head carved in the form of a dog. None wore anything more than a thin blue tunic covering from chest to knobby knees. They perched on soft cushions laid atop wooden frames roughly the same height as the piled stones.

Leander made his way over, smiling despite an unexpected twitch in his left cheek.

"This is Leander, a librarian from the winter palace." Idan pointed at the others in turn. "Leander, meet Yedan my grandfather and the oldest of us all, and Feley my grandfather's sister—"

"Much younger sister." The small, bent-over man wagged a finger.

"And not going anywhere before I get a chance to be eldest, so you'll have to die before me." The woman stamped the dog-head cane against the dirt.

"And Orodan, my father." After making introductions, Idan produced a flagon of perfumed water from somewhere and filled a blue-glazed mug for Leander. "You survived the throng. Congratulations. Have a seat."

"Are they always . . ." Leander settled onto a stone close by Idan and took a tentative sip. Cool, fruity goodness slid down his throat, and he drank more deeply.

"Always." Idan bobbed his head. "Though there aren't always quite so many of us usually. Some of the family who travel try to stop here for fests."

"It started with only three—Feley and me and my beloved, Seloro —of whom all are the fruits." Yedan rolled his cane between his hands.

"So many children, grandchildren and more. So many cousins sent here for fostering." Feley lifted her chin, a mischievous light in her eyes. "Is it any wonder we've grown as we've prospered? Under my leadership, of course."

Yedan opened his mouth, but Orodan immediately jumped in. "And yes, anyone arriving is cause for a mass hug."

"Or anyone departing the same. Or accomplishing something great, or failing, or any reason whatsoever," Idan added.

"What good is being eldest if I don't get to talk when I want to?" The oldest man tapped his son on the head.

"Were you going to argue over who was leader again?" Orodan refilled his mug. "Air our differences before a newcomer, you who taught me that was not the sign of a good host?"

"It is a sad day when one's children quote one to oneself." Yedan smiled as he shook his head. "But you speak truth. Far better to welcome newcomers with hugs and cries of delight."

"Mind, you don't have to be hugged." Idan stretched his arms to either side, fingers brushing his father and great-aunt. "Some of us enjoy space around us. People will understand if you say no to a hug.

You may have to say no twice, but after that they'll remember and ask rather than presume."

"I'll remember that." The quick exchanges between them brought Edrena to mind. He checked on his sister as she followed the children into the shade of the trellised area. The sun beat down on his back, offering warmth rather than heat.

"Leander."

He jumped at the sound of his name, but Yedan wasn't calling him.

"Leander," Yedan said again. "Almost close enough to be one of my line."

"I don't . . ."

"Yedan, Orodan, Idan, Danissa." The old man reached around and patted Leander's hand. "Take the parents' names, mix them up, and come up with something new for a child. Simple and easy."

"Don't believe him. It's never so simple and easy as he says." Feley shook her head, chuckling.

Idan nodded. "It took me months to get Larissa to settle on Danissa."

"Because you complicated it! Simple and easy, the first that comes to mind is often the best." Yedan pounded his cane again.

"He forgets how much he and Seloro argued over naming their children." Feley leaned in toward Leander, cupping a hand around her mouth. "The eldest tend to forget more than they remember."

Before Yedan could respond, Idan coughed. And coughed again. Retrieving his flask, he opened it.

Leander's nose wrinkled at the astringent smell. He squinted at Idan, whose complexion had acquired a grayish undertone, hoping it was a trick of the light.

"You don't look good, my child. Bad in the belly?" Yedan rubbed his own, eyes bright and inquisitive. "Or more?"

Idan knocked back a slurp of medicine, then capped the flask. He tucked it away, glancing around.

Groups of people had begun to trickle back into the open area, but none came near the wall.

"I haven't told anyone yet. I thought I'd start with you. Father, you'll share with . . ." Idan gestured at kitchen.

"With your other father, of course." Orodan sat straight, back stiff and fingers restless.

"No one else, yet. Not until I tell Danissa."

A prickle of unease ran up Leander's spine. He started to rise, but Idan waved for him to return to his seat.

"Stay. Danissa may need your advice, or comfort."

Leander swallowed, hard, but a lump formed in his throat and his feet twitched as though he'd hopped up and pelted off. He preferred the kind of secrets he could unravel or entrust to the bowels of the library for later generations over personal confidences. But if Idan wanted him to stay, thought he might be of service to Danissa . . .

The three elders were all attention.

"What ails you?" Yedan asked.

"I had a bout of the whoops last winter that stayed through spring. I was still coughing when court traveled here, but I thought I was doing better." Idan rubbed his forehead, shoulders slumping. "Then I came down with a summer fever, and it hasn't left me. The healers are puzzled. Nothing they give helps, save this strengthener."

"How bad is it?" Idan's father asked.

"Without medicine, I'd scarce have the energy to make it through a day." He folded his hands over his chest, head hanging low. "It's been suggested I make plans, prepare for death, in case they cannot find a cure."

"And you've kept this all to yourself?" Orodan lurched forward as though to embrace Idan. Stopping so suddenly he rocked, he extended a hand instead. Idan grabbed it, skin graying and showing stark veins where he clasped his father tight.

"I kept thinking the next try would work. That I wouldn't need to. That I didn't risk leaving my daughter alone at court."

A harsh, indrawn breath broke the silence.

Danissa stood before them.

14

"I'm told you would like me to dance."

Danissa barely breathed. The mumbles and bangs from the kitchen, the children yelling as they ran down from the orchard, sounds faded into a distant buzz. A gray fog edged her view, leaving only five faces visible.

A guilty expression on each and every one.

The earth bore her up, steady and unmoving beneath her bare feet. Her tunic and mantle rippled about her calves as a late afternoon breeze twined about. A thin layer of clouds hid the sun and reduced shadows to almost nothing.

Platters of food sat ready for serving on the tables set up under the trellis. The aroma of fresh nutty bread and stuffed fruits overrode the lighter floral scents from the trellis flowers and distant fields. Torches holding stone glows stood at the corners of the yard, covered for now.

Family thronged the square, but kept to the edges. Some sat on chairs or cushions. Others perched on walls or handcarts.

All watching.

All listening.

All waiting for the fest of the eldest to start. It always began with a song and a dance. Always she danced. Perhaps someone else had when she was young, before she could remember. Her father was asked, in those early years, and chose her to partner him. Once she came of age, she was requested directly.

She'd asked her great-grandleether, years earlier, why they chose her, though others danced the start when they weren't around. *"I might not understand what princesses and compeers are,"* Seloro, then the eldest, had said, *"but there's a difference when you or your father dance, especially you. But hush."* They laid a finger across their lips, pretending they didn't know her father looked over their shoulder. *"Don't tell your father."*

"For the first time, the burden is mine to choose. I miss Seloro, but I would not have a dance of sadness or loss. I choose you, and joy." Great-grandfather rose, tottering a bit. Danissa held his hands until he steadied, thanks in no small part to her father and grandfather bracing his legs and torso. "Will you dance joy for me?"

"Of course." The words fell from her lips unbidden. She'd assumed he'd ask. Anticipated partnering with her father, as usual.

Until she'd heard the last words from him. His confession of illness, and the lack of a cure.

His early summer sickness hadn't gone, but returned in greater strength.

And he didn't tell her, didn't share, didn't let her help.

Shared the news with one of his fathers and his grandfather first, rather than her. His other father, busy in the kitchen, would have to hear later as well, but that offered little consolation.

A heavy weight seemed to press on her shoulders. Every bone and muscle grew stiff, awkward.

Yet she had to dance.

Joy.

But first, she needed to choose a partner or two.

Rustles and whispers penetrated the thick fog around her. Her neck refused to move, waist likewise. Feet shuffling, she turned in a circle. Other people's bodies blurred into each other, forming a big mass topped with distinct faces. Aunt Madane. Grandfather Amdrei. Edrena perched on the wall in a far corner next to the cousins who'd traveled around the lake for this fest.

Around, and around, until she once again faced Great-grandfather

Yedan. Behind him, her father didn't seem to understand her hesitation. He watched her with a puzzled expression although, as a born compeer, he should know something of Danissa's mood by how she stood on the earth.

Had his sickness weakened his gift as well?

She wouldn't know. He didn't want her to know. Why? He had let her help care for her mother, feed her and comfort her in her last days. They'd sat watch together on the night her mother breathed her last.

Given time, Danissa would dance with him again.

Not now.

Even as he'd wanted to withhold the news from her, so she needed time to adjust.

She had to ask someone else instead.

"Will you dance with me?" Danissa extended her hand to Leander.

He looked away—at her father, great-grandfather—she didn't. The gray receded from the edges of her vision until he filled it. Stevan had said he liked the way Leander stood on the earth. She'd take that as an endorsement for this dance.

Whispers whipped around the square as her family realized she asked a stranger over her father.

"Are you certain?" Out of the corner of her eye, she caught him setting his hands on the wall and pushing up. "I can—"

"No. Rest." Danissa raised her other hand to him, palm out. Her right she continued to extend to Leander.

Sucking in a long breath, he matched his palm to hers. She hadn't realized how cold she'd turned until their hands met. He rose and followed her to the center of the yard. Yanking off the cloth covering her curls, she tossed it to the wind. Her hair spilled loose, warming her neck and shoulders, as the wind blew the cloth to Edrena.

Danissa had never performed this first dance with anyone but her father.

Always with a compeer.

Whatever else Leander might be, he wasn't a compeer, taught or born.

Princesses didn't require compeers to dance or Dance. Partnering with one merely made things easier.

Leander's fingers, warm as they were, shook within her loose clasp. Maybe he, too, heard Edrena explaining who he was to the children, who passed it along around the square.

"What do you want me to do?" He bent close, voice low.

"We're dancing joy. Joy of . . ." A shudder ripped through Danissa, but she pulled her shoulders back and straightened. The eldest had asked her for joy, and she'd give him that somehow. "Joy of being here together, of a lovely day, of life and living."

"I've never danced like this, only as part of crowds."

"You asked me to trust you." She smiled, a rote movement of lips turning up at the corners. It probably looked ghastly given the concern clear on his face. "Show me you deserve my trust."

Fine words, to hide the truth.

She didn't know how she'd manage the dance, with him or without him.

Then again, this dance involved no set steps. It was always an expression of a moment—and a feeling.

"Stay here. Watch me, where I go and what I do. Whenever I come back, be here for me to hold onto." She squeezed his hand, leaning some of her weight on him to show him what she meant.

"If I do this, you will trust me?" He squeezed back, their fingers now the same temperature. His dark eyes scanned her face.

She broke first, glancing away—down at the hard earth beneath their feet. Then up to meet his gaze again. "If you succeed, I will have more reason to trust you than before."

A puff of laughter escaped him, his belly jerking, but he smiled. Hesitant. Tentative, yet with a hint of joy.

Her lips softened, matching his. Tears prickled the corners of her eyes. A hint of hope warmed her core. If she had to dance joy, she'd chosen a good partner.

Turning her head, she located her great-grandfather and nodded.

"Today we live." He stepped forward, the cause for celebration and the celebrant in one. "We are here. Together. Hold to that, and let there be joy."

Clapping his hands, he set the beat: slow, fast tap-fast tap, slow, slow.

Three times, then the family picked up and repeated the rhythm until the very earth resounded with it.

After another three repeats, he sang. His voice creaked and cracked, but the crisp consonants and elongated vowels of his first language carried over and above the clapping. He sang the verse alone, and the rest of family joined in on the chorus. Their pronunciation was all over the place, especially the children who didn't understand many of the words.

Danissa remained still through the end of the first chorus. The song had nine verses because it came from around the lake where great-grandfather's people didn't believe in the magic of indivisible numbers.

Since she preferred to dance following the rules she'd learned, in ones and twos, threes and fives, sevens and elevens, she and her father had always posed during the first and last verses.

Leander's stance altered. He shifted, sharing his weight evenly on both feet and standing taller. His gaze grew distant as he listened, although his hesitant smile remained unchanged.

Did he understand the words? She only knew only the chorus well, but then she'd always danced rather than sung.

It was enough that she understood what the song was about, what it meant to her family, and to her.

As great-grandfather had said, they were here, together, alive.

With the start of the second verse, she moved.

There were no set steps, no kinds of movements she needed to do to embody fire or rain or wind. It was all improvisation, seeking ways to reflect and project a feeling.

Joy.

First *she* needed to feel it.

Her feet remembered the yard well, the size and scope of the ground. The family ringed the edge, clapping and singing, so that she couldn't accidentally go astray unless she really tried.

She closed her eyes and danced in darkness. Sun on her skin and shifting qualities of darkness—from red-tinged to gray—ensured she marked the directions.

She swayed to the beat.

What movements, what actions, might represent joy?

Her hands rose, as though reaching for stars. Gathering them and bringing them close to her heart.

Turning circles and swirling, she let them fly free to float or land wherever they wished.

Again she reached out. This time, warm motes formed within the curves of her hands. Heat trickled into her fingers, threading along her arms.

More lined her soles and seeped up through her legs.

The fevered rush made her head sway. The claps and voices combined into a single mass of sound the same every way she turned. Unable to distinguish different voices, or loudness versus softness, she lost track of where she danced in relation to the family lining the perimeter.

Head swaying, she let her hands pass over her eyes—miming tears. Of sadness or joy?

Or fright.

The earth beneath her shifted. Slanted. Rising on tiptoes, she followed the incline with an outstretched hand.

Leander's hand brushed her thumb, but he adjusted quickly and slid his palm under hers. She bent, resting half of her weight on him. He hissed and held steady.

Danissa opened her eyes and met his. They'd opened wide, pupils dark and large and gleaming with emotion she couldn't, wouldn't, name.

The earth pulsed beneath her, in time to the claps.

Drawing back, she twirled around and around. Quick turns of her head enabled her to pick faces to focus on. She chose people by chance and whim and found smiles and pleasure everywhere.

Motes of light likewise met her gaze wherever she turned. Some floated above her, close enough to reach and catch. Others swayed at knee-level, ready to pluck and gather.

Stars and flowers.

No one else seemed to notice. Wherever she looked, the faces watched her, not her surroundings.

Yet the more they clapped, the louder they sang, the brighter grew the points of light—and the greater the resemblance to stars and flowers.

She wafted in a loose spiral, as though carried on a breeze back to the center.

This time Leander held out both hands, palms up. Grabbing hold, she wilted.

Energy flowed up from the earth, revitalizing her.

Again she whirled out, this time with eyes open. She ran her hands through the sparkling stars. The motes clung to her skin until she pulled her fingers in then flicked them open. The stars streamed off to either side. They sparkled as they touched her watching kin before fading.

Lazy arcs of her arms to either side gathered flowers of light. These she tossed to her family and scattered back upon the earth.

Every time she reached for Leander, he met her. Supported her. Rooted her—and let her go to pluck stars and harvest flowers.

Power built. Not the crackling energy when with her fellow princesses beneath ground, or the lesser vibrations of practice, but rather a fizziness in her veins.

Light and warmth filled her.

Effervescence set every speck of her being alive with joy.

Faster and faster she whirled about, gathering magical flowers and stars only to scatter them upon the winds—and her family.

She had this day.

Her father.

Her family.

And always Leander there to ground her. Even at the last, when she rested for the ninth verse.

The remaining motes of light moved in. They coated her skin, seeped into her body, and drained into the earth below leaving her whole being light and full of warmth.

Danissa's hand rested on Leander's, and he supported her. Their gazes and smiles meshed as glad voices rang out in the last line of the chorus.

A moment's hush fell over the crowd as the last word faded away, the last clap.

With a whoosh, everyone raced in to press around them. The welcome hugs were nothing to this. It was a mass embrace of all-together touching, holding, hugging.

Her father was one of the first to reach her. He clutched her shoulders, saying words she couldn't hear above the roar of all the other voices. The crowd shifted him, children slipping in front as they grabbed at her and moved on.

Her chest heaved, power still fizzling in her veins—more than she remembered from previous years, but maybe she just wasn't paying attention.

For she had Danced joy.

She'd Danced on her own.

Her fingers still clasped Leander, at the center of the mass.

It was all too much.

Too many changes.

Too many possibilities.

Too many secrets.

At the first opportunity, she pulled her hand from his and ran away.

15

Warmth flowed through Leander every time Danissa rested her hand on his.

The rest of the world faded away, including Edrena, Idan and his family. The sun headed down toward the lake, bathing the yard in golden light. A light fragrance hinting of stars and fresh-bloomed flowers filled Leander with every breath, driving away any vestiges of food cooking. Clapped hands and voices singing registered, but as though far away.

Everything became secondary, a backdrop to Danissa dancing. Sparks of light flared around her as she twirled, rose, and gathered, only to scatter. She danced for everyone in the courtyard.

While only touching him. He remained where she'd placed him, at the center whenever she needed something—someone—to hold onto.

As a child, he'd often crept about the roofs when the princesses danced in the open air. Most of the roof dwellers enjoyed watching, and crowded the lower roofs, leaving no room for children who weren't supposed to be there in the first place. So he'd clamber up a chimney or tower and perch atop for the best view available.

After grounding himself and Edrena, they'd maneuvered around the courtyards and scoped out all available windows without ever managing a view much closer than that from the lower roofs.

How many people in the land dreamed of dancing with a princess? Thousands at the least, and here he was: living a dream and finding it exceeded his imagination a thousand-fold.

He had no illusions about his role. She danced, he supported.

Nevertheless, each time she returned she rested more of her weight against him. Gripped his hand harder. Held on a little longer.

She needed someone. She might have chosen anyone else—her father, another of her family members, Leander's sister.

She'd chosen *him*.

Around the yard she leapt and whirled, strewing glittering, intangible flowers and stars of light. Always returning to him, until some sign he didn't recognize. She came to a stop, both hands resting on his and her eyes gazing straight into him.

One last verse echoed around them, followed by a last chorus. A few of the words registered. They sang in a language he might've studied, but only to read and compose simple sentences.

Their words, their claps, washed over him.

The world narrowed further to encompass only their clasped hands and meshed gazes.

Silence fell after the end of the song. A rush of movement broke it. The still air heaved as dozens of bodies headed for the small space where Leander stood with Danissa.

A massive hug embraced them both, without ripping hand from hand. Instead, the press squashed them together. Their hands remained clasped between them. Their torsos pressed against each other. Their foreheads met, heights close enough for their gazes to still hold, despite the arms wrapping around them and delighted cries of her family plus Edrena.

Danissa let go first. Her fingers flexed and compressed his hand— then slipped off.

A hiss escaped him as he resisted grabbing her back.

Instead of turning to enfold her father or any of the other relatives close in about them, she slipped through the press of bodies.

And kept going.

Leander lacked sufficient height to track her. Ducking low, he followed her as best he could through the maze of arms and legs, torsos and delightedly screaming mouths. How many relatives did she have here? She was more familiar with navigating them, and had some destination in mind, so she moved far more quickly than he.

By the time he emerged from the still-hugging crowd, she'd crossed the courtyard.

He ran after, sandals slapping the ground. His mantle hung heavy on the right, light on the left. His tunic hadn't slipped sideways along his arms or torso, but the hem was rucked up near the top of his hips. Adjusting the balance of the mantle and yanking the tunic hem down delayed him.

She pelted through the trellis-covered plaza.

Darting after her, Leander faced yet another maze more familiar to her than him. Flowered vines grew up from immense vases to produce a thick overhead cover, reducing the increasingly golden sunlight to little more than small patches here and there. Light-stone torches made up the difference, illuminating a dozen or more tables groaning under platters of food ready to be eaten, plus other tables surrounded by benches for eaters to sit on.

He whipped from side to side as he chased her across the dimmer courtyard.

By the time he reached the far end, she'd vanished into an overgrown garden of flowering bushes and more trellises supporting different vines, some overhung with star-shaped fruits.

A wealth of scents assaulted him from the flowers and fruits and breads and roast vegetables on platters nearby. Swaying branches and vines provided movement to conceal Danissa's path.

Blood pounded through his body. Every mote throbbed with life as never before.

All beating with joy.

"Danissa?" he called. "Are you all right? Do you need help?"

"She sh . . . shouldn't . . . be . . . alone."

Leander turned to find Idan had followed them only to stop halfway. The older man clutched one of the trellis posts, knuckles gray as he sagged against the support. His father and another man, perhaps his other father, along with his sister Madane, eased him away. He fell back into their arms, one hand gesturing for Leander to come over.

With a last glance at the flowering garden, Leander hurried to Idan's side.

Fathers and sister urged the compeer to go into the house and rest, or at least settle into a comfortable chair and drink water.

"I'll be . . . well . . . soon. Give . . . strengthener. You—" Idan grabbed Leander's hand, fingers weak but capable of squeezing tight enough Leander winced. "Tell Danissa . . . don't want fuss or worry . . . bad enough . . . she watched . . . mother fade."

"You rest, and I'll go," Leander said, "though I don't know where I'll find her."

"Oldest trees." Idan's head lolled to the side, resting against his fathers' chests. "Better soon. Strengthener."

Orodan fussed with the top of the flask as his beloved cradled their son.

Madane pulled Leander away, though she kept glancing over his shoulder at her brother. "Wait here. I'll have one of the children lead you."

A good decision, for Leander would never have found the way on his own.

A youngling no taller than Leander's waist, including the wealth of tightly curled hair rising about their forehead, served as guide. They wore no mantle, and their red tunic had dozens of tiny tears along the hem, likely from brushing against stretches of thorny bushes. Matching scratches marred their bare feet. Tiny toes dug into the soft earth between flower patches.

The path looped around so many times Leander wondered if there was a straight line anywhere in the gardens. Half of the plants were in full bloom, filling the air with so many competing scents he had trouble distinguishing any.

An intricate web of ditches no bigger than his thumb and holes in the earth, all lined with a substance that gave off a faint greenish glow, suggested the gardens were watered by rain runoff carefully distributed. A few drops lingered here and there. When Leander asked about them, his guide ducked their head and turned up their hands without saying anything.

No chatter, not so much as a single word from the youngling all the long, twisting way to a cluster of three trees. Each tree soared high, with tall, thick trunks and roots rippling outward. Among them, arms wrapped around her legs and head bent, sat Danissa.

The child pointed her out, then turned and opened their arms to Leander.

Clearly a hug was an acceptable reward for having led him. He knelt down and wrapped his arms around the lithe body, getting his back pounded in return.

"Thanks."

The child nodded and skipped back off toward the courtyards—and food.

Hopefully Danissa would be willing to lead Leander back, or he'd likely get lost a dozen times over.

The princess made no sign of noticing their arrival, or the child's departure, or Leander picking his way over to settle on a wide root nearby.

The sun still had a way to go before setting, but the light sifting through the wide canopy of leaves overhead had gold-green tinge that gave the air an unworldly appearance. Oblong fruits in pale green hung amidst the leaves. The overwhelming floral scents of the gardens had reduced, mixed with a brisk, astringent smell from the trees or fruits.

Leander sat within arm's reach—close enough to touch although his arms hung loose at his sides. Even at that distance, the air around her vibrated to the point bumps formed along his arms.

Idan's plea resounded in Leander's ears, but he swallowed it back. Better to wait.

And wait.

And wait.

He shifted his perch as the ridges of the root began to impress themselves on his buttocks. None of his ample experience in waiting seemed to apply. He usually practiced patience in work contexts, choosing when and how to question witnesses.

His sister sometimes woke screaming in the night, even so long on the ground, or got angry at him and stomped off as far as she could get muttering all the while, or yelled until she slurred her words together and mispronounced them so badly he failed to understand anything she said.

Edrena never managed so long a silence.

The quiet, save for birds calling overhead and a breeze whistling through leaves, wore on him. The muscles in his legs began to twitch, and his stomach to remind him how much time had passed since he'd eaten.

He tried words instead. "How can I help?"

One breath, two, three. Right as he braced himself to try again, she finally responded.

"You can't."

Such a flat pronouncement, her words left doubt as to whether she meant he couldn't or no one could.

"I can listen."

She lifted her head, pupils nearly filling her eyes. Her lips were turned down, but one side tightened as a chuff escaped her. "And talk."

"Yes." Nothing else to say to that.

Another long pause, but again she broke it.

"What if I don't want anyone to know?" Danissa's arms rose to rest atop her knees, and she buried her chin against them.

"I can keep secrets." Leander settled his hands in his lap.

"Of course. You're too busy prying them out of other people."

"You're not the first to say that." He flinched, and sought for a way to offer a distraction. "Do you know how librarians are trained?"

"No." She clearly didn't care either, for this pause stretched out twice as long as either of the earlier ones.

Sometimes you must give up information first, to create an imbalance that most people will fill by unconsciously offering a trade. His mentor's advice rang in his head. *Stories are often the best option. Choose wisely.*

"Librarians are trained by degrees. We have many ranks. Each rank brings more responsibilities, more power, more discretion." Nothing she couldn't know if she'd paid any attention on her visits to the libraries.

Her stance didn't change, but she seemed to be listening.

"In addition to being earned, every promotion is contingent on passing tests involving secrets. The first is the easiest: you're given a piece of information to keep to yourself. Then you're given two, one which must be kept secret at all costs and the other doesn't matter."

"Easy."

"We're not told which is which."

"Still doesn't sound bad." She flipped a hand at him, he'd earned that much reaction.

"To become eligible for promotion to librarian—I'm a sub-librarian now—I had to pass a more complicated version." A heavy weight formed at the base of his belly at the remembrance. "I was given three pieces of information. One to keep secret no matter what, and if the merest hint reached anyone I would fail and be barred from trying again for a year. A second that could be shared at will. And the third I was told must be kept close and confidential, but at some point during the weeks of the test it should be shared with one other person."

She moved, raising her head and settling her chin atop her arms rather than behind them. "No doubt you're not told which is which again. How close are the secrets?"

"Similar enough, but there's another twist."

No reply from her, but she watched him through those great, wide eyes.

"There are always a number of us tested at the same time. Some are friends or at least friendly and don't begrudge fellow librarians succeeding whether or not they do so themselves." He linked his hands and shook them. "Others would prefer to rise by climbing over the backs of the rest of us." Turning his hands around, he pressed his knuckles against each other and spat to the side. "The information we're given? It's about each other. Sometimes it's true, sometimes false. But we have to figure out which piece to share with someone who might wish us ill."

Danissa straightened her back and shook her feet and legs as she extended them. "Why would they do this?"

"Because the higher we rise and the more authority we have, the more we need to be able to discern which secrets need keeping, and with whom—and when and under what circumstances—to share."

"You've mastered this?"

"I passed the most recent test, but more lie before me." He edged off the root to sit on the earth facing Danissa. "The tests are easier, in a way, because the secrets aren't necessarily real. In investigations, they are—and almost always hurt someone."

"Why are you telling me this?" A leaf floated down and landed between them. Wide and long, it was light green with spots of red. She leaned forward and scooped it up. Fanned herself. The far edge of the breeze she raised nipped moisture from his face.

"Secrets are hurting you." Many of them, but one in particular— and not only hurting *her*, given the shock and horror on her father's face when he'd realized she'd overheard.

"What kind?" She adjusted her seat, sending vibrations through the earth. Dropping the leaf, she wrapped her arms across her chest.

"At least one that you think should have been shared with you."

Her hands clenched as she drew in a hissing breath. "My father told you before me."

"It was an accident. I happened to be there." Once again, tension poured off her. Leander shifted his seat, moving a tiny bit closer. The air vibrated between them, growing warm.

"He could have asked you to leave." Her voice wavered as she shook her head. "He told *you* before me."

"And his father and grandfather and great-aunt."

"Was he ever going to tell me? Don't answer that." She pulled back, throwing her hands up before setting them against the dirt.

"He sent me after you."

"Hmph."

"How else would I have found you?"

"I wouldn't put it past you to find a way."

Leander blinked, not sure if her words counted as a compliment or complaint. Her body had turned stiff again, and moisture glinted in her eyes.

Yet something about her reaction struck him oddly. Running back over what else she'd said, he straightened and stuck his chin out. Dared her to give him truth. "Did he have to tell you? You already knew, didn't you?"

"I overheard something, before now. Might have guessed anyway, how tired and slow he was climbing up today." Her head hung, hair swaying against her back. "But he didn't tell me. He didn't want me to know."

"Perhaps he wanted to choose another time and place."

"Too late."

"That happens a lot." His turn to sigh and slump. "You know now. What do you plan to do next?"

"I need that codex."

"You what?" Leander shook his head, touching his ears to make certain they were clear.

She drew in a whistling breath and didn't answer for a long time. "The codex has a spell in it that might—if Ylena's right—be a way to Dance healing."

He'd almost forgotten that part of their accidental encounter at the library. No, not forgotten but set aside until he had a chance to spend time there, or Falfor returned. "I'll find it for you, if it's there."

"I don't doubt you." Leaning forward, Danissa ran a finger along his hand. A glancing caress but meaningful because she was the first to break the space between them. "I wasn't sure I'd be able to do it, whatever it is. Ylena didn't believe it when she first read it, because it was a Dance for one princess. Who Dances alone? We're always in groups of five or seven, or three at the very least. Never even two. Oh, there are dozens upon dozens of tales about a wandering princess who works magic and leaves places better behind her, but those are only stories. Princesses have tried, sneaking into the practice room or even down into the underground chamber, but they never work anything worth repeating. No one Dances on their own."

Leander kept his mouth shut. Largely because he wasn't sure what to say, even after having danced with her—but he couldn't help considering how this connected to whatever had turned the Shadow into flowers. One or two princesses?

"But today . . . I Danced."

"This morning?" he asked.

"Now. With you."

"Me?" The intangible stars and flowers had a different cast, considered in that light. The rush of delight rippling through him. He'd supported her, held her, during a Dance?

"It should be impossible." Shivers racked Danissa, head to toe. "Amara, my father, my aunt Yanna, the Terparchon, nearly every princess I've ever known—and I've known many— everyone's always insisted that for true magic you need at least three princesses. But I Danced magic alone. And what did I Dance? Joy. My father is dying and I Danced *joy*."

Tears poured down her face. She bent over, weeping and shaking. She stretched out her hands before her, even as she had during the dance.

He leaned forward and placed his hands under hers. She grabbed hold, fingers clutching at him.

Getting up on his knees, he moved closer. Slipped one hand out of her grasp so as to wrap it around her. She buried her head against him, tears dampening his tunic.

He rocked her, humming for lack of words. Held her as he'd done Edrena every time she woke screaming that she'd climbed the tower and was trying to fix the gap, but her hands were slipping on the ice and she was falling. Danissa's body had a very different shape, more curves and a different combination of muscles and soft spots, so warm against him.

Danissa burrowed, readjusting and tucking her face against his neck and slipping an arm around his waist as she sobbed.

His humming shifted to recreate the rhythm and tune he'd heard while she Danced. The beat had settled into his bones. She started to sing, words he only partially understood especially muffled as they were against his neck. The tension in her body eased and she snuggled close.

The whole evening was beyond his wildest dreams.

If felt so good to hold and be held. Now that he'd had a taste, he wanted more.

16

When miserable, Danissa didn't love company.

Nothing helped ease her mood, not walking in the garden nor long soaks and steams following practice. This morning she'd donned a favorite mantle in bright, sunshiny yellow with moons and stars embroidered along the hem and a large sun emitting dozens of rays where, when she arranged the folds just right, it rested over her heart. Even her tunic beneath had a sunny tinge. A dozen gold bangles around her wrists and ankles chimed when she moved, and her sandals bore bells.

Only to find the chiming annoyed her. It reminded her of time ticking away—and that she'd fled back down the hill while her father remained with family.

Ill.

Perhaps dying.

Too busy pleading with her to forgive his keeping it a secret to offer any real explanation as to *why*.

She'd pled her responsibilities as a princess, and the odds of being needed soon for a Dance, only to end up with an unanswerable conundrum. Wherever she was, she wanted to be somewhere else.

Up on the hill? Better to leave and find the means to face her father.

Down in the palace? Tangled in commitments that kept her from going back up to carry him down herself and march to the infirmary demanding they help.

And at all costs, away from Leander—who had started to trouble her dreams.

She ended up at the infirmary but in attendance on Ylena rather than her father.

Ylena remained in the same narrow room as before, surrounded by the same astringent, medicinal smells and ghastly white bedclothes. The other princess had, at least, improved to the extent she'd cleaned up—or allowed herself to be cleaned up since her leg remained splinted—and wore a lovely sea-blue tunic that complemented her light complexion.

Moreover, Ylena proved far more lively from the moment Danissa entered the room and settled on a stool near the bed.

Alas, the liveliness seemed largely prompted by the fact that Danissa hadn't arrived alone. Jola's carefully wrought schedule had paired Danissa with Gisela.

Danissa regretted more than ever wearing so many bracelets and bells. They chimed whenever she moved, sometimes when she did no more than breathe, and ensured she couldn't fade into the background.

For Gisella bubbled over with happiness. Her every barefoot step fell light and almost soundless. Even the cool tiles of the infirmary floors didn't prompt her to put her sandals on. Her toes peeped out from under her long bird's-egg blue tunic and matching mantle.

The blues of Gisela's attire clashed with Ylena's. A hint of what was to come.

Stevan had escorted Gisela, and hence Danissa, to the infirmary before sneaking off with a promise to return later.

Smart man.

"I see you're enjoying being a princess." Ylena smiled, or rather bared her teeth. Her gaze lingered on the twined gold and silver cords around Gisela's waist.

"Would it make you happier if I didn't?" Gisela's smile appeared more genuine, albeit with a hint of bite, as she settled onto a stool opposite Danissa.

"Of course not, that would be rude. I am happy for you." Ylena rubbed her hands together. "I presume you enjoy dancing with Todor. He's quite accomplished."

Danissa swallowed hard, trying to maintain a polite expression. Although she herself had rarely dealt much with Todor, she considered him somewhat indifferent or absent-minded. She wasn't sure which, and her father had refused to offer any comment—likely since Todor was the Terparchon's second child and only son.

Regardless of Danissa's opinion of Todor, Ylena raising the subject was in questionable taste. Though how often had Todor visited Ylena, if at all? Maybe only on Jola's assigned schedule, which would be a bad sign since rumor had it that Ylena had meant to marry him and become Terparchon after the current one died or retired.

"I'd prefer to dance with Stevan, but alas I do not make the choices." She waved at Danissa. "I imagine you enjoy it."

"Since I must dance with a compeer other than my father, I am happy to do so with Stevan although I know he'd rather be with you." All truth, for Danissa did appreciate being paired with one of the few born compeers rather than a taught one. Though when she thought of it, which she tried not to, she'd Danced well with Leander who wasn't any kind of compeer.

"Wait, your father's not dancing with you?" Ylena turned away from Gisela. She leaned forward, chilly politeness dropping away and replaced with concern.

"Or anyone, apart from occasionally demonstrating steps with Amara." She tilted her head down, playing with her bracelets. Before she headed down the hill, she'd survived a short, stiff exchange with her father in which Idan had explained his spring illness had come back and kept getting worse. No more explanation, and she couldn't plead. The last thing she wanted was to make him worse for worry over her worrying about him. "He's retired. Ill."

"What? Why didn't anyone mention this before?" Ylena sat straight up, only to wince and ease back down as she rubbed at her thigh.

"Maybe because the subject didn't arise? You were so busy feeling sorry for yourself." Danissa clapped a hand over her mouth. "I'm sorry. That wasn't kind or true."

"True enough." Ylena held out her free hand. "I'm sorry. He's always been so full of life, it's hard to imagine him stepping aside."

"Hard for me, too. It happens, though." The stool creaked beneath her as she wriggled, preferring other topics. "I may not have been a princess long, but I grew up around court, and princesses and compeers come and go. Who knows but another princess may retire by the time you mend, and then you may go back to dancing with Todor."

"I won't hope for it." Ylena slapped pallet next to her leg. "If I ever heal. Why haven't you found the steps?"

An ache started in Danissa's head. She rubbed her temples, the chime of her bracelets off-beat to the rapid beat of her pulse.

Puzzlement on Gisela's face caught her attention. Danissa tried to signal the other princess not to step back in, once Ylena was distracted, but too late.

"Steps?" Gisela asked.

Danissa waited for Ylena to answer, but the injured woman was busy massaging her thigh. Or pretended to be.

"Ylena read a book—" After the silence held too long, Danissa broke it.

"Codex," Ylena said.

"What's the difference?"

"It's a specific kind of book. Handwritten, not a printed mess." The corners of Ylena's mouth tightened.

Danissa began again. "Ylena read a codex whose author—"

"Compiler."

"Do you want me to answer or are you going to?"

A giggle escaped Gisela, quickly swallowed when both Danissa and Ylena glared at her and then at each other.

"The chief librarian showed me earlier this summer a new purchase containing all manner of old tales and anecdotes. There was a story about a princess who Danced health into someone else. She did it alone, of all things, but if a princess *could* Dance people back into health ages ago, surely someone could do it for me now."

Danissa checked Gisela at Ylena's reference to Dancing alone, and found the other princess looking back. They both knew Gisela had Danced alone, albeit with Stevan's help. Danissa shivered, comparing memory of that horrid night with her own, recent joyous Dance.

"All you have to do is go and ask the chief librarian to bring the volume out, page about halfway through, and copy it for me." Ylena crossed her arms over her chest, glaring at Danissa.

"Oh yes, that's all. Did it occur to you the chief librarian might go off somewhere else?" Danissa mirrored the other woman, crossing her own arms.

"He never travels anymore."

"Well, he's off now although due back any day." Danissa wove her fingers together, drawing in a deep breath. "And when he is—"

"Bring a copy of the story here, and we'll test it." Ylena stretched out a hand to Danissa. "Maybe it will help your father, too."

"That's what I hope." She'd snuck in a visit to the library, even knowing she might find Leander there after avoiding him as successfully as her father albeit for different reasons.

Unfortunately, although Leander wasn't present, the presiding librarian recognized her and suggested she come back when the chief returned.

One accident with an ink well—maybe a few more. The first spilled over the table rather than an open book, by luck. Only the librarians never stopped watching her every move, so she'd started teasing them with occasional *almost* misses.

Danissa thought she'd escaped further questioning about her father, but Gisela accompanied her when she left Ylena's room.

The other princess kept her mouth shut until they reached a narrow passageway near the princesses' residence. The overhanging roof offered protection against the high, hot sun, even though the space had nothing otherwise to recommend it. No benches on which to sit. Merely whitewash on the walls. Not even a decent view of the floor mosaics and plantings in either of the courtyards it adjoined.

The only thing it did provide, at this time of day, was a relatively private place to speak.

"Is there anything I can do to help?" Gisela patted Danissa's arm.

Even without more specific words, Danissa guessed Gisela meant her father. But what came to her mind immediately after was Leander and the need to figure out what Danissa might tell him while ensuring he stopped asking others and didn't share unfortunate details with the Terparchon.

She should have leapt on Gisela's offer, but she waited too long.

The other princess shifted to block Danissa's path. "What's troubling you most, your father's situation or Leander's investigation, or both?"

Danissa hesitated, swallowed, then tried to recoup. "My father, of course."

"Then let us ease your other trouble."

"Us?" Danissa stepped back, but she misjudged and hit a stone wall.

"Stevan and I are agreed. You said you let a little slip to Leander. Well, if you need to tell him more . . . If sharing what I did, with Stevan's help"—Gisela laced her fingers together, her face serene despite the fast beat of her pulse at her throat—"will answer Leander's questions and mean you have that much less to deal with, then you may."

"May what?" Danissa barely breathed.

"Tell him. Leander." Gisela met Danissa's gaze. "Stevan trusts him to do right by us."

"Stevan trusts him." Danissa repeated the words, trying to keep them as uninflected as Gisela.

She evidently failed, for Gisela's eyes narrowed in irritation. "Stevan is a compeer, able to learn much about people by the way they stand or walk."

"And he's known it for all of a moon or two."

"What does your father think?" Gisela asked.

A rueful chuckle escaped Danissa. "Good question. He likes Leander as well. But he's ill. Doesn't seem able to concentrate as much as he used to."

The qualification didn't trouble Gisela. She smiled again, as even as before, as she repeated her offer for Danissa to share her and Stevan's names with Leander and even the Terparchon.

"No, don't even think about that or breathe it." A series of shivers racked Danissa, and she shrank back against the stone wall. The last of the night's cool leached some of the heat and fear from her. "You've never seen the Terparchon in a rage."

"She might not get angry."

"You don't want to risk it." Danissa grabbed Gisela's hand. "You don't understand."

"I know she's not particularly kind or thoughtful, but I've seen no signs of cruelty." Gisela shifted closer, touching Danissa's shoulder. "And in the time I've been here, so many people have assured me over and over how much better, kinder, gentler the Terparchon is than her mother. Starting with you!"

"What have you heard about the old Terparchon?" Danissa didn't remember what she might have said, much less know what others had shared.

"Everyone was afraid of her." Gisela drummed fingers against the stone wall. "You told me she used to dance on the Shadow, on poisoned ground."

"I'd say she was the one who poisoned it, except my father says the Shadows were like that forever." Danissa dropped her voice, moving closer to Gisela and turning her head around to make sure no one else was anywhere near. "The old Terparchon was known to favor poison. Even after the Terparchon and Marchon overthrew her and imprisoned her in a tower, she still managed to . . ."

Tears stung her eyes, hot as they leaked down her cheeks. For a moment, she stood not in a warming passageway but the infirmary. She pressed against her father's cold, still body as she watched healers feeding her mother and aunt all manner of foul-smelling concoctions. Her aunt survived, albeit weakened.

"The old woman didn't manage to take direct revenge, but she had my mother and aunt poisoned. All because they'd grown up with her and supported the Terparchon against the old tyrant."

For eleven, seventeen, twenty-three days after losing her mother,

Danissa got up in the night two or three times to check if her father was still alive and well. Every time she found him crying.

"She must've been a horror." Gisela wrapped an arm around Danissa, who realized only then she'd been rocking and hitting her back against the stones.

"The Terparchon learned the poisoning was her mother's doing." Danissa huddled even closer, whispering in Gisela's ear. She'd cuddled against her father at the time, able to see the fury on the Terparchon's face. "She stormed off to confront her mother. As they argued, a storm came up. Lightning struck the tower. Only the Terparchon left it alive."

Blinking, she leveled a hard glance at Gisela.

"I'll take your word for it." The other princess swallowed, yet managed to continue. "But if you need to speak, you have Stevan's and my permission."

Nodding, Danissa slipped away.

She followed a light breeze down and over to the lake, the better to drive the memory from her waking thoughts.

Or did memories guide her? Over and over again, the face of the Terparchon flashed before her as she'd appeared right before she'd stormed off—gray complexion, lips drawn back and teeth clashing together, but also eyes filled with horror. Perhaps the Terparchon had raged as she'd ended the threat her mother posed, but she'd also been devastated.

Danissa's feet led her around the dancing pavilion and across the plaza to gaze down over the balustrade at where the old Terparchon's prison once stood.

As before, a group of children played in the water while a few adults waded in to help them practice swimming techniques. Blackened stones served as a backdrop for the rocky beach from which other adults watched. The children's cries of delight drove away bad memories.

Flailing arms produced gouts of water that sparkled in the sunlight, making the air twice as bright.

Danissa settled sideways against the warm stone of the balustrade, lost in the children's simple pleasures.

"Hello?"

Danissa lurched off the balustrade, whirling to find Edrena only an arm's length away. The girl seemed to have grown in the hours since Danissa had seen her last. That, or the light gray tunic and green mantle were old, for neither reached far below Edrena's knees. The girl had a well-worn book tucked under one arm and a cheap tin flask of water in the other.

An instant after realizing who had tracked her down, Danissa checked about for Leander. Then scowled as she realized what she was doing.

Edrena stepped back. "Are you all right?"

"Yes, sorry. A bad memory." Danissa waved a hand at the lake. "Are you here to study?"

"No, I was looking for you." The girl gave Danissa a sideways glance. "Your father told me where to find you."

"He's back?" Danissa leaned against the balustrade, hands pressing against her lips. "Is he . . ."

"He's doing better." Edrena's head bobbed in a vehement nod. "Your cousins brought him down the hill in a handcart, though they had to go right back up again. Your aunt and grandfathers are staying with him. They hope you'll stop by again soon."

"I will." Competing desires flooded through her: to know exactly how he was even though she wasn't ready to talk to him again. Afraid he'd beg forgiveness again, still without explaining why. Yet at the same time wanting nothing so much as to hold onto him and never let go.

She must have missed something, nodded while Edrena talked, for when the girl's voice rang in Danissa's ears again the topic had changed.

"And your family were so wonderful. I love them! They all kept hugging me. It was so much better than anywhere else I've been." A tinge of warmth added ruddiness to the girl's cheeks. "Some of your cousins even told me to write and tell them when I get posted to an embassy somewhere, and they'll be sure to pick up a trading route through and see me."

"That's a compliment," Danissa said.

"But when I do get sent off, Leander will be left alone. He has friends among the other librarians at the winter palace—and some of the other year-round staff, but that's not the same as family." Edrena balanced her book and flask atop the balustrade in a speck of shade and held out her hands. "There'll be no one for him to talk to when he comes home in the evening. No one for him to share his worries or joys with. He's spent so much time watching over me, and making sure I have all I need, that he doesn't always take care of himself."

"He's your older brother, and he loves you. He'll be happy for you." Even as Danissa's father had always encouraged her, although granted she hadn't gone so far from him as Edrena would from Leander.

"He could love you, too."

Danissa's breath caught in her throat.

"I've seen how he watches you. And you him. All the way up the hill, and in the dance, and after." The girl waved a hand at the bulk of the palace, blocking view of the hill.

"He's a . . ." Mouth dry, Danissa only shrugged.

"A good man. Friend. Brother." Edrena's dark eyes stared straight at Danissa, her jaw tight. "But he hasn't seen you since we came back down. Even less than you've seen your father, who at least wasn't here until recently."

"What do you want?" Despite swallowing, Danissa's voice nearly cracked.

"Talk to them, my brother, your father, that's all."

"You don't know what you're asking." Danissa had talked to Leander, too much and not enough.

"You may not have your father much longer, though I hope you do. Leander won't have me even though it's not the same." The girl paused and shifted, planting herself where Danissa couldn't escape her hard gaze. "But you could have each other."

"It's not that simple."

"But what if it's worth it?"

Danissa sucked back her initial response as Edrena's words settled in. She'd never particularly considered who she might someday care for. No image had ever formed in her head, merely a general sense that if or when she ended up with someone it would be a compeer not altogether unlike her father. Certainly not someone utterly unconnected with dance magic. A librarian to whom she'd confided far too much.

And yet . . . memories of meeting with Leander washed over her. His kindness. His hand in hers when they watched the flowers glow at midnight. His reticence with her father at breakfast.

The way he'd managed to support her, though untutored, simply by being there when she Danced.

The feel of his arms as he'd comforted her after.

What if Edrena were right?

17

Leander tasted his future and didn't like it one bit.

No one noticed when he entered his rooms late in the morning. The clop of his sandals broke silence, without the usual competition of huffs and groans and muttered curses as his sister argued with one or another book she had to read in preparation for the big exam. Her bedclothes lay utterly smooth, suggesting she hadn't even sat down on the bed once since rising and setting the covers to rights.

The sun beat down on the roof overhead, warming the room despite the thickness of the walls or the shutters that kept out all but thin slivers of light. Nevertheless, a chill ran through his blood.

A few folded and sealed messages waited for him on the floor. He stepped over them and set the small satchel containing a light lunch for two on the narrow table between the beds. It gave off a whiff of some fruit he didn't recognize—perhaps the starmeg Idan had served him a few days earlier.

Whatever it was, hopefully it would keep. Leander couldn't—wouldn't—eat it all.

He doffed his green mantle as beads of perspiration formed along his brow and shoulders. A more suitable one for midday—of lightweight material and a middling blue in color—lay folded atop a pile of clean laundry.

It would be entirely too easy to become accustomed to this level of care.

Though he'd trade it for assurance he wouldn't enjoy it alone.

Rather than donning the lighter mantle, he laid it on the side of his bed and scooped up the messages from the floor.

He read and re-read them as he nibbled at portions of the meal he'd lugged up the stairs. Consumed half of a savory pastry stuffed with leafy greens and crumbles of a sharp cheese. Drank the yogurt sweetened with mashed chunks of fruit. Left the whole fruits for another time.

All the while sorting through the missives and noting the absences as much as the contents.

A scrawled note from Idan announcing his return, albeit not at his former strength.

A newsy letter from the third librarian at the summer palace library, indicating they'd located additional works on magic for him to review.

A short order from the Terparchon requiring an update sooner rather than later.

Nothing from Edrena to explain where she'd got to.

Nor from Danissa, despite the gentle reminder he'd sweated over before sending her.

He couldn't keep waiting to question her much longer. Over the course of the morning he'd interviewed servant after servant and guard after guard, and managed only to confirm earlier information. No one admitted to seeing anyone around the gardens that evening except Natter—whose name roused reactions from rolled eyes to shivers on the occasions Leander mentioned it—but a few guards mentioned hearing a day laborer say they'd seen a woman with long curls running away.

On his way back out of the building, his lighter-weight mantle slung under one arm and fastened over the other, he dropped two replies into the box for palace communications. A promise to visit, and wishes for better health to Idan on the one hand, and a request for a meeting with the Terparchon at her convenience on the other.

He'd hope to see Edrena in the evening, and allow Danissa one more day. Silly of him to have let his hopes rise.

As for the note from the librarian, he answered that in person.

Merely stepping through the doorway into the summer palace library gave him at once the feeling of coming home—and that home had changed on him.

The building itself was smaller than the winter palace library. Thick walls to keep out heat paired with high windows and protective shutters strong enough to remain in place during summer storms. The windows and louvers in the shutters directed breezes along the shelves. These were spread out wider than he was used to, the better to allow air circulation and prevent mold.

The windows also offered sunlight for reading or copying, as did baskets of luminescent mosses hung at strategic intervals.

Floorboards creaked under his feet. Wooden platforms filled the space between the shelves and provided ample space around the perimeter of the library for tables and benches for reading and copying. Beneath lay a rough stone floor lacking any decoration. Stone supports undergirded the shelves, raising them high enough above to reduce chances of flood damage.

A number of clerks and librarians bent over books or scrolls, their pens scratching against paper and copied pages rustling. Several wore two tunics in the older style, the outer decorative and rarely falling past the knee and the inner one reaching to mid-calf or ankle. Others wore mantles over their tunics, but in the same style as Leander with the mantles over one shoulder and draped under the dominant arm to allow as much free movement as possible.

In clothing, at least, Leander was among his own kind.

The place smelled right as well: parchment and ink; leather and preserved cloth; and the specially treated threads and glue turning loose pages into books.

All the contents might be counted friends of a sort, as each contained knowledge. Subjects varied. So did quality and quantity in any given volume. Still, books helped make a library and libraries were, at their best, places where people came for help.

It was in a library that Leander had learned where to go to turn himself and Edrena in, to obtain sanctuary. He still owed old Falfor for sponsoring Leander and helping him and Edrena settle into life on the ground.

Alas, Falfor hadn't returned from his venture. It was one of his subordinates, Vel, who met Leander. The other librarian was short and stout, dressed in doubled tunics of light gray that dropped straight from shoulders to floor. A few wisps of black hair curled across the top of their dark brown head as they tromped Leander over to a corner table.

"Here we are." Vel set a pile of blank papers and pen and ink next to the books.

"I'm glad you found more." Leander leaned a hip against the table, checking the window and seeing only an empty courtyard on the other side. "I was surprised at how few books discussing magics you have."

"There were more." Vel's whole body rose and fell with a sigh.

"Oh?"

"I was still fresh from having shifted here from the East Sun Library, but when the old Terparchon was imprisoned in a tower here, after the coup, she was allowed certain comforts." Vel gave another whole-body sigh. "She took near half the collection with her, particularly those on magic."

"That doesn't sound much like a prison," Leander said.

"Agreed, and a bad decision as it turned out, for they all went up in smoke when the tower burned. It's half the reason we lured Falfor over when he retired from the winter palace. We dangled the task of rebuilding our collection before him and he bit the whole hook. What I've found to share with you are some of his purchases."

Within moments, Vel set before Leander a small volume with a very ordinary spine, hardly decorated at all. The pages were parchment and quite old, although well-preserved.

Leander sifted through the pages, glancing at the contents here and there. It was written in an old variant of the common trade tongue.

"I've been looking through all our books since we first talked." Vel's voice registered, even as Leander stopped to glance at passages here and there. "I still can't find any kind of magic worth pursuing. There are some smaller gifts that could apply. It turns out stoneworkers developed a technique to roll millstones and other large, round objects to relatively far destinations without damage."

"Wouldn't there be signs the stones were rolled? Flattened grasses, things like that." Leander glanced over, then back at the volume.

"Yes, yes. Interesting, but doesn't fit. Nothing fits. All the same, this"—Vel stroked the top of the book—"seems to have been written by someone wandering around collecting stories several hundred years ago. The dating system is unfamiliar and rather odd. Many of the stories refer to magics such as I've never heard, so I've set a clerk copying it for trade."

The other librarian gave Leander a meaningful glance.

"I'll be sure to mention it when I return to the winter palace library." And its store of copied books for trade.

"That will be most appreciated." Vel rubbed their hands. "But back to the point, the clerk brought to my attention that there's a story . . ." They reached over and opened the book to where they'd placed a scrap of parchment. Soft runnels of sand weighted down the pages to hold them open. "Here. It mentions flowers just such as those blooming where the Shadow was, but in the tale they mark where dancers are buried."

"Ah!" Leander bent to read for himself, barely noting the creaks when Vel trotted away.

The story proved little more than an anecdote under the heading "on mourning flowers." The author had evidently spotted the flowers while strolling through a meadow while visiting a place whose name Leander didn't recognize. An elder explained that the village had recently lost a much beloved dancer, a princess in all but name, who'd kept the fields and woods healthy. The morning after the princess was buried in a favored site for dancing, the villagers woke to find the flowers marking the spot, ". . . and there they bloomed for a year and a day."

Although not particularly useful or applicable to the current situation, Leander jotted down the story on the parchment. The more information the better, especially when he'd face the Terparchon in a day or less.

Then his gaze fell on the following page, and the title of the next story in the compilation.

How the dancer cured the throne-holder and brought him to health.

The description of the dance bewildered him, despite his brief turn partnering Danissa, but struck a chord nonetheless. Several additional stories followed behind, with similar titles, perhaps a sequence on dancers and wellness. He copied them all for Danissa in hopes they were what she was looking for.

While glancing through the remaining tales, two sets of footsteps broke his concentration.

Vel tromped over with Edrena right behind.

"I told you he was still here," she said, voice low but not enough to keep from drawing attention from other clerks and librarians.

"I didn't disagree." Vel directed a speaking look at Leander over Edrena's head. "If you're going to talk much, perhaps you can speak outside?"

Edrena scowled, head drooping, evidently not recognizing the joking note in Vel's voice.

Leander left the book with Vel, on the understanding he might wish to see it again, but took the copied pages as he walked outside with Edrena.

"How did you find me?" He filled a mug at the fountain, similar to the one he'd offered Danissa at their first meeting but a different combination of colors.

"I asked Idan, of course." She scowled, scuffing the tip of her sandal against the base of the fountain. "He's not better but not much worse. His fathers are keeping care of him . . . but that's not why I'm here. Danissa will meet you on the plaza overlooking the lake an hour before dinner." She beamed at him, as though expecting a pat on the head and ample praise.

Danissa on the plaza in late afternoon. He gulped down water, whole body feeling lighter.

Although, he couldn't put his finger on why Edrena was telling him it.

"Because I'm the messenger." She kicked the fountain again. "You've been moping so much I figured the sooner you talked to her the better. So I asked Idan to help me find her, which he did. She got all weird and soft-eyed—not that you're much better—though she pretended she didn't want to until I gave her enough reasons to say she would."

"You talked her into meeting me?"

"Of course I did. You weren't doing much to track her down, only checked for messages dozens of times a day. But don't you know sometimes you can't just wait, you have to go out and make things happen?"

His sister had done this for him.

"It's in all my books about the ambassadorial service." She grabbed his hand. "We're supposed to go and watch and learn, but also help people realize that it's in their best interests to work with us. And convince our people back home to be careful what they ask for . . ."

She kept on, but her words went in one ear and out the other. Already she'd grown up enough to practice ambassadorial manipulation, if not diplomacy. The date of her exam edged ever closer, and she was ready. She'd surely pass, which meant soon she'd go off for training and then an appointment somewhere far away.

"Why are you looking at me that way?"

"I'm going to miss you." He wrapped her in a tight hug, as good as any given by Danissa's family.

"I know." She beamed up at him as he let her go. "That's the whole point. So don't you miss out on talking to Danissa!"

Yet for all Edrena's confidence and hope, Danissa's choice of place concerned Leander.

They met in the same spot where she'd slipped and given him the clue that one or two princesses were involved in the Shadow switch. While not the same time of day, it was still a moment of heat, the bright sun reflecting off the water, and blackened stones in the near distance.

She arrived first, her slim body near glowing in yellow and gold tunic and mantle as she stood in one of the few spots of shade. The thick foliage of a tall tree allowed him to see her without squinting.

Soft chimes rang out as her bracelets and anklets brushed against each other, indicating she wasn't as still as she seemed.

A satchel hung by his side, carrying little more than his usual wax tablet and stylus—except the copied stories. Awareness of them made the spot where the satchel rested against his torso grow damp and slick. His fingers twitched with the urge to give them to her, but he rubbed his wrists instead.

He didn't want the stories tainted with the discussion of the Shadow and flowers. Everything else had to be subsidiary to that, because it stood between them and even the dream of having more.

Their greetings were tentative, followed by an awkward silence.

"Are you ready to answer my questions?" Leander dipped a hand into his satchel, brushing the papers not the stylus.

"It depends." Danissa clasped her hands together, chin high.

"On . . ."

"On what you want to know."

Fair enough. He swallowed, mouth dry, then ticked off the core matters on his fingers. "Who you saw. What they did. What happened."

"You mean everything."

"It's hard to pick out what's important without as many details as possible."

Danissa turned her head to the side and stared at the lake. "I need more time. I haven't even talked to them yet, not enough. They don't understand the danger."

"What are you afraid of?" he asked.

"The Terparchon coming down hard. Not on me,"—she whirled back with a pleading gaze—"but on the others."

"My duty is to document events for the library records." He stretched a hand toward her, in the same way as in the dance.

"Not to get an answer for the Terparchon?" She watched his hand as though it were a snake about to strike.

"The two are not the same thing. I am charged to provide the Terparchon with the answers she needs. I believe I can do this, with your help, without giving her any names or even her asking for them."

He didn't move, breathing only to speak. "But the library records need a more complete truth."

"How complete?"

He watched her. Nervous energy ran up and down his spine, and sparked in his toes and fingers, but he kept his hand outstretched.

Danissa finally broke the silence, but without taking his hand. "I trust you more now than I did yesterday."

"But not enough." He wiped his damp hand against his mantle and let it hang by his side. Tried to keep his shoulders straight and chin high.

"Not yet. Give me time. Don't . . . At least don't talk to the other princesses and compeers for a little while longer." She moved close enough for her breath to brush his skin. "Let me do so first."

"One day." He doubted he'd speak with the Terparchon before the next afternoon, and even if he did, her concern was primarily for safety.

But he couldn't let the other details slip. Every oath he'd made to the library and his fellow librarians involved ensuring the library held as complete as possible accounts of events. If he were to make an exception for Danissa, he'd break faith with them and give her reason to suspect he might someday do the same for her, above and beyond proving himself untrustworthy.

"One day it is." She brushed a finger across the back of his hand.

"Here, then, this time tomorrow? Or somewhere else?

"Here is as good as anywhere."

The air between them grew thick with all they hadn't said. He broke it with the crinkle of papers as he drew the stories from his satchel.

"I found these in a compendium of stories about magic. They may be what you were looking for."

"You found?" She blinked, then glanced at the papers. Her breath caught, and her eyes shone as she read the first lines and then pressed them against her chest.

"I'm in your debt. How can I ever—" Her jaw shut with a snap.

"They're a gift, not a bribe. You owe me nothing for them." Leander retreated a few steps, putting more space between them.

"Finding stories and books and information, that's what I do when not conducting investigations."

"If this is a gift, do me the courtesy of allowing me to want to give something of value to you as well." She followed, so close her breath caressed his cheek.

"Then consider this a thank you for your kindness to Edrena."

"It's easy to care for your sister, but that's between her and me more than you and me." One of her hands still clutched the papers, but the other grabbed him and held tight. "When your investigation is done, when there's no chance of questions, then I'll find something to give you in return. Let me be that much of a friend."

It wasn't a friend he wanted in her, but he'd take what she was willing to give and keep hoping.

anissa blamed Leander for her restless night.

Bits of grit clung to her eyelashes despite washing her face twice over. She'd thrown on the nearest tunic and mantle at hand, in shades of blue, and pulled on only one bracelet, a simple braid of gold and silver cords that matched the cloth wound about her head. Her sandals scuffed the floor with every step. Walls and doors were no more than a distant blur as she shuffled down the hall toward her father's chamber.

A plain satchel hung across her chest, the contents light and heavy at once. Light, for how much could a few pages weigh? Yet heavy for despite too many hours reading over the stories inscribed on the pages —in Leander's exquisite writing—she couldn't quite piece out how the princess in the stories had Danced healing.

No doubt Ylena would figure it out in a trifle, but the healers had denied Danissa entry to the infirmary the previous evening. Thus she'd been left on her own to read and ponder the stories.

Not to mention Leander's gift of them to her, when she'd done nothing to earn it.

Small wonder she'd slept ill.

And dreamt. Over and over Edrena had appeared, much as she had the previous day, with her earnest face asking why couldn't Danissa love Leander. It would be so simple.

Love Leander.

Why hadn't that occurred to Danissa before? She'd had to have a girl several years her junior so much as introduce the notion!

Which suddenly explained so many things. Why Leander's image had troubled her sleeping even more than Edrena. The new and unexpected aches in her body, the hot rush of blood and trembling of nerves when she saw him. When she as little as *thought* of seeing him.

Even in the cool of morning, inside of thick walls, she stopped and leaned against chill stones but could not quench the warmth in her cheeks, at her throat, and various other places.

All new.

Love and sex were everywhere around court, even for those who didn't take the time to look for them. The other princesses and compeers all had lovers or would-be-suitors, or people with whom they enjoyed a night's pleasure. The same was true of Danissa's family. On her mother's side, her aunts Sounia and Yanna were devoted to each other. Her father still cherished memories of his beloved, though back when he and Danissa had still shared apartments at the palaces she'd known him to return very late after a court event smelling of someone else's perfume. Moreover, no one who spent as little as a few hours with her father's family on the hill could miss the constant kisses and caresses that were distinctly different from hugs, the latter distributed to any interested but the former reserved for one or a few.

That wasn't counting the giggles and sharing of information among others Danissa's age, even before she'd come of age. In which she'd participated, albeit mostly listening to others extol the delights of their latest crushes.

She'd never looked for love, never sought sex, although sometimes she wondered what they found quite so exciting. While she enjoyed court events and casual, non-magical dances with all manner of people, she'd never lost breath or composure at the sight of anyone regardless of how attractive.

Never dreamed of them.

Until she'd Danced with a man who had no experience of partnering a princess.

A man who gazed at her with warmth in his eyes. Who'd lured secrets from her lips.

And gave her the stories she carried.

Most unsettling.

Pushing away from the wall, she hurried down the hall. If any noticed the heat in her cheeks, she'd blame it on rushing.

A knock at her father's door brought not him but Aunt Madane. The skin around the older woman's eyes hung heavy, suggesting she'd enjoyed as little soothing sleep as Danissa, but otherwise she was up and dressed in a gray tunic. A mass of rolled up blankets sat in a far corner, next to two large satchels of clothes.

The room had been rearranged so that the two sofas lay alongside each other. Danissa's grandfathers rested on them, Orodan snoring slightly while Amdrei emitted soft whistles. Thin sheets covered their bare bodies, but couldn't hide that they clasped hands even in their sleep.

For an instant, the image shifted and Danissa saw herself and Leander instead, but she pushed that away. Turning to her aunt, she kept her voice low. "How is he?

"He slept well but in fits and starts." Madane accompanied Danissa across the few steps separating the outer door from the entrance to Idan's bedroom. "Seems much better."

"I am better." Her father's voice creaked halfway through, and he broke into a short coughing spate after as though something had gone down wrong.

"And he's still as stubborn as ever." Madane's voice remained low, as she glanced back to see her fathers remained asleep.

Open, west-facing shutters allowed in a light breeze and enough ambient light to reveal Idan sitting up in bed in an orange tunic. The warm shade highlighted the ashy tinge to his skin. Worse, it hung loose across his chest.

"What are you planning to do, go off somewhere?" Madane crossed her arms over her chest and clicked her tongue at him. Her body partly blocked Danissa's view.

"I will meet the day face to face, not recumbent." He'd shifted up so that his back rested against the wall, but for all his brave words, his legs stretched out on the mattress. The grass stuffing in the mattress remained fresh enough to perfume the room.

"How far do you plan on going?"

Idan pointed at the main room.

"That can be arranged, but no further yet," Madane said.

"When did you get so bossy? I'm older than you." He wagged a finger at her.

"Right now, I have more sense than you. And if you'll take a dose of advice, you'll throw yourself on your daughter's mercy." Stepping out of the way, she shooed Danissa in and closed the door behind.

Danissa leaned back against the door. Her conversation with Edrena the day before echoed in her ears, encouraging her to ask straight out. "Why didn't you tell me you were sick?"

"What, no easing an ill man in?" His shoulders rounded and head drooped, though his eyes were bright as he glanced sideways at her.

"You just said you were better." She crossed the few steps to the bed and sat down at the far end. The mattress creaked beneath her, followed by a waft of grass-scent from the filling. She tucked her fingers beneath her, to keep from grabbing him tight.

"Caught by my own words." He sighed and leaned back against the wall, shoulders straighter and head up although the slope of his body proclaimed resignation. "I wanted to spare you."

"Spare me what?"

"The heartbreak, the hope and disappointment when you try new treatments and they don't work." He closed his eyes tight, moisture glittering at the corners. His hands fisted around tufts of his bedding. "What we went through with your mother and Sounia. I didn't want to put you through it."

His words rang true. All the same, Danissa stayed at the far end of the bed. One leg twitched, toes tapping against the floor. She'd been much younger then, but she recalled the hustle and hope as each new healer tried something new. The disappointment when attempts failed, at first searing then half-expected.

The arguments over what to try next, her father and Yanna grimly optimistic while her mother and Sounia suffered pain and nausea from each new treatment. By the end her mother turned her head to the wall, declining to even consider anything more, and died.

"And this way you kept all decisions to yourself."

"Perhaps."

"Was I the last to know?" Prying one hand from beneath, she traced aimless circles on the blanket, head down.

"Neither Sounia nor Yanna knows."

"They're not here." Her mouth tightened as she watched him. "Was I the last to know *here?*"

"No, but I'm not sure who's guessed. I only know who I've told or who's asked me." Her father reached forward, grabbing her hand in his. He pulled as he sank back, yet her fingers slipped through with ease and fell instead upon his knee. "I didn't think it would come to this. I truly thought . . . the medication helped with the fever on the way here . . . until it didn't anymore."

Danissa's throat hurt from all the shouts and angry words she kept down, but she might only have her father a little longer and didn't want to lose the time remaining. A hint of pique tinged her voice as she kept her head low rather than glare or plead. "I wish you had trusted me."

Her father didn't reply. A breath later, he sniffed. When she glanced up, tears trickled down his face. His hands were shaking.

She dropped her satchel at the foot of the bed and decided not to mention the contents and the possibility they might help. Her belly jerked, irony flooding through her. She didn't want to raise his hopes unless warranted—just as he desired to protect her.

"I know you don't like hugs much." She shifted up to the head of the bed, leaning against him.

"I like one hug at a time. Everybody at once is too much." He wrinkled his nose, tears still flowing. "But I'll never turn down your hugs."

She wrapped her arms around his shaking body, helping him lay his arms over her shoulders, and they held tight without words. The embrace said all that was necessary.

Danissa remained in her father's rooms long enough to greet her grandfathers, then snatched up her satchel and rushed out. Feet tapping a rapid heartbeat against the paving stones, she marched over to the infirmary—arriving at the door a few steps behind Jola.

The other princess wore a muddy green mantle, only slightly softened by her pale green tunic. The colors emphasized her red hair, trimmed short and held back from her face by strip of gold and silver-colored lace, and the red spots on her cheeks. The thick, humid air and rising warmth of late morning had covered her face with a layer of perspiration.

Likewise Danissa's tunic clung to her skin in places beneath her mantle, breath coming fast but even despite her rush.

"What are you doing here? You're not due again for two more days." Jola blinked and waved a hand.

"I have something for Ylena. For you, too, if you're interested. Stories of past princesses who danced more than storms and fires." Danissa pulled the rolls of parchment from her satchel.

The other princess took them, glanced idly, then tilted her head. Her eyes flicked as she did more than skim the first pages.

"Where did you get these?" The parchment rustled as Jola flipped through them. "They're like . . ."

"Like lightning turning the Shadow to flowers?" Danissa kept her voice low, although the courtyard as usual was empty. "I got them from Leander."

"What did you tell him?" Jola handed the stories back, chin high and gaze challenging.

"That I was looking for something like this. Ylena remembered seeing them." Danissa tucked the stories back in her satchel. "He found them for me."

"Very nice of him," Jola said, lips pursing.

"It was a gift. A kind deed." And he'd taken such care to give the copies to Danissa without asking anything of her.

"If you say so. I wonder if Gisela and Stevan will agree."

"I've given no names, though you're tempting me to drop yours." Danissa slapped her hands together. "Besides, Stevan already said he liked Leander."

"That's not quite the way I remember it, but let's see what Ylena thinks about the stories." Jola opened the door and waved for Danissa to proceed before her.

"They're not just for Ylena, if they work." Danissa swallowed hard. "My father needs healing, too."

"I'm sorry to hear that." Despite entering second, Jola led the way through the corridors, nodding and waving at healers as they went by. The route was familiar by now. "If we're to try the dances in the stories . . . The one I read wasn't very detailed. No steps, no set beat, and we'll need a compeer."

"If necessary, one of us can compeer for the other."

"It doesn't work that way." A harsh chuckle escaped Jola. "But we can ask Todor."

Todor? Danissa shaped the name but didn't speak it as she belatedly spotted the compeer standing outside Ylena's room.

Tall and solid, Todor's face proclaimed his relation to his mother. He had the same long, narrow face as the Terparchon, with deep, dark eyes and thick brows. His purple mantle over a silvery tunic complemented his burnished skin—but his thin-lipped mouth was set in a decided downward curve.

Giving Danissa a speaking glance, Jola spread out to box Todor against the door. "Leaving so soon?" she asked.

"Ylena doesn't want to see me." Todor was too polite to push his way past them, but his eyes narrowed and lips bared sharp teeth. The short phrase left so much unspoken. He and Ylena had kept close company since shortly after Todor had become a compeer. They were exactly the kind of pairing Danissa had always vaguely expected to be part of: a princess and their compeer.

A year and a season of togetherness. They'd seemed happy, or at least content, and an example for her to someday emulate. Why had Danissa been so caught in doing likewise when she was the result of a very different type of pairing—a compeer and someone barely capable of dancing?

"She may change her mind." Danissa winced at the weakness in her voice. Ylena was nothing if not decided.

"Why not come along with us right now to see if she'll change it."

Without allowing him breath to refuse, Jola swept Todor and Danissa into the room in her wake.

There was room for them around the bed, but the air quickly turned harder to breathe despite the regular inflow of air from outside. The humidity thickened everything.

Ylena's shift from sullen, slumped shoulders to eyes flashing at Todor didn't help. The injured princess looked much as she had the day before, neither better nor worse.

"There's nothing for you here." Ylena glared at Todor.

"Don't be so sure of that." Jola shifted to block Todor's retreat even as she waved Danissa forward.

Danissa pulled the parchments from the satchel. She stroked the smooth rolls, then laid them on Ylena's lap. The other woman's hands shook as she unrolled them and began to read.

"What're those?" Todor asked as Danissa retreated to stand against the cooler stones of the wall.

"Old stories about Dancing healing."

Todor nodded, face relaxing into lines of sorrow rather than resentment. "I heard about Idan. It's hard to take. He's always been such a force, and a friend and counselor to my parents. Is he . . . ?"

"He's well enough this morning, but if the stories help us heal Ylena, maybe they can work for him too."

Todor squeezed Danissa's shoulder. She nudged him with her elbow in thanks, an old way of communication from when they'd grown up together in the children's palaces.

"Are those the stories you remember?"

"Dancing of healing to restore the body to its natural state? Yes!" Ylena's face glowed as she clutched the pages to her. "This is even better than I recalled." Then her face fell as she studied the copied words. "But there aren't enough instructions. Dance windwards? What kind of direction is that? What is the music?"

"That's all Leander found to give me." Danissa spoke his name to ensure he received due credit, but it meant nothing to Ylena. Jola made a grumpy noise from the far corner.

Todor, on the other hand, drew back to study Danissa. "Leander.

The librarian summoned from the winter palace. He found these and copied them for you?"

"It was a gift." Her cheeks heated, and she couldn't meet Todor's gaze. She, who was always so collected.

"A caring gift." He gave her another pat on the shoulder, eyes bleak.

"A hopeful gift." Despite Danissa's correction, his words resonated in her bones. Caring. A sign of affection, for why else would Leander have taken the time to find them, inscribe them, and then present them to her without seeking to place her under any obligation.

He hadn't said any words, but perhaps Edrena was right.

He could love her.

19

Next to the faces of Edrena and Danissa, one of the most welcome sights greeted Leander when he returned to the library: his old mentor.

The cool morning air had already begun to burn off when he wended his way to the courtyard. He stopped inside the door to readjust his clothing, a corner of his mantle hem having got caught awry. His fingers loosened the soft cloth as he drew in a deep breath, savoring the scent of parchment, ink, and leather.

Only to stop as a raspy voice spoke just loud enough for someone very near to hear.

"My dear boy!"

The library served as a backdrop for a familiar shock of white hair topping a face shrunk to a mass of light-brown wrinkles. Three tunics in different lengths and graduating shades of green covered the elderly man from shoulders to ankles. Lengths of matching green cloth covered his feet beneath the straps of his sandals.

Although no younger than when he'd left the winter palace to come here, Falfor, the chief librarian, seemed to stand a little taller than Leander remembered. The other man's fingers fumbled as he fastened a thick leather belt three times around his waist, the center loop hanging low as it supported several rings of keys. As soon as he settled the last buckle on the belt, he opened his arms wide.

Leander rushed over to embrace his mentor. Falfor seemed much improved since coming to the summer palace. His arms squeezed Leander tight. The older man might have filled back out, despite wearing fewer tunics. He'd always favored wearing layers as warmer than mantles—sometimes donning so many in the depth of winter that he couldn't match the colors as well as he liked.

Another librarian, with matching key rings hanging from their belt but clad in two tunics rather than three, watched. An expression of dry amusement stretched their smile wide. Their complexion was a ruddy tan and only a few gray hairs glittered among the short strands falling no farther than the bottom of their ears. No doubt the librarian who'd accompanied Falfor to Erevestis.

"Boy?" The other's nostrils flared in a snort. "Hardly. He's likely been shaving a good five years or more."

"Details." Falfor waved an airy hand as he drew back. He studied Leander's face, patting his cheek. "I fear you'll always be a boy to me. Though how you've grown! A librarian yet?

"Only a sub-librarian, still, but I have hopes." The hug had pulled the fastening of Leander's mantle down to his elbow. He yanked it up just in time for a second embrace.

"That you are here now suggests you undertake the query into the Shadow, in which case, I would think you are soon to rise higher." Falfor withdrew, nodding and beaming at Leander. "Though I cannot dictate ranks from a distance, I fancy I have some insight into my successor's thinking."

"I am here for just that." Leander took a deep breath once the older man's arms loosened. He kept his voice low, as did the others, but they attracted smiles and the occasional raised eyebrow from the clerks already in place copying works. "I brought my sister with me, and I know she'd love to see you."

"Dear Edrena, of course." Falfor rubbed his hands together, eyes narrowing. "The exam is only a month or two away. Is she ready?"

"Readier than I." Leander sucked in air and winced. When she passed, and he couldn't envision her doing anything but, she'd be off on the first steps of her journey away. Leaving him alone. With friends, of course, among whom he now could list Danissa, but friends were no substitute for family. Straightening his spine, he turned to the business at hand. "I have an appointment to speak with the Terparchon this afternoon, and I hope you have brought information for me to help solve the mystery?"

"Yes, indeed, though as is too often the case, mystery rarely proves singular." The elder led Leander to a table in a far corner, away from most of the clerks. "So many answers that in turn reveal more questions and mysteries, but we have brought much of value with us."

Falfor stopped in his tracks, so suddenly that Leander nearly crashed into him, and the other librarian, following behind Leander, stepped on his heels.

"You have met each other, right?" The white-haired man glanced from one to the other. "No? Rhoda, this is my last protégé, Leander. Leander, meet Rhoda, an earlier protégé, who will take the title of chief here before the Terparchon departs, and kindly let me fritter away my last days helping build up the collection."

They exchanged acknowledgments, then hurried after Falfor who'd barely waited a moment before hustling along. He whisked around, waving his hands at a thin, wide box. A blue-and-white enameled wave pattern decorated the edges of the box, bright against the smooth wood of the table.

The top of the box resisted Falfor's efforts to open it, wood crackling but not separating. His fingers grew pink with effort, until he gave up. "Swollen from the travel."

Shaking his head, he stood back with grace but lips decidedly downcast as Rhoda took his place.

"Did Vel tell you about their discovery yesterday?" Leander asked, in part to distract the elder.

"No, they listed the clerks and others working here, and the volumes they copy, then were called off to help locate missing pages." Falfor's eyes sparkled as he leaned in. "What news?"

"Old stories that describe flowers such as the ones that appeared in place of the Shadow as growing over the graves of dancers."

"Truly?" Rhoda glanced up, fingers prying the top off with care.

"Another twist." Falfor tapped the tips of his fingers against each other.

"Is this different from what you discovered?" Leander laid out his ever-present tablet and stylus on the far end of the table.

"Possibly." Rhoda laid the top of the box to the side, revealing an assortment of loose pages. "Did the source name the flowers?"

"No. Here, I'll get it for you." He darted in among the shelves, the platforms creaking beneath his feet. Within moments, he returned with the small volume.

Falfor nearly snatched it from his hands as Rhoda laid out the loose pages across the length of the table. Most were decent quality paper and bore assorted copied lines, each carefully labeled with the author and title of the work from which it came. At the center she placed a larger page of high quality parchment. None of the ink inscribed on it had smudged, and the contents appeared fresh although dry to the touch. It featured several colored drawings of the flowers—and a word written in larger letters at the bottom.

Nightbells.

"An odd name." Leander traced the outline of one bloom. A hint of the glorious scent wafted through him. He bent to sniff the paper, getting only the metallic tang of the inks. Excitement flickered in his veins.

"Likely inspired by the color. I couldn't replicate it, but the oldest botanical compendium the Erevestisi have features a shade of ink I've seen nowhere else." Rhoda stroked the central image, a single detailed flower. "It shows the petals as the blue of the sky at midnight on a clear night with no moon."

"They're roughly bell-shaped if you look close enough, and supposedly they ring." Falfor lifted his head from perusal of the stories.

"No one's reported hearing anything of the kind." Leander grabbed his tablet and stylus to make notes.

"Only one source mentioned that they sometimes ring," Rhoda said. "Supposedly they do so when earth is purified, and only bloom in land that princesses have cleansed.

"All of which means they are most definitely magical flowers." Falfor laid the compendium next to the copied pages.

"They appeared out of nowhere, in full bloom. I don't think that was in much doubt," Leander said.

"Ah, but one can never assume." Falfor wagged a finger. "What did I teach you?"

Leander tucked his stylus behind one ear and ran a hand through his hair. "Very well. They could have been ordinary flowers merely transported and brought to full bloom through magic."

"Exactly." Falfor rewarded him with a nod while Rhoda, behind him, shook her head and gave a wry smile as the old man continued, "except in this case they likely were magic."

"Your work? It's beautiful." Making a quick, rough sketch of the bloom, Leander nodded at Rhoda. Falfor didn't paint or draw.

"Thank you. It pales in comparison to the originals, both the compendium and the actual flower."

"You must have spent much time with the Erevistisi sources."

"The Council resisted at first, but when they realized we'd seen these flowers in life . . ." Rhoda waved at the drawings. "Many doors opened.

"When we left, several of their librarians and gardeners and one of their governing council were busy planning a visit here to see for themselves." Falfor removed a sealed missive from the bottom of the box and held it out to Leander. "They entrusted me with a message to the Terparchon requesting permission to come. I'm charging you with delivery since you already have a meeting scheduled, if you don't mind."

Leander lifted the missive. At first glance it was a single piece of paper much folded, but the paper quality proved extremely thin and fine. For the weight, it must be several pages long. It bore a thick blob of wax scented with the heavy fragrance of sonnewood, and imprinted with the Erevistis seal. The complex folding pattern was as likely as the wax to keep anyone from prying into the contents.

"Do you have any more information for me about the flowers, the nightbells, or how they appeared after a lightning bolt?" He slipped the missive into his satchel.

"Are you sure there was lightning?" Falfor pursed his lips and rubbed his chin. "I saw the bolt, from the blue, but don't see how it could have created the flowers."

Blood pounded through Leander's veins. Danissa's visage passed before his eyes. "There's a witness."

Falfor and Rhoda exchanged glances, then turned to him with matching expressions of inquiry.

Leander laid a finger against his lips, wishing Danissa might know, wherever she was, how he kept his promises.

"How much are you not telling us?" Falfor's voice dropped.

"The libraries, summer and winter, will receive all I know." Leander set down his tablet and laid hand over his heart. "Just . . . not quite yet."

"Fair enough, as you haven't completed your task." Falfor said, all traces of humor or entreaty gone from his face. "But don't forget we serve the interests of what lasts over what is transient. Our records must be complete."

As if Leander needed prompting, though to be fair, Falfor had always been fond of repeating himself and offering unnecessary reminders.

The leading librarians rarely spoke about it in public, but one of the most basic tests for whether a person would advance in the hierarchy was how they ranked their priorities. From all Leander had heard, this held true for librarians outside Codaros as well as within.

Family first, but libraries and library records a close second. Always.

Lands and rulers came a distant third, and all else far behind.

And even though librarians were allowed to consider the interests of their families first, even there, interests were circumscribed. Dedication to one's family involved supporting self and loved ones through and past survival to the point of thriving, but not to the point of profit.

Edrena counted as Leander's family. Danissa did not, as far as the libraries were concerned.

Leander could dance around her name and any details identifying her as witness while he spoke with Falfor and Rhoda—it was a practice of sorts for his meeting with the Terparchon.

When the time came to entrust the truth to the library records, that would be the true test.

All the same, his nerves jangled as he returned to his room and changed into his best attire. This time he donned tunic and mantle, and calf-strapped sandals, without Edrena's help. She was off studying and visiting with Idan and his family, based on the note she'd scribbled on a scrap of paper and left on his bed.

His fingers fumbled and he fastened the broach on the mantle through luck more than skill.

No Rik guided Leander from door to door this time. Retracing the steps through the maze, he made his way back to the crowded formal court rooms. The Terparchon wasn't anywhere in sight, only officials and scribes dealing as best they could with the press of petitioners.

Although he remembered the way to the back door, he wasn't sure he could retrace it on his own. A sour taste bloomed in his mouth as he gazed around at the dozens of others waiting, hoping, for an audience or some favor. Sweat accrued where his satchel rested against his side.

Where should he go?

Fortunately, Rik spotted Leander and escorted him through the throngs to the same chamber as before.

Little had changed. The walls remained clear and almost bare of art, brighter now with the warm, yellow glow of the early afternoon sun on the lake. The Terparchon again wore only a plain, slightly wrinkled tunic of light yellow. A bejeweled purple mantle lay over a simple wooden bench to one side, with gold bracelets and a necklace atop. Matching earrings swung at the ruler's ears, bright against her hair.

She sat on a cushioned bench, beside an oblong wood table with an inlaid design of seashells. It held a red clay plate covered with crumbs and a half-empty goblet of a clear liquid. A partially empty platter on a higher table against the wall still held two pastries oozing a savory green filling and a slice of meat wrapped in a wide green leaf.

Leander's stomach rumbled, from hunger as well as nerves, for he'd barely eaten anything since breaking his overnight fast.

Two of the Terparchon's earlier attendants were missing: Idan ill, and Leander had no idea where Amara might have gone.

Rik offered to leave, but the Terparchon asked them to stay with a tired smile, offering their pick of the remaining food. The eleee bowed and retreated to stand against the wall. They selected the meat wrap, teeth crunching as they bit in.

Swallowing a lump, Leander bowed when the ruler turned her dark eyes on him.

"What news have you brought?" She dusted her fingers over the plate, minute crumbs catching the light as they dropped through the air.

"My inquiries are not yet complete, but I can assure you of some things." Leander shifted his weight to both feet, the better to keep his calves from twitching. "First and foremost, I do not believe the change from Shadow to flowers poses any danger to the realm or to you."

"You don't?" She sat back, hands resting on her thighs—but fingers curved.

Leander held up one finger. "There is no evidence anyone from outside the palace complex was involved—"

"So it was someone already here." The Terparchon's elbows pressed against her sides, creating new wrinkles in her tunic.

"We have identified the flowers that replaced the Shadow." Leander added a second finger. "All references are old, as these have not been seen for centuries, but the accounts are distinct and speak of the flowers as gifts."

The Terparchon jerked, head lifting and puzzlement clear on her face. "Gifts?"

"The flowers are called nightbells. They evidently appear—full grown and blooming—under a number of different circumstances. Some sources suggest the flowers mark places where princesses dance a circuit, or transition, or cleanse land." Leander swallowed, mouth dry and longing for a drink of any kind. "Other sources suggest they mark where princesses are buried."

"I've never seen them over graves of princesses." The Terparchon huffed, then shook her head. "Whatever does dancing the circuit mean? Transition? There's no dance called that."

"I can only repeat the wording we found in ancient sources." Leander spread his hands wide, palms up. "More research will be required if you wish me to seek the meanings. But while the circumstances under which the flowers appear are unclear, all sources located agree that the blooms should not be plucked or cut down. They are not poisonous, but picked blooms dissolve into thin air and new flowers form. The flowers cannot be removed by any known means. They will last for a year and a day, then vanish."

"I've never heard of such magic." The Terparchon turned her head, stretching out a hand toward Rik.

The eleee placed their palms together and pressed the tips of their fingers against their lips. Their head tilted to the side and they shrugged.

"In short, I do not believe the flowers to be evil. I cannot—yet or possibly ever—say for certain why they manifested in place of the Shadow . . ."

The Terparchon sucked her breath in and held it, hands braced against the bench cushion.

"But they appeared after the lightning strike many mentioned. The sole strike that hit following the storm."

Whatever she was expecting, this wasn't it. Her torso swayed, but her face showed only puzzlement mixed with a trace of sadness. "You're certain?"

Leander bowed.

She leaned forward, grabbing hold of the cushion and gaze fixed on Leander. "What are you not telling me?"

"I have enough of the story to believe that this is not a danger, not a threat, not something you need be uneasy over. It has, by the way, piqued the interests of the Erevestisi. Some of their gardeners and librarians and officials wish permission to visit." The corners of the folded paper scraped Leander's fingers as he withdrew it from his satchel and handed it over.

The Terparchon barely had to glance at the complex folding. Her fingers unwrapped it in a matter of breaths. She read the contents, then handed the pages over to Rik with a request they arrange for a scribe to come the next day to write up her answer. Rising from the bench, she paced over to the open window and gazed out.

A line of sweat trickled down Leander's spine.

"You're treading a fine line." She turned her head to stare at him. "What else? That cannot be all."

"I swear that the library records of this incident will be complete, and that all information necessary to answer your questions and ease your mind will be provided." Leander tangled his hands, fingers pressing hard against his skin as his palms grew damp.

"Trust a librarian to give such a slippery answer." Even without her jewels and mantle, she exuded authority. "I ask a third time, what are you not telling me?"

"Do you need the whole tale, or enough to move forward?" Leander locked his knees and lifted his chin. Fear filled the air—his? Or hers?

"Do not presume to tell me what I do or don't need to know. What happened?"

"My inquiries are not complete, but I believe this to be something of an accident." He'd promised Danissa to keep her name confidential as long as he could.

"Accident?" The Terparchon gave a dry chuckle, but she swayed. Her fingers twitched, and she grabbed hold of the wall.

"I lack the exact circumstances, but I will have them soon and ensure the entry in the libraries' records is as detailed as possible." He held his breath. Waited. Hoped.

"An accident, destroying the Shadow, replacing it with magical flowers that purify the land, or some other unknown purpose." Pushing away from the wall, she paced the length of the room. "You expect me to accept this?"

Before Leander could come up with a response, Rik pushed away from the wall and planted themself at one end of the Terparchon's path. "It seems to me the kind of accident that would be well to have happen to all the Shadows."

"You know anything about this that you haven't shared?" she asked.

Rik glanced Leander's way, lips quirking in a gentle smile. "I believe him when he says that it is not a danger to you, not now. It may well prove to be of benefit."

"You think I should accept this?"

"I would not presume to tell you what to do . . . still, merely because this happened in a night, it does not mean then that you need respond equally fast." They waved the opened missive. "Allow the Erevestisi envoys to visit. Spread the news and see who else asks permission, or sneaks in without. You'll be leaving here to process to the winter palace soon. Wait to make a final determination until next summer."

The Terparchon stared out over the lake for a long while again. Turning around, she pointed a finger at Leander. *I am relying on you.*

The door opened with a bang, and whatever else she might have added was left unsaid.

The Marchon burst through. He wore half-armor over a plain tunic, although his head was bare and he bore no weapon. His sweaty skin gleamed in the sunlight, and a hint of smoke wafted in with him.

He took in the occupants of the room with a glance before focusing on the Terparchon. "A messenger from the hills arrived. Fires have started and are growing. I've already sent guards to alert the princesses and compeers."

"Are you ready?" She wrinkled her nose as she squinted at his armor. "You'll be needed for the Fire Dance."

The two swept out of the room together, taking nearly all the air with them.

"Do make the library records complete." Rik patted Leander's back as they ushered him away from the royal apartments. "I doubt she'll ask for much more in the way of detail unless she has too much time on her hands, but she'll want it there if she does."

"They'll be complete, but she may not be able to read them." If Danissa trusted Leander, just enough, he'd be able to ensure that.

"For now, she trusts you. That should suffice." A huff of relief escaped the eleee. "You've at least eased her mind about danger, for which you have my thanks at least."

Tension drained out of Leander, along with much of his energy. He slumped against the wall halfway down the circular stair away from the royal rooms. He'd kept his word to Danissa and she was safe.

All that remained was to get the last info from her.

And find out whether he'd ever see her again, or speak or dance, after.

❧ 20 ☙

A hard beat drummed in Danissa's blood. She ran, sandals pounding against the stone walkways. The hems of her Dancing tunic and mantle fluttered around her—lightweight undyed materials, easy to launder. Summer palace or winter, she'd never yet emerged from a Dance *not* soaked in sweat. She wore no jewelry, and had wrapped a cloth around her head so that all her hair tumbled from a single point at the back, cascading away from her neck to brush the base of her shoulder blades.

Each breath dragged in warm air, sluggish and thick with moisture. Her muscles already ached from earlier exertions, but she pushed through twinges. Her lungs labored as she pelted toward the dancing pavilion with Jola, similarly clad, hot on her heels.

Only to come to an abrupt halt.

Leander stood to the side of the entrance to the dancing pavilion, as she'd never seen him before. His court attire became him, the creamy yellow tunic and bold red mantle bringing out golden undertones in his warm brown skin. He'd planted his feet far enough away from the door to leave a clear path. Other princesses and compeers darted through the door with barely a glance his way.

She was the only one who stopped and stared of her own volition.

Her face and front heated. The admiration in his eyes, despite her plain clothing, roused awareness prickling along her body. Her breath caught in her throat as ripples of electricity flowed along her limbs and through her torso.

In contrast, her back grew cold. Jola, who'd followed a few steps behind—although usually the leader—shifted to stand shoulder-to-shoulder with Danissa. The movement roused a slight breeze but left her chilled.

The other princess drew in a deep breath, body straightening.

"Why are you here?" Danissa asked to keep Jola from doing so, possibly in ruder words.

Two musicians passed them, both carrying drums and neither giving them more than a sideways glance.

"I was meeting with the Terparchon when the news came." Leander directed a slight nod at Jola, keeping his gaze otherwise fixed on Danissa. "I wanted to wish you well."

"Oh." She clapped a hand over her mouth to still the unexpected giggles threatening to emerge. The warmth along her front intensified, wrapping around to enfold her back and ease sore muscles. No one had ever come to see her down to Dance before. True, no one else had ever been in a position to do so except her father, who was usually ahead of her. Still, the gesture sent further flutters through her body, helping keep back the cold awareness her father would not be down in the chamber this time. "Thank you."

"There's no time." Jola glared Leander as she tugged at Danissa, pulling her away and down.

Danissa followed the other princess into the pavilion and down the narrow stairs. The thick stone walls focused her vision on the smooth, steep stairs and Rik standing at the first landing with a lantern raised high. The soft yellow light revealed the many slight depressions in the stones left by centuries of passage.

Instinct and familiarity guided Danissa. She rested a hand atop the thin wood railing affixed to the right wall as she continued down the second set of stairs to the bottom.

All the while, possibilities whirled around her head. Leander had met with the Terparchon. A simple statement of fact, that he'd spoken to her. Shared what he knew, the progress of his investigation.

Or a warning? He'd asked her to trust him—and let her enter the pavilion to join the ruler. Surely because she ran no risk. She had to trust.

Though her breath caught in her throat and her lungs struggled to adjust to the drier, cooler air below. The dancing chamber's design drew air from above, but somehow filtered it so that it never carried more than a hint of the outside. Storms could, and had, pounded overhead without Danissa smelling or tasting other than the merest tang.

The room matched the one above for space, complete with a lofty ceiling. Despite well-positioned baskets of luminescent mosses casting light, the overall impression was always of gray shadows. Alcoves carved into the exterior walls contained soft couches and food stores so that dancers might rest and recover during long Dances. Long, thin fountains affixed to the walls ensured an ample supply of water.

For all the room's space, as soon as Danissa emerged from the stairs, her shoulders hunched and body drew inward. All the princesses and compeers who'd preceded her down the stairs clustered there. None showed any inclination to step onto the dancing floor.

Only the musicians pushed their way through to settle into their alcove. Then again, although former princesses and compeers, *they* didn't have to set foot on tiled mosaic that filled most of the chamber. A thousand small tiles formed the dancing floor, embedded in stone so as to ensure a completely level surface.

Usually the floor gleamed a dull silver gray—today it held instead a sullen, ruddy cast.

Of fire and flame.

Or blood.

Danissa slipped to the side and backward, settling against the cool stone wall. Low drum rolls marked the musicians readying to play. Amara and Rik checked the condition of the water closets, food stores, and fountains.

A sharp elbow dug into Danissa's side. Jola turned a glare on her. "Stretch!"

The other princess passed through the crowd, rapping princesses and compeers as she repeated the instruction.

Rolling her shoulders, Danissa began a course of stretches to prepare her body for the labors ahead. She ignored the condition of the dance floor, or rather tried to. Sooner or later, every single stretching sequence forced her to look there at least once.

The ruddy cast on the tiles deepened. Hazy clouds of gray floated amid the seething redness—primarily at the center where the Terparchon stood. She wore the same tunic and mantle as the rest, as did the Marchon at her side. His presence marked the importance of the Dance. He did his part by rote, worse than any of the other taught compeers, and the Terparchon had excused him from a good half of the Dances well before Danissa became a princess.

The Terparchon became the center of the Dance. All others faded in comparison.

The last dancers rushed down the stairs, adding to the crowd at the bottom as the door clicked shut and locked.

No way out until the Dance ended.

"Welcome." The Terparchon turned in a circle, focusing on each dancer in turn for a breath or two.

Three for Danissa. Or four or five, for she lost count. She froze under the shadowed, watchful eyes of her ruler, whose face she searched for any sign of anger or concern.

Nothing.

No indication Leander had dropped Danissa's name to the Terparchon. He'd said he wouldn't.

She had to trust him.

With a nod, the Terparchon's gaze moved on.

Danissa dropped to the floor and continued stretching, taking every opportunity to bury her face against her chest or arms or legs. Her whole being turned inward despite the slight burn as her muscles warmed.

Trust Leander?

She'd Danced with him, the first Dance she'd ever done with someone other than her father or a born compeer he'd selected for her.

Her father liked Leander, and she usually took his guidance.

Stevan liked the librarian. Gisela, too.

Danissa liked him, maybe even more than liking, so why did she not trust him?

Or perhaps she did, but wanted to deny it. Extending trust to him meant change and opening herself to someone else, someone new.

Facing life without the stalwart presence of her father at her side.

But she already did that. Idan wasn't here. He'd continued to attend Dances after his retirement earlier in the summer.

This was the only Dance since she'd become a princess that he'd missed.

A sharp clap shook Danissa out of her reverie. The Terparchon had completed her rotation and faced the closed, locked door.

"Circle up." The Terparchon clapped again.

Danissa stepped up to the edge of the Dance floor. The toes of her sandals brushed the tiles, sending a rush of warmth up followed by a gout of bitter smoke. The burnt taste of scorched leather made her gag. How could the Terparchon and Marchon bear to stand on the floor? Danissa moved back far enough to see the gap between sandals and tiles.

Stevan, Danissa's usual compeer since her father's retirement, slipped into place at her side.

"Ready?" He bent and whispered the question.

She grimaced at him, shaking her head slightly, and won a soft chuckle that turned into a gasp a moment later.

The ruddy cast on the tiles vanished. In its place appeared hills and dales, streams and forests, fields and houses little more than small squares. None bigger than a toe. Even the occasional city and castle took up minute space compared to the flowing landscape.

An instant later, fires manifested among the trees and fields. Some spots smoldered dark red amid blackened embers. Elsewhere gouts of flame and smoke rose above the floor. None higher than the Terparchon's ankle, but present nonetheless. The air grew hotter, hazy with enough smoke to make eyes water and each breath taste of ashes.

Stevan trembled, raising resonance in her bones.

"It's not burning here. We get only a hint of what it's like, but we're safe." She bumped his shoulder. Of course he'd be uncertain, as he'd never Danced fire before.

But he shook his head and pointed at a manorial complex near where they stood. "I grew up in the Silver Hills. Most of my family are still there."

Whether or not he meant to keep his voice down, his words resounded around the room. Others cast glances at him, and a few offered similar worries for friends and families who lived in the area.

"Fire is a force of nature." The Terparchon raised her hands. Flames roared up, surrounding her but leaving her unconsumed.

Danissa leapt back, as did everyone. Stevan's longer legs carried him farther. Even the Marchon flinched.

A clap dispelled the conflagration. The landscape still covered the floor, but flattened into a two-dimensional image. The haze in the air remained.

"It is friend and ally—and implacable foe. It hungers, so it eats. It comes where it is fed and goes when it has consumed. We cannot stop it, any more than we can forbid storms from lashing us with winds and rain. Instead, we seek to shape this fire. We will offer guidance. Show flames places where they may burn as they will, and those we would have spared. Bring available moisture to the surface for the earth and plants to draw on and resist being consumed. Give to all those living in its path, human and not, calm in the place of panic, and the chance to find a way out or a place of sanctuary."

"Chance?" Stevan's voice broke, rising high at the end. He stepped back up to the edge of the dance floor as Gisela grabbed his hand and leaned against him.

Danissa took her place on his other side, offering what support she could.

The Terparchon bowed her head, hands pressed tight against her midsection. "We cannot offer any guarantees, only possibilities."

"Keeping calm gives people better odds of escape or finding places to hunker down." The Marchon wrapped an arm around the Terparchon's back. As she had done before, he gazed at each dancer, nodding at Stevan in his turn.

"Let the Dance begin."

A hard, fast, raging drumroll echoed through the chamber. It vanished as quick as it started, replaced by two pulsing beats—one predictable and the other random.

The Terparchon seemed loath to leave protection of the Marchon's arm as she assigned the first to take the floor with them.

In a gesture of mercy toward Stevan, the Terparchon gave him and Danissa the task of Dancing calmness. Other pairs took on the roles of flames, wind, and moisture.

Stevan hesitated when it came to actually stepping onto the floor. He trembled, moisture beading his forehead.

A thin coat of sweat already covered Danissa's body, too. She filled her lungs with the smoke-tinged air and let it out slowly. Hands pressed over her heart, she pushed out fear and worry and every distraction.

She must *be* calm to Dance it. The earth beneath her feet lent her serenity. The stones forming the chamber knew change—and how to remain what they were.

One foot raised and lowered. One step onto the floor, then another. She no longer stood on stone. The land over which they Danced welcomed her. The smells of crops ripening, deep woods, and cooks laboring over meals mixed with the stench of smoke.

"Let the earth lead us." Danissa offered Stevan a hand. The same gesture she'd made when she asked Leander to join her, but so different in partner and circumstances.

Stevan's gift let him follow her into the overlapping landscapes springing up around them. He drew tranquility and comfort from the earth through Danissa.

Unrestrained fire reached them all too soon. Flames arced over, raging this way and that. Animals trampled grasses, crashed through forests, broke burning fences, seeking escape. Voices shrieked. Babies cried.

Drums beat on, at odds.

Danissa Danced hope in the midst of fear and desperation. Calm allowed her to spot lines of possible escape, places of refuge. She leapt across rivers of fire with Stevan in her wake. Their passage eased humans and animals alike. Rushing feet followed the paths she and Stevan Danced.

Nor were they alone in the chaos. Other dancers twisted their bodies as they bent flames this way rather than that. Jola and her compeer, Nefeli, redirected winds, shifting gusts from feeding fire to holding it back. Gisela and Todor imbued skin and fur, bark and leaf, with moisture to aid survival.

The Terparchon swirled through everywhere, with the Marchon supporting her and barely holding her down to earth, as they guided the dancers across threatened lands.

The earth's serenity filled Danissa to the brim. No tears or cries escaped her when she and Stevan were tapped to swap out of the Dance and let others take their place.

She dropped onto a sofa, feet aching and thin sandals nearly worn through. A creak alerted her to Stevan settling onto a nearby sofa.

Amara pressed a goblet of water with sweet herbs into Danissa's hands and bade her drink it all. She did in a series of gulps, blinking and surprised by the stench of burnt hair lingering in the air—until Amara trimmed off some crisped ends from Danissa's curls.

The Dance itself continued. Seven princesses darted about the floor with their compeers. Flames and smoke wreathed around the Terparchon and Marchon, shielding their movements.

Despite the chaos continuing on the floor, calm welled within Danissa.

Her worries fell away as ashes scattering on the earth, whisked away by wind, and drowned in rain.

Indeed, tranquility allowed her to note the hints of rain manifesting at the far end of the dance floor. To hope for an end to the raging flames before too long.

And to believe in Leander. Accept he hadn't mentioned her name to the Terparchon. Appreciate all the signs of care he'd shown her—finding the stories and supporting her in the Dance of joy, but also little things such as sharing bits of his past, though it hurt, and coming to wish her well.

Giving her time to decide whether she trusted him.

Time to understand she could.

She did.

Calm settled into every inch of her body throughout the Dance and beyond. A buoyant feeling eased her climb up out of the chamber after it was over, despite aching muscles. The same joy that she'd Danced before infused her.

Cleansed and clad in clean attire, she left the baths wanting nothing so much as to see Leander and share this with him.

Only to find someone else waiting for her. Her grandfather Amdrei, his face drawn and eyes bloodshot.

"Your father's in the infirmary." Amdrei wrapped his arms tight around Danissa in an almost-bone-cracking hug. Tears dripped onto her shoulder, dissolving her calm drop by drop. "The healers aren't sure he'll live."

L eander hustled through courtyard after courtyard.

The slap of sandals against stone affirmed that Edrena followed behind, hot on his heels. Every time she caught her breath she used it up asking one question or another.

"How is Idan?" "What happened?" "Where are we going?"

In one ear and out the other. Leander either didn't know the answer or refused to waste time telling her, again, that they headed to the infirmary.

A few drops of sweet pepper lingered on his lips from the dinner he and Edrena had enjoyed with Falfor and Rhoda, before the messenger located him.

All the beauties of the twilight went to waste on him. He noted the soft breeze shifting the temperature from hot to merely warm only because the change allowed him to walk faster without working up additional sweat. He turned his back on the streaks of gold, red, and purple across the sky.

He rubbed his hands and wrists every couple of steps, particularly when he had to divert from a straight path.

The masses of humanity emerging to enjoy the glorious evening proved impossible to ignore. They, too, were beautiful, skin of all shades glowing in the radiant light and many wearing jewelry along with fine mantles and tunics.

All the people got in his way. Where had they come from? Passages and corners that he'd ducked through and found empty during the day now teemed with crowds talking, drinking, courting—and blocking his way.

The loose ends of his green mantle flapped as he curved around a group chatting in the middle of a path across a courtyard. Some called after him, but he ignored their angry words.

Even the courtyard outside the infirmary was half-full with people standing around. Five guards in gilded leather armor over knee-length tunics formed a line before the wide, arched doorway. Short swords and daggers hung at their belts. No one challenged them. The others in the courtyard clustered in and around the alcoves lining the walls, or rested on the rim of the fountain at the center.

Most of the princesses and compeers. Servants. Courtiers.

Not Danissa or any of her family.

Edrena's stream of questions finally quieted. She hung close behind him. A slight tug and the shifting weight of his mantle on his shoulder betrayed she'd grabbed hold and wrapped her fingers tight around the cloth.

Without stopping his forward momentum, he reached around and swapped his hand for the cloth. Her cold fingers trembled within his grasp until they started to warm.

None of the soldiers wore helmets, leaving their faces plain to view. One or two familiar, but not the central guard.

Leander strode straight up to him, stopping with ample space between. Edrena bumped into him, and he stumbled forward another step.

"I'm Leander. Idan sent for me."

"We have your name, but no one else's." The guard peered around and pointed at Edrena. "Is she with you?"

"Yes."

"You'll take responsibility for her?" they asked.

"Of course." Leander laid an arm across Edrena's shoulder as she slipped up next to him.

"Then enter. Turn left at the first hall, then all the way to the end." The guard stepped aside, leaving enough room for one person to pass at a time.

Leander shooed Edrena ahead, nodding at the guard as he passed.

Even this early in the evening, the hall proved comfortably cool. It was wide enough for four to walk abreast. Delicate landscape mosaics decorated the uppermost sections of the tall walls. Plain tiles covered the rest, and the floors as well. A mixture of very light shades of blue, pink, green, and gray, they gleamed with cleanliness, but here and there the grout between showed stains. Five corridors led off from the central one, two on the left and three on the right. Baskets of luminescent mosses provided ample light by which to see.

Astringent smells hung in the air. The back of Leander's mouth and nose prickled and he sneezed twice before adjusting.

At regular intervals, small pipes emerged from the walls at waist level. Each dropped tinkling streams of water into scalloped bowls just big enough for a person to wash their hands. Water dripped from the bowl rims into narrow channels lining the edges of the walls, flowing down toward the garden courtyard at the center of the infirmary. Bright green leaves and yellow blossoms suggested a place of respite.

The floor underfoot was almost level, with a slight slant at the edges.

Fewer fountains graced the walls of the first corridor on the left. It was narrower, half as wide, but otherwise decorated with the same combination of pale tiles in a random array topped by landscapes along the highest reaches—showing distant hills and valleys. Instead of leading in a straight line, it had a gentle curve.

Voices sounded in the distance, but the chimes of the flowing water concealed words save for occasional loud consonants.

All the doors along the narrow hall were formed of shutters, with separate upper and lower halves plus an additional window above. Most of the upper halves were open, pinned back with curves of metal inset into the walls. The doors to the left revealed narrow chambers with thin windows overlooking courtyards, bare pallets covered in white fabric, and one or two stools or benches. The doors on the right were closed, but with the windows at the top open to allow air circulation.

Following the curve of the corridor, Leander stopped in his tracks as the source of the voices appeared. The Terparchon and the Marchon sat side by side on a bench. The sheen of their skin along their necks suggested they'd come straight from the baths. Both wore plain clothes and little jewelry, but their profiles were unmistakable.

Two handfuls of attendants lined the walls near them, half guards in attire matching those outside. The rest included Amara and Rik, and three who so closely resembled the Terparchon or Marchon that they were surely their children, compeers all.

"Oh!" Edrena's soft gasp carried.

The dozen heads all turned, the guards stiffening.

"Whatever are you doing here?" The Terparchon rose but didn't otherwise move. One hand remained tucked in the Marchon's.

"I received word Idan was asking for me." Leander swallowed, licking the last drops of pepper from his lips, and continued forward at a slower pace.

The top half of a door a short ways beyond the crowd opened, and Orodan peered out, his resemblance to his son, or vice-versa, particularly pronounced in the soft light.

"Excellencies." Orodan nodded at the rulers, a strained smile stretching his face at sight of Leander and his sister. "Ah, Leander, good."

"I came as soon as I heard."

"You're in time. Enter, please, if you would." The older man's hands fumbled at the bottom of the door, opening it fully. He nodded at Edrena, keeping close enough to Leander to be his shadow, and allowed her in as well.

A narrow bed filled the center of the chamber. Idan lay still, his upper half raised by several pillows. A thin sheet covered him from the waist-down, clinging to his gray-tinged skin thanks to a gleaming layer of sweat. A rectangular swathe of darker gray cloth rested heavily on his chest, dripping moisture and exuding a pungent aroma. Something floral, but sharp and with a strong hint of salt. Oblong reddish blotches marred Idan's throat as he turned to blink heavy eyelids at Leander and Edrena.

The temperature rose several degrees, prompting perspiration to bead Leander's forehead and neck. Idan's fathers stood on one side of the bed, Danissa and Madane on the other. All wore clothes showing wrinkles and sweat stains. Danissa's hair hung loose from the back of her head, a glorious fall of curls that under other circumstances Leander would enjoy marveling at.

Danissa glanced at Leander and Edrena, then turned away. Her fingers fumbled as she clutched her father's hand. A sniff escaped her.

Edrena's hold on Leander tightened.

"I'm so sorry. I came as soon as I could, but . . ." Leander stopped right inside the doorway. Even with Edrena at his side, he didn't belong.

Idan lifted his free hand and gestured with a finger. A small movement, little more than a flick, but most definitely a command.

"You made it in time." Idan dragged in a deep breath in three distinct gulps. The blisters on his neck brightened slightly. "I'm not going anywhere yet."

"I'm sorry you're ill." Leander bit his lip. Edrena's hand shook within his grasp, or his hand trembled holding hers, or both. "How may I serve you?"

"Give me cause to rejoice before I die." Idan rolled his head to the side and smiled at his daughter.

Leander blinked, jaw dropping. Signs of surprise on the others' faces suggested he hadn't misheard. Orodan whispered to his beloved, their arms wrapped around each other.

"Is there anything you want to share with Leander?" Idan asked his daughter, then coughed and dragged in another long, halting breath.

"I don't . . ." Danissa trembled head to toe, eyes wide.

"You wouldn't want an audience, if all were well." Idan hissed and coughed, then shook his head. "But since I may not be about later, may I have the pleasure of being present?"

"For what?" Danissa glanced at Leander, their gazes meeting across her father's limbs. She looked away first.

"Did you think I wouldn't feel the change in how you stood on the earth, how you Danced, just because I wasn't underground with you?"

"Change?" Danissa asked, voice more hesitant than before. Her head curved as she looked down, though she peeped across at Leander again and again.

Each glance sent as clear a rill of delight through him as though she'd given him the kiss of a butterfly. Hardly appropriate for the bedside of a dying man, but Leander accepted what he was given as his own breathing shallowed.

"You've given me permission to check on you every time I've asked. I try not to abuse it, but I couldn't resist seeing how you were in the Dance." Idan's head fell back, his expression one of pure delight. "The peace in your heart, the trust . . . it eased me."

"You know that?" Danissa straightened, shock clear on her face.

Leander's heart beat stronger, louder, faster in his chest. Dragging in a deep breath, his head swayed. A hissing breath near him and the sudden pressure of Edrena against his back helped keep him upright.

"Come now." Idan pointed at her without lifting his hand from his side. "You know better than most what born compeers can do if we wish. Not just align ourselves with princesses for the best use of their power, but find people, even know their hearts by the way they touch the earth."

"It's not a choice I've made." A soft huff escaped Danissa. "Not yet."

"It's closer than you've gone with anyone. I'll take it, and I think he will, too, for now." Idan lifted his free hand, barely a finger's length above the bed but clearly reaching out for Leander.

One hand still tangled with his sister's, Leander laid his free over Idan's. Energy sparked at their touch, then it settled into a rhythmic pulse from Leander through Idan to Danissa and back. Flickering lights above their joined hands, and across Idan's body, traced the repeating circuit.

On the far side, Danissa sighed as her shoulders straightened. She met Leander's gaze straight on, a hint of added color in her cheeks.

"You asked me to trust you, and I do." Each word resounded

distinct within the hushed chamber. "It's too early, too fast, for anything more, but . . ."

"It's a start." His body felt light, as though he could rise and bump against the ceiling. "It's all I asked you for." Despite the elation filling him, an element of sorrow twanged within him. That she hadn't shared of her own choice, but at her father's prodding.

"All you asked, but not all you want." Danissa's lips quirked to one side.

"True, but we can discuss the rest at another time." Her trust buoyed him, but this was not the place to ask questions, either about the extent of her trust or, more particularly, the full story of Shadow.

She swallowed, throat muscles working, but nodded.

Still more warmth flickered across Idan's body, from his hand to hers and back.

"Is that what you wanted?" Leander asked Idan. "Or do you need anything from me?"

"Not from you now. I saw you dance together the other day, that will have to be enough to go on." Idan's fingers twitched within Leander's loose grasp as the older man turned his head toward his daughter. "I always hoped I'd be here to see who you'd choose. I'm not telling you to choose Leander, but that you trust him is something."

Sniffs and muffled exhalations rippled around the room. Madane had her arms around Danissa, who leaned into her as both trembled. Idan's fathers clung together, one muttering under his breath that it wasn't fair or right for children to die before their parents.

A harsh cough racked Idan. He jerked, his hands coming free of both Leander and Danissa, before subsiding flat against the mattress and pillows.

"Don't just say something like that, stay so you can see it." Danissa pulled free of her aunt, producing the flask of Idan's strengthener from somewhere and removing the cap. The sharp smell turned Leander's stomach.

"I'm trying." Idan coughed again. "I can't keep anything down."

"Just a sip." Danissa and Madane between them raised him and held the flask to his lips long enough for him to take a swallow. "You're fading just like mother. You didn't want her to die young, allow us not to want you to either."

"Not like your mother." Idan lifted his hands a little, waving his fingers. "She had splotches all over her body and pains in her belly, and I've neither."

Danissa seemed to accept this, but Madane and Idan's fathers shook their heads.

So much pain and sorrow. Hope turned to hurt when left unfulfilled.

Hope. Leander had met Danissa in the first place when she'd run to the library in a burst of yearning for a way to heal him.

"Didn't the stories help?" Careful words, holding meaning only for her or anyone else to whom she'd confided. Based on the looks of puzzlement among her family, that was no one but him.

Danissa turned away and gazed down at the floor. Her shoulders slumped.

"Stories?" Idan licked his lips, head rolling to the side to see his daughter.

She glanced over at Leander, eyes big and pleading and mouth open without uttering a sound.

"Old tales I found for her in the library." He waved a hand. "Stories of dancing and healing."

"Nothing much." Danissa closed her eyes and drew in a deep breath, head hanging low again. "They could have been more, but they weren't." Her monotone voice and dispirited attitude warned her listeners not to get their hopes up.

Piercing him with her disappointment.

22

Why did Leander have to mention the stories?

Then again, he didn't know Danissa's father well. Idan loved stories. He'd put her to sleep many a night when she was a youngling by recounting tales of derring-do, people venturing out to right wrongs, princesses and compeers gathering to save countries from war or famine—all with happy endings. No sad tears allowed those nights, long before her mother sickened. He'd sat next to Danissa as she curled on her pallet and recounted stories from memory or read from books.

He'd come by his joy in stories quite honestly. Every time she'd ventured up the hill to spend part of the summer with her relatives, she wound up spending evening after evening listening as they took turns topping each other's tales.

There'd be no stories from him now. His energy lasted for at best a sentence or two at a time, and he'd already used much pulling an admission of trust from her.

The narrow confines of the room pressed in on her. Too many people, all breathing in the warm air, all crowded around a bed containing a dwindling loved one pretending not to know that they were saying goodbye—seeking a few more days, hours, of hope and possibility.

All looking for distraction, and finding it in Leander's ill-timed mention of stories.

Too late to warn him.

"Nothing much." Dropping her head, she sought to depress any unwarranted hopes. "They could have been more, but they weren't."

"Were they new, or ones you've heard before?" Idan shivered and rubbed his fingers against the sheets, raising a whistling sound.

"New."

All but Leander's ears pricked up. Clear interest shone on her grandfathers' faces—although they watched their son, not her—her aunt's, Edrena's. Even her father, weak as he was, turned to her with clear anticipation.

"Once, very long ago when the world was new?" The ritual phrase, one of several ways to begin telling tales, fell readily from Grandfather Amdrei's lips. Idan's mouth silently shaped the same words.

"Would you like me to tell you?" She wrapped her hands around her father's, careful not to press too tight.

He nodded, eyes closing. His pulse still beat at the base of his palm. She kept light fingers pressed there, as a precaution.

She'd memorized the most relevant of the stories, after working with Ylena and Jola to piece it apart. Enough to recount it without consulting the scrolls, though she could not recite all the lines word for word, particularly those not to do with dancing.

She'd have to muddle through.

"Long ago and far away, when the moon had not yet kissed the sun,"—a different opening, but enough ritual language to feed listeners' anticipation— "there lived a ruler who, in a moment of carelessness, swallowed a golden seed. For him, no amount of gold was ever enough. Though the precious metal covered his throne, piece by piece he ate it. His people brought him all they could spare from feeding themselves and their loved ones. All they had, that he might acquire ever more gold. Never did it suffice."

Idan's chest jerked as a bitter huff escaped him. Her aunt made a similar sound, and her grandfathers exchanged glances.

"Anyone who passed by the city, or was so careless as to venture near enough to encounter the throne-holder's army, was summoned to render tribute." Danissa rocked, rooted to her father's bed by point where their hands met and his pulse pounded against her. "They might give of their goods or themselves, but give they would or be locked in the deepest pits and highest towers until they found something to satisfy the throne-holder's everlasting hunger for any and all things gold." For all Danissa had skimmed the first half of the story, she found the words and phrases coming readily to mind. "Now, you might wonder why his people obeyed and did not rebel."

Edrena nodded, crossing her arms over her chest. Leander nudged her, then again he had copied the story for Danissa and knew how it went.

"But they knew not what they'd wrought until they were trapped in service to his hunger." Her father rubbed her hand. No doubt this was in some part familiar to him and all the others since they'd all, even Edrena, lived part of their lives under the old Terparchon. "They took pleasure in his might, and the way gold filled his body and gleamed from his eyes and teeth, seeing themselves reflected there. The greater he became, the greater they considered themselves. To do otherwise risked facing the chances they'd had to protest, to set bounds upon his appetites before they grew insatiable. To say no and deny him gold. Few are the people with such courage, and few there were, there and then."

"That's stupid." One of Edrena's heels tapped against the tiled floor. "They should've just said no. Sooner is better, but . . ."

"The longer one lets things slide, the harder it is to say no." On Edrena's far side, Grandfather Amdrei gave her a half-smile. "And in tales of old times, things are often magnified from reality and matters simplified. It's much easier, and more engaging, to speak of horrendous tyrants. Less so for the middling we are more likely to face and less likely to recognize."

Edrena's lips tightened and her shoulders rose up to her ears, but she didn't argue.

Idan's smooth, even pulse throbbing against Danissa's hand indicated he was enjoying the story, so she went on.

This continued, forever and a day, until it so happened the guards brought a small group of travelers into the great hall. The strangers marveled at gold-bedecked and gold-infused ruler, and bowed before him.

His eyes passed over them with disregard, for all were dressed simply and carried their worldly goods in worn satchels.

"What do you bring me?" he asked.

"We have nothing but ourselves," the oldest answered, a woman who stood proud and strong before him. She had with her her beloved and her partner, as well her partner's beloved and their young child—who, alas, had hair the color of gold.

"All who come here must pay tribute. If you have nothing else, then give me one of yourselves. The child with the golden hair will do."

He thought himself generous to make the offer instead of keeping them all— and having to feed them.

Oh great kindness, cried his people, to take only one.

"We came together, we will leave together as we are to the last hair," said the woman, drawing herself up, "but I see now that you have a hunger in your belly that nothing can satisfy. It is a sickness that came upon you, and you embraced it and made it part of you.

"I will make you this bargain: I will dance for you, and if my dance does not please you then you may keep me, and cut and keep the child's hair, so long as you let her and the others go."

"A wandering princess tale?" Idan jerked, hand nearly slipping from hers as his eyes opened in wonder.

"A what?" Edrena asked.

After a moment's silence, Amdrei answered. "There are many stories that involve a princess wandering, alone or with a compeer or other companion, who lands in trouble or finds people in trouble and Dances magic to make all right."

"But isn't that what princesses do?" Edrena's foot tapped faster.

"We don't wander, except when walking between the winter and summer palaces." Danissa snuck closer to the head of Idan's bed, never losing hold of his hand.

"In the tales, there's only ever one wandering princess and she never manages big Dances unless she finds other dancers to join her." Idan coughed, then lay back limp and eyes flickering closed.

One of the rules taught to every new princess was that Dance was additive magic: the more princesses, the greater their power. Indeed, it was so much a truth at court, where Danissa had grown up, that she had taken for granted that individual princesses couldn't Dance on their own.

Until she had. Joy. A small thing, though not unimportant, and in keeping with the wandering princess tales.

Except Gisela and Stevan had Danced the destruction of the Shadow on their own.

But better not to dwell on that, since she still had to fulfill her trust in Leander and share details of what she'd witnessed.

And hope her trust wasn't misplaced.

"She isn't called a wandering princess, but yes, she is one," Danissa said, then continued with the tale.

The throne-holder puzzled over her words, thinking them strange but finding in them no way that he could lose, so he agreed. For which his people praised his generosity.

Her companions were not so pleased, but rather fearful for her though her partner, a young eleee, knew gratitude for her offer to protect the child from forcible removal of their hair, and the eleee's beloved clasped the babe to their chest.

"This will not be easy," the woman told her partner and beloved. "I shall need your support."

So many people crowded into the hall that only a small space remained for her, but she stepped to the center and performed a Dance to no sound but her heartbeat and the earth's response.

Windward she went as she woke the earth."

Danissa's head ached for a moment, in memory of the time she and Ylena, Jola, and Todor had spent the day before trying to figure out what this meant. Some dances included instructions to blow as the west wind, or east or some other direction. Alternatively, they might be told to dance angry winds, happy breezes, or blustery gusts.

Never windward.

They finally decided it might mean following whichever way the wind was blowing at the moment. A faint prickle of power had bloomed in Danissa's fingers and toes when she tried it, only to fizzle moments later.

Then the stranger danced in circles, pulling out what wasn't natural and retaining what belonged.

This was even worse than windward. Todor and Jola had pulled Ylena's bed out from the wall so they could circle around it. But how did one pull out what was natural and retain what belonged? From whom or where? They'd tried plucking gestures to no avail. Touching Ylena hadn't helped. Indeed, to the extent power had begun to gather in Danissa, at least, anytime she brushed Ylena's hair or arms it turned into static energy that made them both jump with the crackle.

Such was the beauty of her movement that no one noticed. Even the throne-holder was caught, spell-bound, as the stranger danced while her beloved anchored her and her partner extended her reach.

This at least made a little more sense. While princesses usually danced paired with a compeer, on occasion the Terparchon, or Amara, had them practice other combinations: threes and fives, with one, two, or three princesses, and one, two, three, or four compeers. Three dancers linked—they'd tried it with Danissa and Jola on either side of Todor—certainly could stretch farther, but they hadn't figured out what they were supposed to do.

Within the very seat of the throne-holder, wood and earth felt her and responded. Out they came, blossoming and taking from the ruler the golden seed and insatiable hunger that he might at last be satisfied.

The people were not pleased with the result, for they were left with a man lacking any tinge of gold, and he did not long remain on his throne before he was cast down.

Nevertheless, when the wandering dancer left, she took with her all of her companions, and every last hair on their heads.

Edrena nodded, satisfaction clear on her face at the ending. Danissa's grandfathers and aunt seemed caught still in the tale, savoring it in their heads, no doubt, to recount later when they went back up the hill.

Leander smiled, but his gaze fixed on Idan, not Danissa. Her father's eyes had opened wide and his fingers twitched in circles. His pulse speeded, thrumming against her touch.

He, at least, had seen to the heart of the story: that it told of a princess Dancing a sick person into health.

"We tried. Jola, Todor, and myself, with Ylena. Over and over, failing each time. Ylena's no better now than she was before." She stroked her father's hand, head down and wishing she had better news to share. "Ylena thinks that if the story is true, that the throne-holder had some unnatural thing in his belly that the princess drew out. That the spell won't work for regular illnesses.

"I'm sorry, Father." She bent to the side, burying her face against the corner of the pillow under his head—the better to avoid seeing understanding and disappointment in him and their family. "We failed."

⚘ 23 ⚘

Leander was on the wrong side of the bed, and too far away to offer any comfort.

Danissa bent over her father, shoulders heaving as she sobbed. Her father winced as he raised a hand to stroke her back, the splotches on his neck growing brighter. Sniffles echoed around the room as Edrena and Danissa's family joined them in sorrow.

Although Leander's eyes dampened as well, Danissa's words resounded in his bones. Mingled. Shifted. Became possibilities and patterns swirling and connecting. Idan had dismissed any similarities with his beloved's death. Fair enough, as one far more familiar with both situations.

Yet the bits of familiarity nagged at Leander.

With one last glance at Danissa's tear-marked face, he pulled his hand from Edrena's grasp. "Stay with her. I'll be back. I need to check on something."

Edrena's damp eyes brightened, but she didn't hold him back as he slipped from the room seeking more hope for Idan and Danissa.

Loath as Leander was to leave Danissa, he slipped out into the hall.

He leaned back against the cool stone wall and filled his lungs. As he let the air out, slowly, he pushed away the excitement and joy of

Danissa's admission. Calm filled him, followed by certainty that there was no harm in pursuing the possibility—so long as he didn't raise false hopes.

A sharp breath had him snapping his head around. The Terparchon and Marchon still crowded a little way down the hall, along with their children and attendants. Nothing betrayed who'd gasped, but the Terparchon rose and stepped forward. Her plain tunic and mantle fluttered around her ankles, lacking any belt to constrain them.

"Idan isn't—"

"No." Leander raised both hands, shaking his head. Better to interrupt and give the good news—or at least the lack of bad news—first.

The Terparchon settled back onto the bench, head down. A few locks of gray-streaked dark hair slipped to brush her cheeks. The Marchon laid a hand on her shoulder, fingers rubbing and raising a faint whistling.

None of the small group clustered around the rulers showed any sign of being a healer, though surely one or more was about. Leander didn't want to wait until one came to check on Idan, but the layout of the infirmary differed enough from the winter palace that he wasn't sure which way to go.

"Do you know where the healers are?" he asked.

The Terparchon and Marchon barely glanced at him. Their attendants frowned or looked puzzled, no one answering until the rulers' older daughter moved forward.

"This way." The woman—his age or a little older—lacked her parents' height. Nefeli by name, and a quiet, sensible person by all accounts around the winter palace. Of solid build, her gold tunic was a few shades lighter than her skin while her red mantle brought out ruddy highlights in her short black ringlets. She moved with ease, sandals barely raising a whisper as she proceeded before him.

They didn't go far, taking only a few turns to end in front of a small office. The chamber lacked any view of the outside, but had short, wide windows set atop each of the walls. Two were closed, the others open to allow movement of air.

The room resembled Falfor's office, crammed full of wooden

shelves loaded with scrolls and papers. Other items were tucked in among the writings: bits of leaves, flowers, and bones.

A person several times Leander's age perched on a stool as they poured over a scroll unrolled atop a beat-up wooden table. Two bones, a stone, and a flagon half-filled with liquid kept the scroll from rolling up. The surface bore few words, but drawings of . . . blotches in shades of purple, blue, and pink.

The healer was hardly less colorful than what they studied. Clods of dirt and bits of leaves stuck out from their short, tousled gray-brown hair. Streaks of mud marred their light-brown face and arms, though their hands were clear and clean. So too was the dark green tunic tied over one of their shoulders, only partly covering a small, drooping breast. A lighter green mantle, well-daubed with mud along the hem, lay abandoned on the floor in a far corner.

"Compeer Nefeli." Their voice held a deep burr that resonated in Leander's bones as they turned bright green eyes on him. "And . . ?"

"Leander, sub-librarian at the winter palace library," Leander said.

"I'm Varhas." Thin gray eyebrows arched as they rose and nodded at Nefeli then him. "What brings you here?"

"You're wondering about poison and Idan." Nefeli waved at the scroll. "Why?"

The healer set their palms together and pressed the tips of their fingers against their lips, letting no word escape.

Nefeli turned and asked the same question of Leander.

"Little things," he said, turning his own hands out. Hoping they added up to enough. "He mentioned his beloved dying of poison that included spots over her body. Although he said it was different from him, he has spots on his neck now. He said was getting better, then took a turn for the worse that his strengthener couldn't help with. A strengthener that smells awful and tastes worse." He licked his lips, swallowing to dispel the remembered taste.

"That's a common complaint of medicines, no matter how much honey we add." Varhas wrinkled their nose, then tilted their head to the side. "Yet one in truth that Idan never made. If anything, he said it tasted better after he got a fresh batch here than the staler one he brought with him."

"You mean his strengthener changed when he got here?" Nefeli asked.

"Not at first, only after he started feeling more ill." The other settled back onto their stool. "We tried other combinations. For every day of improved health, he spent two sliding backward."

Leander waited, but the compeer didn't ask more so he stepped in. "What goes into it?"

The healer stared at him for a long moment without speaking. Turning toward Nefeli, who leaned against the doorframe, they raised an eyebrow. The compeer waved a hand, perhaps granting permission or overriding some unspoken concern, and a moment later the healer listed off ingredient after ingredient. Most were little more than strings of syllables to Leander. Maybe he'd seen them somewhere, maybe not. But others . . .

"Are those plants?"

"What else? Few types of dirt have enough healing power of their own to warrant eating or drinking." Varhas tapped the spines of the books resting on a near shelf. "Most cures come from roots and leaves, flowers and berries."

"Where do you get them?" Pieces fit together in Leander's head, filling out inklings into full-blown supposition.

"Some come from a distance, those we trade for, but most are grown here." The healer's eyes narrowed and they rested their head on their hands as they stared at him. "If anything, we send away more than we purchase. At least half the supply at the winter palace comes from our gardens."

"There's a gardener who has a grudge against Idan. Natter."

No sooner than the name dropped from Leander's lips than Varhas leapt to their feet, hands pressed against the scroll.

"Natter? Wild beard, missing teeth, bald?" At Leander's nod, the healer lifted their hands and slammed them back against the table. "He brings in herbs and leaves that grow wild where they will in the gardens, and distills some of the liquids we use as bases for potions. Including that for Idan."

Nefeli shifted her stance, planting both feet flat on the tiled floor. Her gaze turned abstract. "Tell me more about this Natter."

Varhas described him and the cottage in which he lived, a small dwelling in a far corner of the gardens, Leander offering a few additional comments, but not much was needed before the compeer raised a finger.

"I've found him. He's happy." She snarled, lips drawn back to reveal bright, sharp teeth. "Pleased that Idan's ill. I cannot say for certain Natter poisoned Idan, but he exudes a sense of . . . completion."

"If he did, what would he have used?" Varhas scrambled around the table.

"I can't get that level of detail." Nefeli turned on her heels. "But we can get him."

In a matter of moments, she led the way back to her parents.

"Poison?" The Terparchon paled, then flushed at the word. She clenched her hands and teeth as she ordered all assistance necessary for the gardener to be brought in.

A few words resulted in guards accompanying Nefeli on a hunt for Natter. The healer and Leander trailed along behind, as did the Marchon. The ruler came last, though Leander kept trying to offer him a place ahead. His neck and back itched knowing the older man followed behind.

They made good time, yet at the edge of the gardens Nefeli stopped and threw out her hands.

"Natter's left the cottage. He's learned we're on our way, somehow. He's fleeing." She grabbed the hem of her mantle and wrapped the ends around her waist as she ran off. Most of the guards followed.

Varhas continued on to the cottage, muttering about possible clues and evidence of what Natter could have used. Leander remained with them, as did the Marchon and three guards.

They hurried through along a path through thick bushes and trees. Birds called in the distance, and the sounds of the palace faded away. After twisting back and forth several times, the trail led to a single-room building, half-stone and half-wood with a small latrine tucked around back and a chimney on the far wall. The house sat in a clearing twice the house's size. Stepping stones outlined the opening, with more stones circling oval plant beds.

The healer hissed at the sight of the beds and scuttled over to examine them.

Lacking sufficient knowledge of plants, Leander headed for the door gaping open.

One of the guards stopped him, went in to check, then nodded for Leander to enter.

A mess met his eyes. Another guard let slip a curse at the sight.

The table was overturned, and two stools had rolled to the sides. The bed frame sat square against one wall, lacking mattress and covers. Clothes and the rotting innards of a once-sweet grass-stuffed mattress lay scattered everywhere. Broken glass sparkled against the packed earth floor and lengths of cloth. So too did broken plates and goblets of the kind used for most meals served from the palace kitchens. Light and dark green leaves, red leaves, berries in different shades of pink and blue, and soft petals in nearly every color under the sun clumped here and there, all mixed together with fresh ashes in the narrow stone-lined fireplace.

The combination of scents made Leander sneeze again and again. He lifted his mantle and held a fold of cloth over his nose and mouth.

What good to find Natter acting so suspicious if they couldn't figure out what he might have used to poison Idan—and the cure?

The guard poked at a pile of clothes.

"No, leave it." Leander turned around.

The guard dropped a dirty tunic, glancing behind Leander.

"Agreed." The Marchon's deep voice almost echoed. The tall man bent as he entered the doorway and stopped one step after. "What do you see, Librarian?"

Sub-librarian, but this was hardly the time and place to correct him.

"This is hardly the work of an innocent. It speaks of guilt, though it's best not to leap too fast to conclusions over what." Fine words, but better than making guesses or cursing the gardener's escape. Bringing Natter to justice wasn't Leander's task, that fell to the guards, but they needed him to admit if he'd added anything to Idan's medicine. "The timing, though, is suspicious. Why else destroy his home and flee just as we sought him out?"

"How did he know we were coming?" The Marchon slapped the doorframe, the hard thud echoing.

"That I can't guess. Could someone have sent word ahead?" Something about the far wall called to Leander. He tiptoed through the scattered belongings and bent down next to the fireplace.

"If so, we have bigger problems." For a big man, the Marchon had little trouble walking in near silence despite the mostly covered floor.

Leander startled as the other squatted next to him.

"What are you looking at?"

"Why burn a fire in the height of summer?" The ashes were still warm when Leander held a hand over them.

"Cooking up a dinner?"

"Could be. Or destroying something of value. In which case . . ," Leander passed a hand over the ashes, making circles with even strokes. Three. Five. A prickle of power set his fingers twitching at seven. When he reached eleven, the air started to sparkle with bright dots.

At thirteen, a circular breeze whisked up the ashes. Leander continued his movements, fighting the pain trailing up his arm. Then stopped at seventeen.

The ashes continued to swirl, glittering as they brightened into the soft tan color of much-used parchment. Bit-by-bit they settled back onto the hearth, forming an irregular rectangle. Incomplete, for the top and bottom had burned more thoroughly, or the ashes floated up the chimney. Yet enough remained to recreate three lines of spiky writing.

Kill all born compeers at court.

Start with Idan.

This will please you.

The Marchon flinched. He reached for the parchment scrap, drawing back at the last minute.

"Let it sit a moment or more, then you can pick it up." Leander shook his aching hand and arm. "He must have poisoned Idan."

"What did you say about leaping to conclusions?" The Marchon stretched and rose, frowning down at the parchment. "Not that I disagree. Poison. Again. Will it never end?"

"But which one?" The healer's pained cry had them both whirling around. The other stood in the doorway with their tunic turned into a sack to hold a dozen different leaves and blossoms. Their knobby knees knocked as they stared around at the destruction. "Natter grew at least four lethal plants not native here, and with no known medicinal value, in addition to the thousand species with poisonous parts that grow here naturally."

If they couldn't find the cause, how could the find a cure?

Leander bent and scooped up the parchment, the smell of ashes lingering in his nose.

He'd helped unsnarl the cause of Idan's illness—but not enough to save Danissa's father for her sake, her family's, and his.

$$\begin{array}{ccc} \text{❧} & 24 & \text{❧} \end{array}$$

anissa had doubted on occasion that the court appreciated her father's many contributions. He always walked at least one step behind the Terparchon as her counselor, and refused bribes. Although celebrated as the longest serving of the compeers, the rulers and court considered this less important than the service of the princesses.

Her uncertainty dissolved under the outpouring of affection as he weakened in his bed. Though no one was so crass as to break in upon his bedside and insist upon a place with her and his other relatives, still the Terparchon, Marchon, and others of the court made clear their concern, as the numbers of those who cared spilled out of the infirmary into the surrounding courtyards.

Indeed, their numbers grew to the point they impeded normal activity in the infirmary. The healers conferred, then sent one to ask if Danissa and Idan's family would consent to move him for the evening out to a secluded courtyard. Although accessible only through the infirmary, it was a simple route and the square large enough that others might pay their respects without crowding.

The clear sky offered a glorious, high roof of light blues slowly darkening toward night. Warm air swirled around as small eddies of a south wind found the courtyard and twirled in lazy circles. Luminescent plants overflowing from baskets fastened to the surrounding walls gave enough light to note the delicate ivies and savory herbs flourishing in raised beds spaced around the edges. Gray flagstones set into the earth offered a smooth surface, almost level save for slight slants to direct rain runoff to discreet drains.

Most courtyards boasted a decorative element at the center, whether a fountain offering water and cool or an elaborate mosaic portraying some historic moment. This enclosure had once boasted an immense tree, but it had fallen at some point—Danissa didn't remember ever seeing or hearing of it, so perhaps before her birth—and only the trunk remained. The smooth, polished surface offered a seat suitable for a ruler, though the Terparchon elected to remain standing and allowed Idan's fathers to sit there instead, right at their son's side. He hadn't had to move a muscle, for infirmary attendants carried the bed through wide doors and corridors to settle it near the trunk.

Danissa stayed close, keeping hold of her father's hand and marking the steady beat of his heart. Madane and Edrena remained near. The latter seeming to believe her brother had left the rest in her care until he returned, for she brought them water and simple fruits to nibble on, and coaxed even Amdrei and Orodan to eat.

Counselors, servants, clerks, and others, most clad in simple, everyday attire—no doubt having heard of the Terparchon and Marchon's lack of decoration—waited their turn to pay their respects. Only the rulers, princesses, and compeers lingered as the others passed through.

One by one, two by two, three by three, but in no larger numbers, the crowd took their turn to come and speak, expecting no reply and receiving at best a smile and a word or two. Voices remained low, and the movement of the crowd was marked by the beat of many footsteps.

Even Ylena got up out of her bed, with the help of two compeers, to come and bear witness. She resisted at first when Amdrei offered her a place on the trunk, but was persuaded to settle down with him and Orodan when admonished by one of the healers.

Idan conserved his strength, but he was failing. To Danissa's surprise, and she thought his as well, the Terparchon had yet to make her approach. Rather than come near, she lingered where she had a clear view of the entrance, and glanced often in that direction.

"Make way!" The Marchon's deep voice carried across the hushed conversation and shuffle of sandals against stone.

Whispers rose as the crowd parted to let the Marchon through, with Varhas and Leander in his wake. The Marchon headed straight for the Terparchon, but Varhas and Leander continued to Idan's bedside.

"Poison. We don't know which, but there are antidotes to try." Varhas scowled as they turned this way and that, searching for something. "Where is your strengthener? If we can figure out what he used . . ."

"He?" Idan blinked, body going rigid. His fingers pulled from Danissa's hold, knocking the flask that lay nearby.

"Natter," Leander said.

Varhas grabbed the flask and passed it over to other healers. They remained, checking Idan's condition, while the others headed into the infirmary.

"Natter? Why?"

"We haven't got him yet." Leander glanced away, arms tight against his body, then shifted to look over Idan's body at Danissa. "Have you tried Dancing him well?"

"It didn't work with—" She nodded at Ylena. The other princess frowned, head tilting to the side as though she'd heard although Leander and Danissa hadn't spoken loud.

"But if he's been poisoned, then it's not something natural and you might be able to draw it out," Leander said.

Danissa froze. Her whole body felt so light she might blow away on the wind as hope rushed through her, followed by fear. It could work, but what if it didn't . . . Still, it wasn't her decision. Dragging in long, unsteady breaths, she searched her father's face and found a similar mix of hope and fear.

"May I try?"

He pressed a shaky finger against his lips, mutely asking for time to think.

Person by person, a greater hush fell over the crowd. Whispers here and there suggested the news of poison spread, or even shards of the stories.

"Yes. Once." Idan touched her cheek, hand falling back onto the bed.

Danissa stepped back from the bed, wobbling, mind blank of what to do next.

Sharp hand gestures caught her eye. She turned to Ylena even as Jola rushed over to Danissa's side while Todor and Stevan helped Ylena up off the tree and brought her close.

"Dance to your heartbeat." Ylena grabbed Danissa's hands, squeezing tight. "Follow the wind, which is balmy tonight, so don't move too fast, be calm and tranquil."

Easy for her to say.

"Circular movements. Repeat anything that sparks power as often as needed, fives and sevens worked best for me when we tried yesterday. I didn't rouse much power, but I felt something." Jola stepped back and glanced over Danissa, who was still in the plain tunic, mantle, and sandals she'd donned after the Fire Dance, her hair a long weight against her back. "Would you like a cloth for your hair?"

Danissa hefted the mass, letting curly strands spill over her hands. "Yes."

The other princess made a quick circle, then shrugged and grabbed her thin red mantle. Her teeth flashed as she cut a few strands and ripped off a wide swathe. Her hands were gentle as she helped Danissa pile her hair atop her head and wrap it with the soft swath. Without the weight, her neck and back cooled quickly. A soft breeze wicked away the sweat soaked into tunic and mantle.

Despite Jola's kindness, the press of people around Danissa made it harder to breathe. "I need space, air."

A clap from the Terparchon moved the crowd back to form a tight mass around the edge of the courtyard. They cleared a rough rectangle around the bed and tree trunk.

"You'll need a compeer." Ylena gritted her teeth, glancing between Todor and Stevan whose hands kept her from falling. "Born is likely better than taught for this. If Stevan's willing . . ."

He nodded. Gisela moved to take his place. Ylena gave her a wry look, but accepted the assistance as she hopped back to the trunk.

Everyone drew back except Stevan. Leander, Edrena, Danissa's grandfathers and aunt. Varhas.

Only her father couldn't move on his own. He remained, still and quiet on the pallet. Face calm, but hands twitching against the cover and the spots on his neck brighter than ever.

No one had left. The crowds seethed around the walls, leaving room but not much. Quite unlike the conditions in the practice chamber in the pavilion, or the dancing room far below. On the other hand, this reminded her, in space and press of people, of the square high on the hill.

She'd Danced joy there. Surely she could manage another Dance here.

Except she hadn't known what she was doing up there, or taken time to piece apart how she'd managed it.

All she knew for certain was what she'd wanted the dance to represent. Joy then, and now . . . Healing.

She nodded at Stevan, but waved for him to step back. As a born compeer, and one who'd partnered her since her father's retirement, he would know when she needed him, but she wanted to start on her own and feel her way.

Find her own heartbeat and pace.

Forcing deep breaths into her lungs, she shifted to stand at the base of her father's bed.

An easy breeze turned in circles as it passed through from west to east.

Dance windward—did that mean tranquil, or follow the same progression?

Her pulse calmed, a steady beat throbbing at her neck and wrists.

A faint echo thumped under her sandals. Kneeling, she rested her fingertip against a flagstone.

A matching beat resounded against her fingers and the knee touching stone, unmistakable and aligned with her pulse.

When she stood back up, only the echo remained.

On a whim, she removed her sandals and tossed them to the side.

They didn't hit stone—people caught them. Dancing on the flagstone barefoot would be hard on her feet, but without the sandals the beat resounded in her bones from heels to head.

Even the whispers stilled. Silence surrounded her, broken only by breaths.

And the thrum beneath her feet.

Circles.

Dance circles.

Draw out what wasn't natural, leave what was.

How would she know?

She couldn't stand still forever.

With a whistling breath, she walked around the bed once. Each footfall matched the earth's beat.

The second time around she added arm movements, imperious waves of hands meant to summon. Those, at least, were familiar, as she'd spent plenty of time practicing guiding flood waters, directing winds, coaxing flames.

Around and around, again and again.

Nothing existed except her father, the bed, and the space through which she moved.

Something touched her fingers, a thick, unpleasant substance with an oddly sweet, early spring-flower smell. She twined her fingers in the goo, pulling at it—but there was too much, too heavy. Worse, the scent went to her head and dizzied her.

Why?

An answer resounded up from below—because she was alone. Unrooted.

No sooner had the thought passed through her head than a body aligned with hers. Arms matched hers. Hands dug into the substance, and took it from her. Doing something with it, *what* she wasn't sure, but the weight eased as they Danced around the bed and trunk.

Stevan had removed his sandals as well, and his skin slapped against the stone in time with the beat and her movements.

Dizziness still plagued her. The more her head spun, the more difficulty in feeling and keeping to the earth's beat. Her arms grew heavy, her ability to pull the substance slowing.

Why?

She was following the directions in the story. The lousy, simplified description that missed so much. Windwards? Draw out what was unnatural and send it somewhere else? Aided only by her compeer and beloved.

Ah! The wandering princess had two partners. A compeer who helped deal with the substance—and a beloved to anchor her to the earth.

Beloved.

Without considering the matter more than a moment, she called for Leander.

He answered.

"Here." She set him at the foot of the bed. "As you did before, support me."

"Always." His voice echoed in her ears as she and Stevan made another circle.

With every round she grabbed Leander. Leaned her weight against his. Drooped into his hands, and rediscovered the earth's pulse.

How many circles had she made? She'd lost count, but they weren't enough. Not yet.

One more round.

Two.

Three.

Then something beneath her cracked when she reached Leander.

She stopped, hands clutching Leander. Stevan swayed nearby. She and Leander reached out to brace him.

Only to discover Stevan wasn't looking at him, but Idan and the bed.

New green shoots sprung up from the tree trunk and cracks between the paving stones. They twined up the bed and wrapped around Idan.

Within moments they grew thicker and stronger, multiplying with incredible speed. They lifted his body high in the air. The cover slipped and fell back onto the bed. Her father's withered body, clad only in a simple loincloth, was exposed to view.

Puffs of pale, sickly green air blurred him from view. A stiff breeze whipped about, carrying the green away.

The sprouts shifted, combining into a single massive strand wrapped around Idan's body. It curled down, setting him gently back on the bed, then straightened into a solid tree trunk—young and slender, but tall for all that and boasting a wide leafy growth that hid the darkening sky.

The tree grew from the center of the old tree trunk.

Danissa ran forward, clutching Leander's hand and tugging him after her. The silence shattered. With gasps and thuds, other family members rushed forward as well, and the Terparchon and Marchon and everyone with reason to want to touch Idan.

A healthy, hale Idan. Limbs a bit withered and in need of a good meal or three—but manifestly recovered.

Well enough to grab Danissa and Leander into a tight embrace.

"You did it," Leander whispered in her ear, squeezing her hand.

"No, we did it." Danissa held father and beloved close.

$\maltese$ *25* $\maltese$

One solo dance, one of joy, one of healing.

Three Dances to win Leander's heart, whether or not Danissa intended as much. Even a day later, after a long sleep filled with glorious dreams, he nearly walked on air. Perhaps his sandals slapped against stone or earth, but he heard none of it.

He lingered on the steps of the library. The golden hours of early evening left the air luminescent and warm rather than hot. Savory smells from the kitchens mingled with sweet floral perfumes, neither of which distracted him. Neither did the distant chatter of crowds come out to enjoy the best part of the day. Most gathered in other courtyards away from the library, allowing Leander to ignore them. The skirt of his clean, fresh blue tunic fluttered about his calves, beneath the heavier weight of the matching mantle, as he paced back-and-forth across the arched entryway.

Waiting.

Whenever he stopped, faint images stirred. Memories of Danissa dancing the first time he'd ever come close to her. Talked to her.

Never dreaming they'd come so far.

He trusted she'd meet him here, as promised.

One moment he delighted in the memory of her dance—then the

real person strode through. Danissa, too, wore blues, her mantle paler and tunic darker than his. These were merely backdrop for her, especially as she'd let her hair fall free. Most waved down her back, but a few strands danced to either side of her face. They framed her shy, bright smile.

His mouth turned dry, he swallowed and tried to come up with words to greet her. "Your father?" A silly query, since he'd seen the older man earlier in the day—as well as a person might be.

She broke the silence first, grabbing his hands and pressing close. "Well and happy. I owe you so much. The stories, the support in Dancing—"

"You owe me nothing." A chill swirled around him, as though a blast from winter had snuck free into summer. He didn't want her acting out of any sense of debt.

"No." Danissa pressed a finger against his lips, keeping him from saying anything more. "I'm not doing this out of any trade. You say it's right that the truth be someday known. Well, here I am."

"Then let us be done with this." Taking her hand, he led her into the library. Rather than continuing along the wooden walkways, he turned to the side. Danissa glanced at him as they walked along the wall, but said nothing.

In the far corner sat a small room filled nearly to bursting. Wooden shelves set up off the floor lined the walls to either side, all overloaded with scrolls piled atop small volumes resting on larger volumes. None were piled on the floor, fortunately, as watermarks on the doorway indicated floods had reached a finger's height.

Directly across from the door was a window with a westward view. The shutters were adjusted to allow in the cooling air and golden light of the early evening, while preventing anyone in the courtyard on the far side from looking in.

Between door and window sat a plain table of dark wood almost bare. A small pile of blank pages, a feather pen, and an ink bottle rested to one side. The uncapped glass bottle was less than half-full, but the smell filled the room.

Danissa wrinkled her nose and a line appeared between her eyes, likely in response to the burnt undertone of the ink.

Or perhaps due to the items on the table: a clean rag and a small knife. The blade glittered in a ray of sunlight.

Alternatively, given the twist to Falfor's smile, she reacted to the presence of the elderly librarian. He wore his usual layers of tunics in graduated colors, all shades of red with the top the color of freshly spilled blood. Having unburdened himself of his opinions on the forthcoming testimony, and Leander's dubious wisdom in allowing it, hadn't made him any happier.

He had, however, prepared the ink.

"You know Falfor, of course. And Falfor . . ." Leander met the older man's hard gaze, and wasn't the first to look away.

"Princess Danissa is well known to me." Falfor inclined his head in her direction.

She straightened, rising up on her toes and dropping hard in a huff. "Once. I spilled ink once."

"And how many near accidents?" The older librarian rapped his knuckles against the table.

"Do they count?" The princess crossed her arms over her chest and lifted her chin.

"No. Especially when you were careful not to risk actually upsetting anything." He assumed a gentle smile and beamed at Danissa. "We're grateful for your information. You're certain you won't share the full tale now, to the open air?"

"This is what she agreed to." Leander shifted sideways, catching Falfor's gaze and meeting it. Much as he respected the elder, he let some of his irritation at being second-guessed show. "There's no need to ask."

"It rarely hurts to try one last time. But if you're sure, then . . ." Falfor picked up the pen. The sharp point flared as it passed through a beam of sunlight. The burnt undertone to fresh ink in the bottle strengthened. Turning his gaze back to Danissa, he said, "I need three drops of your blood."

"Why . . ." Danissa recoiled. Only a step, but the movement sent air currents swirling around Leander.

"This magic is reserved for librarians." Leander hoped he'd guessed right that she wondered why Falfor was present. "I'm only a sub-librarian."

"Though likely to be promoted on return to the winter palace," Falfor said, in tones soft enough to ignore.

Likely to be promoted didn't equal reason enough for Falfor to teach Leander the spell prematurely.

"I cannot prepare blood ink." Leander caught Danissa's hands and pressed them, then let go and stepped away to leave her clear room to stay or go. "Falfor has promised to leave the room after the ink is ready to write with. You will be able to read as you write, but when you are done the page will shift and all the words become indecipherable. No one will be able to understand what you have written until your death breaks the spell."

He counted his breaths in the silence, waiting to see if she'd stay or go.

How much was her trust in him worth?

⚜

THE BURNT TANG TO THE INK MADE DANISSA'S STOMACH TURN. Worse, with the sharp point of the feather pen flashing before her, she already could smell her own blood joining the smoky, ashy odor. She grabbed hanks of her tunic and mantle to keep her hands from trembling.

She hadn't realized blood would be required.

Then again, she hadn't asked. She'd only told Leander he could make the arrangements he'd promised, the way for her to both share the secret and keep the details confidential.

He'd kept his promise. Time for her to do the same.

Biting her lip, though gently so as not to spill more blood, she untangled her right hand from the soft folds of fabric and held it out.

A sigh from Leander whiffled her hair. Falfor's lips quirked, but he made no other sign of noticing as he took her hand in his. He laid the pen against her finger and pricked her so fast that she barely flinched. He kept hold of her as he laid the pen down and picked up the ink bottle.

Twisting her hand, he applied gentle pressure against the sides of her finger to produce one bead, two, three. She swallowed against the harsh smell of blood as the drops fell into the mouth of the ink bottle.

He handed her a clean rag, the fabric soft as it pressed against the small wound.

When he waved a hand over the bottle, every remaining drop of blood in her body shook thrice, as though something crawled through her veins.

A puff of smoke rose above the bottle's mouth, dissipating in the air. The burnt stench vanished, replaced by the usual smell of ink with a faint hint of copper.

A rush of air drew her attention to Leander, who extended his hand just as she had.

"You're determined? You might outlive her." Falfor held up a finger, wagging it at Leander as he set the ink bottle down.

"Make the cut," Leander said.

Falfor sighed, but picked up the pen and added three drops of Leander's blood to the ink.

Leander shivered next to Danissa as another puff of smoke rose above the bottle.

"Why did you add your blood?" Her finger had already healed, leaving only a smudge of red on the rag. She folded it and pressed a clean section against Leander's finger.

"Now it cannot be read until both of us are dead." He bent his head over their joined hands, as she held the cloth close. "You need not fear librarians assassinating you for the information, for they would need to kill me as well."

"I didn't think of that. I wouldn't . . ." But the idea of their blood mixing in the bottle eased her nerves.

At the scrape of wood against stone, they whirled around. Falfor pulled a bench from beneath the table, offering Danissa a place to sit while she wrote her tale.

Letting go of Leander, she slipped around and settled down. Lines of sun through the shutters warmed her back.

Falfor left the room with a final nod. Leander turned to follow, after a gentle smile at her.

He wasn't staying to watch, had too much honor to try and read any of what she wrote while it remained legible. He'd promised to give her a way to preserve the story while keeping it secret—even from himself. After all he'd given her, she needed to do something for him.

"Stay." The word escaped her before she could call it back, but she didn't regret it.

Leander turned, one hand braced against the doorframe. He didn't say anything, watching her with wary eyes. A moment later, he bit his lip.

"I'll write, you read." She waved at the pile of blank pages.

A host of expressions passed over his face. Some she wasn't sure of, but he started with surprise and ended bright with pleasure to realize she trusted him with the full tale.

She pulled the first page over to find someone had already written a few lines at the top in the minute script of scribes and clerks, using the common trade alphabet. The page bore the date and a title "The tale of the Shadow turned to Nightbells, preserved in blood ink."

Blood ink.

Hand shaking, she dipped the pen in the ink, not sure what she'd see. The fluid resembled regular ink, save for a deep red glint when it caught the light.

Leander's body blocked some of the sun as he stood behind and read over her shoulder. Bit by bit, word by labored word, she inscribed the tale not once but twice. Her writing was far less neat than whoever had written the title, but legible enough. Then the ink seemed to shiver on the pages.

A moment later, everything save the first line had shifted into strange, unreadable characters.

Danissa slipped her hand into Leander's as they entrusted the copy to a special chest kept under the table. It held several others, all as illegible as the one she'd just finished.

Without saying anything to each other—eyes and glances and pressure on hands were enough—they left the library and wove their way through courtyards and gardens to visit the nightbells.

The evening was so sweet and lovely, air warm rather than hot or cold and the golden sunlight only starting to tinge pink in a hint of sunset. They should have encountered others, if not along their way then at the site of the former Shadow. Yet Danissa noticed no one, and never after was sure if they were truly alone or her focus on Leander had excluded all else.

Save, of course, the uplifting perfume of the flowers and the glorious blooms gleaming midnight blue-black with a touch of gold.

They stood side by side before the flowers. She turned to him and they both started to speak at the same moment using almost the same words.

Then a pause, and ripple of laughter. Danissa waited, allowing Leander to speak first this time.

"May I hold you?"

With a nod, she wrapped her arms around his waist as he enfolded her. Her head rested against his shoulder, more comfortable than she'd have thought when they first met, only days earlier. "This is . . ."

No words came to mind.

"I could get used to this." Leander said, mouth close and warm against her ear.

"We've known each other all of, what, five days? Seven?"

"So short and so long." One of his hands traced circles along the top of her back.

She pulled back enough to watch his face without leaving his embrace. So easy to stay close. She'd leapt first and thought twice many a time, but there were some steps she refused to take without due consideration. "I'm not ready to make my choice. I need to learn more—"

A shadow passed across his face, muting his pleasure without taking it all away. "I understand. You—"

She laid a finger over his lips before he could go off in the wrong direction. "But the possibility becomes ever more real."

"I'll wait." Light and hope radiated from his face, warming her to the tips of her toes.

"Don't wait." A giggle escaped her. "Learn me as I learn you, so if—when—the day comes, we choose each other."

"So wise so young."

She smiled, laughed. Neither of them moved first. As with the dance, their bodies enjoyed a moment of full harmony. The embrace deepened and their mouths met in a first, sweet kiss.

A faint chime rippled through the air, as though the flowers rang in celebration. Danissa noted the sounds, but checking on the source would require ending the kiss, which she preferred to continue.

She didn't need the flowers to ring for them.

She trusted him. That was enough to go on.

❧ 26 ❧

Idan settled onto a wooden bench. Nearly ripe redberries adorned
the vines covering the trellis overhead, their peppery scent all the
sweeter for his never having expected to smell it again. He wore
no sandals, the better to rub his feet against the earth and dig his toes
into small holes, well aware he would end the day with dirt covering his
skin. It would be a pleasure to rub the soil off.

He'd left his mantle in his room despite the cool early-morning air.
In addition, he'd fastened his oldest tunic around his waist so his
shoulders and back might absorb any sunlight that chanced to fall
upon him.

At least once every summer that he and Larissa spent time with his
family, she'd accused him of loving sunlight more than her. Always with
a laugh and a sparkle in her eyes that dared him to prove her wrong.
Which he did, gaining joyful memories to warm the cold years without
her.

He'd never told his daughter, but he liked to think they'd conceived
her after one such mock argument, with its celebratory resolution
conducted out in the fields under the open sun.

Summer lasted longer here, well into what other parts of Codaros
considered autumn. No matter how cool it was now, it would heat up

soon. He hadn't stayed here past the turning of the seasons, when the court headed back to the winter palace, for a long while.

This was a good time to change that.

The warming sun intensified the scent of the redberries ripening nearby. Someone should be out picking them. He was surprised they hadn't done so already, but perhaps they'd overslept after last night's fest. Most of the family and almost all of the visitors had.

Ironic that he, the cause for celebration as the fest honored his return to health, had tired little, danced well into the night, and was still among the earliest to rise.

At least two had beat him, though they'd danced even more than he the night before. They did wear the same green tunics and mantles as the night before, notable for the colors almost-but-not-quite matching, not that anyone had mentioned the slight clash more than fifty times. Perhaps they had never gone to sleep and instead danced through the dawn into morning proper?

If so, they were decidedly an exception. Even Idan's grandfather, who so often complained about inability to rest in his later years, slept on. His snores burst through the air from his bed in a cozy room nearby with one of the best views of the lake and city below.

Danissa and Leander used Yedan's snores as the beat for their dance.

Or Danissa did. Kicking her feet, she traced circles around Leander. She was trying to teach him how to be a compeer, even though they both knew he'd never serve as one.

A good thing too. Some people could be taught to mimic what a born compeer did, although never so well as the born, and Idan would admit to bias but insist he was correct all the same.

But Leander would never be a true compeer, born or taught.

His attention, his focus, centered on Danissa. That worked when she Danced alone, as she had when she'd Danced joy and Idan's health, but for the kinds of Dances the princesses wrought together . . . No.

Princesses needed compeers capable of focusing on the energy and alignment between princesses and power.

For the first time, Idan had some glimmering as to why the old Terparchon had forbidden compeers and princesses from Dancing with their parents, children, siblings, or lovers. The current Terparchon had lifted the ban, despite Amara's arguing against doing so. Idan had always considered that a good decision. It allowed him to partner Danissa for her first year as a princess, and they'd done well together.

Yet watching Leander's focus on Danissa, Idan couldn't but wonder if he'd erred, and at any time put her wellbeing above the purpose of the Dance.

Too late now to make any change.

Or was it? He could return to the ranks of compeers and partner Danissa again or take a turn at partnering others.

Or try something new.

So many new possibilities.

Watching Danissa and Leander together, turned his thoughts in directions other than Dances. Every press of their feet against the earth sent tremors of their growing affection spiraling out. They weren't lovers . . . both seemed cautious and concerned about rushing forward only to fall back.

Still, they were well matched. Idan rubbed his hands together, anticipating watching them dance together for as many years as they might.

Larissa would likely approve if she were here. She wasn't, but for the first time in years the thought of her didn't bring stabbing loneliness. She hadn't been a princess any more than Leander would be a compeer, but Idan had loved dancing with her, moving with her, talking, touching, holding.

Wherever she was, surely she joined him in wishing the same for their daughter.

He could be happy and lonely at the same time.

Lost in regarding his daughter's tentative movements toward love, he almost missed the soft pad of steps. He noted Edrena's approach only moments before she settled on the bench across from him.

He pretended to not have noticed until she waved.

She hadn't combed her hair with anything more than her fingers, given the hanks hanging on either side of her head. Might even still wear her nightclothes, for despite the blue mantle hanging around her, the white tunic beneath showed rents carefully mended. Her bare feet dangled, toes brushing the earth.

"They look happy together, don't you think?" she asked.

"Yes."

Both chuckled as Danissa linked hands with Leander and tried to whirl under their arms, only to get tangled when Leander failed to let her fingers rotate within his grasp. Then again, this led to a kiss, so perhaps it was as much intended as accidental. Indeed, the firmness of Leander's stance made Idan sure.

"Do you mind?"

"Mind?" Idan rarely opened fully his ability to draw information from the way people stood or strode. Much easier, for him and others, to take only tidbits as needed. Yet he couldn't block Edrena and monitor Danissa. Concern seeped from her with every brush of her feet against the earth—not for Danissa or Leander, but for Idan and his ability and willingness to adapt to the change. "This," he nodded at Danissa and Leander, trying the whirl a second time, "is her choice. Their choice."

"But it means you'll be more alone. I mean, you'll all be together most of the time, especially since the Terparchon's letting you and Danissa stay here with Jola and Nefeli to wait on the Erevestisi embassy . . ." She waved her hands, the gesture encompassing all the other details she didn't mention, including that Leander would remain with them as he investigated Natter and Idan's poisoning. "Still, it'll be the two of them and you, not you and your daughter. You might be lonely."

The way bits of his thoughts echoed in her words prompted him to take a closer look at her. Nothing changed from his earlier determination. She wasn't a late-blooming born compeer, just a clear-eyed youngling moving from youth to maturity and seeing more of him than he usually betrayed.

"Being alone doesn't mean one is always lonely," he said.

"Well, not for me. But you miss . . . That." She waved again.

"How do you know?"

"I saw your face, watching them." Edrena crossed her arms, chin high. "People can lie with their faces, but they're more likely to lie when they know they're being watched."

"I'm happy for them." Idan settled his feet firm against the earth, letting his soles soak up Danissa and Leander's joy—and Edrena's worry.

"So am I. I wouldn't mind being happy for you, too."

"I was happy. That's enough." His voice sounded weak to his own ears.

"So you can't be ever again?" Dark eyes watched him unblinking.

He turned away first, gaze falling on the dancers. Somewhere deep inside, the various parts that the earth had cleansed and returned to him shifted. Made space. There was room there for something new. Maybe love, maybe not. He didn't want to look too close just yet.

Edrena proved canny enough not to push further. She too shifted her seat to watch Danissa and Leander.

"I won't be here soon." A sniff escaped her. "Leander got me a place with the Marchon's progress back to the winter palace, to make sure I don't miss the exam. I won't be able to do anything if they mess up. Which they will. Everything I've read says everyone does. Will you help them?"

"Of course. If they need it." And were willing to accept advice.

Idan and Edrena watched as Leander messed up another step. Danissa fell on her bottom. She hissed as she leapt back to her feet and faced him with her hands on her hips, then they burst into laughter.

"Trust them." Idan smiled as the sun warmed his back and shoulders. "Danissa's mother and I did as well, starting out in no better circumstances."

"The way they look at each other makes me feel warm. But I won't remember that when I'm away, not enough." Edrena sighed. "I'll have to wait until all of you come back to the winter palace."

"Which we will, in hope and love."

In the yard before them, Danissa and Leander's laughter ended with a kiss.

SNEAK PEEK

Be among the first to learn of new releases: sign-up for her newsletter at https://BookHip.com/PCSWMCK. Book recommendations, updates on stories, and snippets from works-in-progress—plus a free Dancing Princesses story for signing up!

The world of the Dancing Princesses continues—read on for a peek at *A Royal Princess* . . .

Nefeli longed to be anywhere but the heavy silence of the infirmary.

The surroundings offered the potential for serene rest and reflection. The room held a bed, small table for drinks and medicines, stool for guests, and a mosaic of fish decorating the white-washed walls. Narrow windows in the walls and above the door allowed free circulation of cool evening air, whisking away all but hints of the medicinal tang inherent in the infirmary.

Breezes tugged at the hem of her soft yellow tunic and gold mantle, whisked along the sash that tamed the fabric at her waist, and ruffled through her close-trimmed black ringlets. She leaned against the cool stone wall and shifted her weight from one sandaled foot to the other, setting her bronze anklets chiming.

A lovely sound, because it was a sound. Likewise, she appreciated the trickle of water in the fountain in the plaza at the center of the infirmary, and the distant laughter and happy chatter from down the hall where a family gathered around a different patient.

Oh, to be among them or elsewhere in the palace.

Her brother, Todor, had asked a favor, which he rarely did. She granted it, and this was her reward: heavy, loathsome quiet.

A fitting punishment for not stopping to ponder why he wanted her with him while he visited his lover. He'd kept their budding estrangement too close a secret—Nefeli had caught no hint of it, oddly, or she'd have questioned his request.

Alas, she now kept company with two who studiously stared at their laps and said nothing. The three of them all as still and silent as blocks of wood—one of the land's magical Dancing Princesses, who guarded against natural and unnatural disasters, and two of the three royal-born compeers who partnered the princesses, and no one spoke a word!

Todor sat on a solid wooden stool. Informally clad in dark blue knee-length tunic and no mantle, or jewelry, he'd run his fingers through his black hair—a match for Nefeli's but without the curl—so many times that his hands bore half the pine-scented oil he used to keep it in place. His thin lips pressed tight together under a steep nose and thin black brows, his burnished skin warm.

He should have appeared strong and stalwart, a broader version of their mother, but the position diminished him. It reduced his height and breadth to the slumped posture that their tutors had tried to train out of him as a youngling. For his own good and protection, Nefeli had nagged him about it too. Their grandmother—their mother's mother —hated any such sign of weakness and slapped him whenever she caught him slouching.

Though grandmother never had much to do with him otherwise. Fortunate him.

Ylena, the princess Todor avoided looking at, sat straight upright despite an ample supply of grass-stuffed pillows to lean against. She'd pulled her blonde hair back into a loose braid, the ends trailed over her breasts beneath her simple green tunic. Brown eyes dominated a round face, glowing above a thin nose. Her hands clasped together, light beige fingers resting on her soft belly. A white sheet covered most of the bed, tented over the thick lengths of wood that held her broken leg straight.

A pair of crutches leaned against the corner near the hallway, opposite Nefeli and far enough away that Ylena couldn't reach them on her own.

A just reward, considering the other woman had walked across the palace a few weeks earlier, with her leg only partly-healed, and put her recovery back. Still, at least she was allowed to walk again even if only under strict supervision.

If Jola, Nefeli's lover, were in the same situation Nefeli would celebrate her returning health. Bring her favorite goodies, offer tales and reassurances. Cuddle with her on the bed.

Anything other than this heavy nothingness.

Todor's dark eyes flashed as he threw a pleading glance at Nefeli.

She'd seen that look before, though not for nearly a decade. Not since their grandmother's death from a strike of lightning . . . or a ball of fire fallen from the sky. No one was quite sure which except that her blackened body had been recovered and suitably buried if not exactly mourned.

So many years dead, yet the old woman's poison lived on. Even now, her summation of Todor rang in Nefeli's ears unbidden.

"Fodder for the troops. He'll never make an officer."

Harsh and extreme, but she'd got the core of Todor right. He showed no sign of leading.

Ylena on the other hand . . . She'd pursued, courted, and won him. Though, true, she'd done so with grace and honesty and given him time and space to choose. He could have declined, but Todor never had been good at saying no. Then again, he'd flourished as her partner. Her compeer in the dance, her lover off the dance floor.

Or so Nefeli had always assumed. Yet their postures suggested little of love, more of exhaustion.

Reason enough not to speak—but not for Nefeli to remain.

"Enough." She pushed away from the wall, dusting her hands. The clap of skin against skin broke the thick stillness. "If you're going to sit in silence, you don't need me watching you."

"No, don't go." The stool legs squeaked against the stone floor as Todor leapt to his feet.

"So you can speak." Ylena crossed her arms over her chest and clicked her tongue. "I was wondering if a fish had eaten your tongue."

"I greeted you when I arrived and you said nothing, so I thought you wanted quiet." Todor edged further away, blocking the door.

Nefeli leaned back in her former place and rubbed at a faint ache in her temples.

"'Well, I'm here,' you said." Ylena turned up her nose. "Some greeting."

"I promised to come, every day, and I've kept that." Todor said.

"Every day, yes. Later every day. At first you were here in the morning, now the evening. What next, you'll visit at night when I'm sleeping?"

"Why come when you're awake when you don't want to talk to me?" Todor stamped. Most people would see his foot hit the floor, guess at his sullen anger from the thud, perhaps even catch the vibrations in the air from the movement.

Those born to be compeers, such as Nefeli, got more. The press of his weight against the stones, and the earth below let her read his true feelings. Anger and resentment, yes, but mixed with fear and hurt.

Ylena's bed frame kept her from touching the floor. Nefeli received from her nothing but an awareness of her presence, her location. The imbalance led to nibbling pains on the side closer to her brother.

The princess lifted her chin, elbows tight against her sides. "I never said I didn't want you to visit."

"You didn't have to." Todor said.

"Pleasant as this all is, you hardly need me here for it." Nefeli left the wall again, but Todor shifted to block her. His anger subsided beneath a swell of fear and desperation.

His gaze never left Ylena. "If you don't want to talk to me, at least talk to Nefeli. To someone."

"I speak to everyone in turn." Ylena lifted a stoneware mug from the table next to the bed and drank deep. She coughed, or chuckled, as she cradled the mug against her chest. "I believe Jola wrote up a schedule to make sure that I'm never left alone for long. Two or three princesses or compeers visit every day."

"Do they bring you all the news?" Todor's shoulders slumped again, his body drawing in on itself. Although the movement opened room for Nefeli to slip by, she stopped at his side and rubbed his shoulder.

"They talk of little else. Who Danced with whom, who slipped, who messed up, who angered Amara and made her order everyone do a second practice." Ylena tossed back another swallow. "They tell me everything."

"So you don't need me for anything." Todor's shoulders rose and fell as he sighed. A ripple of hope surged within exhaustion where his feet rested on stone. "Not even word of the upcoming Erevestisi visit?"

"They especially talk about the possibility of a formal visit, since the Erevestisi haven't come this way in decades," Ylena said, eyes narrowing. "It's official?"

"Mother received the formal request from their Governing Council and has agreed to allow it."

"I hadn't heard she'd decided." Nefeli licked her lips to hide a smile at Todor's flicker of pride in having something truly new. "They won't get here until after the Court usually leaves for the fall progresses across the land."

"She's sending word tomorrow, once she decides how to host them, but it's certain." Todor stood taller.

"That's all well and good, but I asked you to find out one thing." Ylena stuck out her chin. "Do you have an answer?"

"Not the one you want." Todor's anxiety seeped into the stone and up Nefeli's legs. Bumps formed along her skin.

"Then what?" The other woman asked.

"A fault was found in the flooring, a plank with a slight depression."

"No." Ylena hissed, spine crackling as she straightened and glared at Todor. He stepped backward, filling the doorway. "No, someone tripped me."

His discomfort made Nefeli's bones ache. Her mouth was dry, and blood pounded at her temples.

She pushed the sensation away, focusing on the stiff length of Ylena's broken leg under the sheet.

"Mother ordered an investigation, you know that. But no one saw anything." He swayed, raising a breeze that whipped around Nefeli's feet. "The dance floor was crowded, and we were doing an elimination dance—the second in a row. Everyone was getting tired, and several people dropped out with aching ankles. It must've been the flooring."

"The flooring." Ylena thumped the mug down on the table and glared over Nefeli's head at Todor, though her gaze seemed to pierce Nefeli as well. "Do you believe me?"

"Yes." He shifted his weight from one foot to another. The weakness in his voice matched the doubt emanating through his feet.

"Go away." Ylena said.

"What?" Todor asked.

"Leave." Ylena flapped her hand. "Go away. Anywhere I don't have to look at you if you aren't willing to believe me."

"But . . ."

"Go!"

Nefeli turned around. The evening sunlight had begun to turn orange with the sun's descent, and the shift made his skin a deeper bronze. Mixed emotions emanated from him in every way possible, so clear to Nefeli that Ylena had to be in little doubt either. "Todor, she asked you to leave."

"I don't want her to be alone." Guilt and relief warred on his face, and in his feet. He turned big, dark eyes on Nefeli.

She let herself read deeper than usual. Truth leaked into the stones, who shared it with Nefeli. This was why he'd wanted her company—not for him but for Ylena. He nearly floated above the floor except for a solid dose of awareness that Ylena might not mean it. No shame at all in having tricked Nefeli.

"I'll stay as long as she needs company." She clasped his shoulder, gripping tight. Some of his guilt over Ylena drained away, but he cast Nefeli a sideways glance and flinched.

"Such generosity." A sharp bark of a cough escaped Ylena. "I accept."

Todor's departure made the room bigger, emptier. Nefeli pushed the stool into a far corner but declined to sit. She stretched her legs and feet, then leaned back. The stones here were far warmer than the other wall, having soaked up afternoon sun, and felt good against the tight muscles of her back.

Ylena mirrored Nefeli's pose, except tilted back against the piled pillows. "What about you?"

"What about me?"

"Do you believe I was tripped?"

Despite the heat of the stones, a chill ran through Nefeli's veins. All the fuss, all the worry, and the official investigation—yet until this moment no one had asked her that question or even anything close. No doubt her mother's doing, as so often the case. Protecting Nefeli, perhaps, or from a fear of learning whatever Nefeli might know. "There was something strange in the air that night."

"Do tell." Ylena huffed. "There've been a lot of those this summer."

"True enough." There were three that Nefeli knew of: Ylena's injury, the lightning strike that had changed a famed outcropping of stone into unknown flowers, and the night that a fellow princess had healed her father through a Dance once thought myth rather than fact.

The latter two were magical—the first?

Swallowing hard, Nefeli met Ylena gaze for gaze. "You won't ever get the answer you want about your broken leg, not from Todor or any of us."

"Why not?"

"Because no one knows. Whatever happened, it was impossible." Or so Nefeli preferred to remind herself whenever she woke shivering and dripping with sweat from nightmares where she relived the dance —and dreamed she was the one to fall, or Jola, or both, breaking more than their legs.

"It wasn't impossible because it happened." Ylena said, waving a dismissive hand.

"Who would do it?"

"Who might actually trip me or who'd want me tripped, injured to the point I may never Dance again?" Ylena asked.

Nefeli shrugged.

"I can list dozens off the top, who'd see me brought down that they may rise. Any princess with ambitions to be Terparchon after your mother dies." Ylena held up one finger. "Or it could have been you or your sister, for you'll have to admit your mother would be a fool to choose Todor as heir if he is not wed to a princess capable of ruling." She raised two more.

"Or anyone who wants to see a princess other than you as my mother's heir, which widens the circle even farther." Nefeli set her hands on her hips. "It wasn't me."

A new silence fell on the room. The light shifted further, loosing orange and turning pink. Footsteps down the hall sent rills of happiness through the floor to Nefeli as the princess who'd healed her father left his side with other members of her family.

Nothing emanated from Ylena. Her lips pressed tight together, then she nodded.

Nefeli exhaled slowly, her own relief flooding through her.

"But you hardly welcomed me." The other woman sniffed.

"You're wrong about that. I admire your competence and determination. Always have." Nefeli inclined her head. "You're a great princess."

"You didn't like seeing me with Todor." Ylena inclined her head in the direction in which Todor had escaped.

With a hissing breath, Nefeli offered Ylena the greatest compliment she could: the truth. "It seemed to me you did all, or most, of the deciding. Todor went along. I hardly think that's a solid base for two who might lead the land."

Ylena opened her mouth, a gleam in her eyes, but Nefeli raised a hand and forestalled her.

"And do not say you resemble my parents. My father defers to my mother, yes, because the right to the throne comes through her—but he pulls his weight rather than let her bear the full weight of governing."

"I wasn't going to compare Todor and myself to your parents," Ylena said, head held high, "but to Jola and you."

"Jola is a princess, and the epitome of competence, but she is otherwise nothing like you." Nefeli straightened, fingers digging into her hips. Her teeth clenched and her temples burst back into full pain.

"You have it the wrong way around." Ylena wagged a finger at Nefeli. "You're like me. You go after what you want—and you wanted Jola. She goes along with you, just as Todor does with me, or did, but how much of the deciding does she do?"

"You know nothing of our relationship if you can say that." Inclining her torso slightly, Nefeli asked "do you need something for your pain? I would be happy to summon a healer."

"No need," Ylena lay back against the pillows, pulling her sheet up. "I thank you for your company, but I would prefer to rest."

"Of course."

Nefeli was half-way through the door when Ylena called after her in tentative tones. "I'm sorry."

One hand wrapped around the wooden frame, Nefeli glanced over her shoulder. The other woman seemed smaller in the early dusk. Tired, no doubt, and still in pain.

Though she hadn't said what she apologized for.

Nefeli didn't ask.

She swept out of the infirmary. Passed her guards in the hall, but they responded quickly and fell in a suitable distance behind her. Both had warded her long enough to leave her sufficient space.

Nefeli moved fast, impelled by desire to be away from Ylena and to not have to face anyone else until she recovered her equilibrium. She left behind Ylena's hard words about Nefeli and Jola, and pushed aside considering the implications of the hard silence between the princess and Todor.

Most of all, Nefeli sought a place to be alone, as alone as she might ever be. Space to move without the weight of other people's steps pressing against her.

Usually the summer palace offered her that much. A swathe of buildings spread in the form of the rising sun along the lake's edge, it was filled with quiet nooks, open plazas boasting greenery and water fountains, and the thick growth of gardens.

Her feet carried her across courtyards and through halls, a back way to the lake that she'd long ago memorized. No one stopped her, although more than one gesture—hands extended, smiles—dimly registered. Training allowed her to lock Ylena's words behind a calm facade.

Push them back. Set them aside for another day. Nefeli's relationship with Jola had nothing in common with Ylena and Todor other than that each involved a princess and their compeer.

Nothing.

A sudden gust of wind heavy with moisture whipped around Nefeli. She stopped and discovered her unthinking path had led her to an immense plaza overlooking the lake. The palace center stood behind her, the array of arches and windows separating the plaza from the great hall. Beneath her feet stretched an immense mosaic that covered most of the surface. Tiny squares and circles in jewel colors formed the image of the first Terparchon selecting her consort and naming him the Marchon to rule at her side.

Step by step, Nefeli passed over the oval frames around the central figures until she stood atop her ancestors with one foot on each.

The sun had set, but glorious pinks and purples arched across the sky and reflected off the waters. Light breezes danced about, bringing sweet scents from the myriad plants blooming on the terrace below the plaza.

So different from the night Ylena was injured.

The mosaic was open to the elements, rather than covered with a wooden floor for dancing as it had been that night. No musicians played nor did a crowd seethe around the edges, alive with chatter. The quiet let her appreciate the crash of waves against the beach below, and the call of birds overhead.

Flickering torches had lit the space, with little aid from a crescent moon. Nothing hung in the sky this night but the first of the stars, for the moon had yet to rise.

Nefeli didn't want to believe Ylena, not about her fall or her insinuations.

But that Ylena would break her leg in an elimination dance? Fall, yes, most people did but usually on their backsides or rolling and taking out a half-dozen others with them.

Accepting Ylena's surety of being tripped hardly required doing the same for her comparison with Nefeli. They were two separate accusations.

Nefeli couldn't say for certain where anyone had stood when Ylena was injured. So many had crowded the floor. Nefeli and Jola, Ylena with Todor, Nefeli's mother and sister with their chosen partners, and others beyond.

Rolling her shoulders, Nefeli stretched her arms and back. They'd done so many dances that night—court dances meant to show off clothes and jewelry and graceful movements. At the last they'd done the tachino, a fast elimination dance that mixed sections of intricate, exacting steps with spates of whirling, with an ever-increasing tempo.

Without any attempt at recreating the tempo, Nefeli repeated the steps. Memory recreated Jola's beloved form in thin air opposite her as she swayed and curved her arms in exacting steps where partners mirrored each other. Little chance there to lash out and trip someone, even if done at speed. This was all about demonstrating control and one's ability to keep time.

The whirling, on the other hand, required keeping balance and not getting so dizzy as to go astray. A foot could easily go astray, accidentally or on purpose, and knock another dancer off-pace.

A shiver racked Nefeli and she stopped atop the image of her ancestors.

It could have been a faulty plank with a dip. The tiles remained solid beneath her feet, but the wooden dance floor had occasionally creaked underfoot.

That was it. Ylena just didn't want to admit that for once she'd stepped wrong.

Except . . .

The slap of sandals against stone barely registered above the call of birds overhead—but Nefeli noted the approach. Only one person walked quite that way, or rather one body. More than one distinct individual shared the short, slight figure who rounded the corner and made straight for Nefeli.

Zora, Nefeli's youngest sibling, wore a blue mantle edged with thick gold-colored fringe over a cream-colored tunic, pulled in at her waist by belt of twined gold and copper links. A matching circlet topped dark brown hair pulled back in a braid. She rarely went anywhere without those signs of her rank, perhaps worried she'd be overlooked or dismissed as a child without them.

But anyone who considered her young and malleable failed to truly take in Zora's face. Dark brown eyes filled with intelligence shone to either side of a sharp nose and thin, mobile lips. Each person living inside her walked slightly differently and had overlapping ranges of expression, however the keen mind behind remained the same.

"Whatever are you doing out here alone? Shouldn't you at least have a guard?"

"I'm not safe here?" Nefeli waved a hand at the distant shadows of her guards over by the far wall. She had never been sure exactly how many siblings shared Zora's body—at least three or four, but their presences blurred together in a way that confused Nefeli's senses. This time, however, she didn't have to wonder who faced her, for that particular sister, the primary one, different from the others.

"You're one of the people who discovered that gardener who wanted to kill all born compeers." Zora waved a hand in the general direction of the main gardens. "No one's caught him yet, or if they have I haven't heard."

The reminder stung. Forget their limited success, no one had even considered that a fellow compeer was being poisoned for months. Worse, when the crime was suspected the poisoner had managed to escape beyond the senses of Nefeli and the other born compeers. She clenched her hands, a growl escaping. "He's run far enough, or is hiding in a thick enough crowd, I can't find his footfall and neither can the other born compeers."

"Then surely it's not wise to be so exposed." Zora twirled in a circle around Nefeli, footsteps light and graceful and completely lacking in magic.

"He can hardly poison me for standing here, and I will know when anyone approaches." Nefeli set her hands on her hips and tilted her head at her sister.

"Fair enough. What if he embroils others in his plans?"

"Again, I will know when they approach." Nefeli checked, just in case. No one, not even at the second or third floor windows with a view of the plaza.

"If they are strangers, yes, but he might suborn those you know."

"I am not without defenses." Nefeli said.

"Good. What about Jola?" Zora stopped whirling, back to the darkening sky and deep waters of the lake. The long fringe on her mantle swirled about her wrists and ankles.

"What of her?"

"I wonder at your allowing her to go into the city today."

"She's her own person and needs no permission." Nefeli pulled back. Her sister's wording stung, too close a reminder of the many times both had wondered at their brother's seeming to need Ylena's permission to do or even be. "It's born compeers who are his targets."

"You forget Natter worked here, in the palace. Grew his poisons in our gardens, where who knows what he saw or heard. Even those who rarely see you and Jola together know of your love." Zora grabbed Nefeli's hand. "If Jola were to be captured, endangered, what would you not risk to see her free?"

"She has guards when she goes out."

"Two, no less than any other princess—but no more either. Have a care for yourself and her. She looked quite distraught when she returned earlier."

"Distraught? How?" Nefeli stiffened.

"Oh, worn, tense, twitchy." Zora let go and shrugged. "You know how she is when she worries."

Nefeli did know, though she tended to consider Jola more as apt to startle than twitchy when ill-at-ease. Or worried. Jola had seemed so lately, though she'd settled in the last days. Extending senses wide, Nefeli searched for her lover. Many others occupied the palace buildings, not least her parents and other princesses and compeers, guards and servants, but even among the familiar crowds Jola's step was unmistakable.

No one lurked near her. She stood safe within their suite in the royal wing—but pacing back and forth. The weight of Jola's worry pressed against the floorboards heavily enough Nefeli couldn't miss it, although she tried to restrain reading Jola's steps to keep them on an even balance.

"I'll take your warning." Nefeli threw her sister a smile as she turned away.

"Have a care for both of yourselves." Zora said.

The younger woman stepped out of the way as Nefeli hurried off to see Jola face-to-face.

FATE OFFERS!

Nefeli dislikes secrets. They lead to mistrust and discontent. Better to face problems straight on, admit weaknesses alongside strengths, and build trust. Only Nefeli's lover and dance partner, Jola, offers a respite from the plots, treacheries, and fears plaguing her family, the rulers of Codaros. But her family's troubles threaten to entangle her one more time when Nefeli's mother offers her true power.

Jola ranks among the princesses who protect the land from danger and disaster, but remembers her common origins. Determined to help other commoners understand the power of dance magic, she led retired princesses to build schools fostering dance training across the nation. She fears losing magic, place at court, and most of all her beloved Nefeli, if her dancing ever fails. One fine evening, she sees the first signs . . .

Two loving, fearful hearts. Two sets of secrets capable of binding them together—or parting them forever.

With characters poignant and fierce, *A Royal Princess* is a joy to read.

ABOUT THE AUTHOR

Alea Henle writes non-fiction by day and fiction by night. Contemporary and historical fantasy, fantasy romance—and more! Check out her website www.aleahenle.com.